Love's Broken Vow

Love's Broken Vow

Honey

www.urbanbooks.net

Urban Books, LLC
300 Farmingdale Road, NY-Route 109
Farmingdale, NY 11735

ISBN 13: 978-1-64556-092-0
ISBN 10: 1-64556-092-9

First Mass Market Printing August 2020
First Trade Paperback Printing March 2019
Printed in the United States of America

10 9 8 7 6 5 4 3 2 1

*This is a work of fiction. Any references or sim-
ilarities to actual events, real people, living or
dead, or to real locales are intended to give the
novel a sense of reality. Any similarity in other
names, characters, places, and incidents is entirely
coincidental.*

Distributed by Kensington Publishing Corp.
Submit Orders to:
Customer Service
400 Hahn Road
Westminster, MD 21157-4627
Phone: 1-800-733-3000
Fax: 1-800-659-2436

Chapter One

"Good afternoon, Sister Ellen Marie. We have a one o'clock appointment to see the senior priest. I know we're late, but this little *angel* decided to take a detour after school," Royce said, yanking her eleven-year-old nephew's arm in frustration. She moved his lanky body from its position behind her to stand at her side.

Tyler frowned and freed himself from his aunt's grip. "Ouch! What did you do that for?"

"You know why. Now, zip your lips, boy. I'm going to let the priest deal with you."

The nun flashed a knowing smile and waved her hand, inviting Royce and Tyler to follow her down the corridor of the church's office area. "Come right this way. He's been waiting for the two of you."

"God bless you, Sister."

Sister Ellen Marie knocked once on one of the massive double doors before she opened them wide. She stepped aside. Once again, she gestured with a wave of her hand, causing the long, flowing sleeve of her habit to sway. "Father Nicholas Gregory, meet Royce Phillips and her nephew, Tyler."

The priest turned around slowly from the bookshelf and flashed a smile so wickedly enticing that Royce instantly felt warm and lightheaded. She saw his hand extended as he walked closer to her and Tyler, but she didn't want to take hold of it. Even in the holy confines of the priest's office, Satan had managed to flood her mind with lustful thoughts. Royce fought the urge to throw herself into Father Gregory's long arms and taste his full and sexy lips. They looked luscious underneath his thick, curly mustache. As a registered nurse turned certified fitness instructor and trainer, Royce could thoroughly assess a human body in detail with just one quick glance. The priest's black, tailored cassock couldn't hide his well-toned physique, standing tall and erect underneath it. His body was simply divine. And his flawless complexion reminded Royce of sweet, rich milk chocolate. Her taste buds began to betray her on sight. She nearly drooled. The new priest had enormous hands and feet, her wandering eyes couldn't help but notice. If it hadn't been for the flaring skirt of his cassock, Royce would've surely inspected the area between his thighs. That thought made her cringe with fear and shock. Undressing a man of God with her eyes in the church had to be a spiritual offense worthy of fire and damnation.

"I'm Father Gregory," his deep baritone timbre rumbled. "It's a pleasure to meet you, Ms. Phillips."

Royce blinked a few times to clear her head from its ungodly thoughts. She smiled and finally took the offered hand. "Hello. Where is Father McGreevy today? Tyler's appointment was supposed to have been with him."

Sister Ellen Marie touched Royce's shoulder lightly. "He's gone on to lead another parish. The archdiocese reassigned him to a church up in rural Pennsylvania. The move had been postponed for a few months until two weeks ago."

"I had no idea. We haven't been to church since New Year's Eve."

"I've heard lots of amazing things about you and your family, Tyler," Father Gregory said, addressing the youngster directly. "Father McGreevy left notes describing you as a wonderful kid with an abundance of energy and creativity." He offered Tyler his hand in a friendly shake.

"He did? He was a real cool dude. I hope you are too." The boy shook and released the priest's hand. He shot him a sharp stare. "You are cool, aren't you?"

"I'd like to think so. Why don't you and your aunt have a seat so you can tell me why you're here today?"

"Um, I have to run," Royce announced, glancing down at her watch. "I usually leave Tyler here with Father McGreevy and the nuns for a couple of hours or so to do chores around the church while I teach my afternoon Zumba class. Will that be a problem?"

"As long as Tyler is comfortable here with the sisters and me, it'll be fine with me."

"So, what do you think about the new priest? Is he nice?"

"I like him. He's smart. He helped me with all my homework before we did anything else. Then after we finished updating the membership roster on the computer and helped the nuns fold blankets for the homeless, we walked around the corner to the park and shot hoops. Father's got an outrageous jump shot, Auntie Royce. I never knew a priest who could play basketball before."

I've never met a priest that damn fine before! The words almost slipped from Royce's lips, but she swallowed them and smiled at her nephew across the kitchen table. "Where is Father Gregory from, sweetie?"

"He was born and raised in Chicago, but he moved down here to Atlanta from Boston. Can you believe he once lived in Barbados for an entire year? I saw the pictures in his scrapbook. He's been all over the world."

"That's interesting." A vision of the handsome priest dressed in a pair of skin-tight swimming trunks while relaxing on a white, sandy beach as waves from the crystal blue ocean crashed against the shore swept Royce away. She imagined beads of sweat glistening against his smooth skin under the bright Caribbean sun with the sound of seagulls squawking in the distance. In his hand he held a fruity, tropical beverage adorned with the cutest tiny umbrella of many colors. There were two straws in the cold, refreshing drink. One was for Father Gregory and the other for Royce. He leaned over and kissed her cheek, causing her nipples to become sensitive and as hard as a pair of marbles. Then in his deep, hypnotic voice, he invited Royce to share his thirst-quenching beverage with him and promised to satisfy her hunger for him later in the privacy of their oceanfront villa.

"So, is it okay with you, Auntie? I promise to be on my best behavior."

Royce had heard Tyler talking to her the entire time she fantasized about a romantic beach rendezvous with their new priest, but she couldn't pull herself out of the daydream, nor did she want to. The scene was much too mesmerizing. She grabbed a napkin from the dinner table and wiped her lips. The very idea of kissing Father Gregory and sharing a cool drink with him had teased her taste buds, causing her mouth to become overly moist. Royce's sinful thoughts had also brought on a sudden gush of moisture in the intimate spot between her thighs. She crossed her legs against the dampness in her crotch and the warm sensations down there, all while hearing Tyler's voice but not fully understanding his words. Her mind was reeling from the aftermath of her erotic vision. She was actually aroused. It had to be an abomination before God to lust after a priest. Royce was pretty sure she was going to hell if she didn't check her thoughts about Father Gregory.

"He only has seven tickets, so I'll have to let him know soon if I can go, Auntie."

Royce's senses finally left the beach and returned to her kitchen. She took a stabilizing breath and gave Tyler her undivided attention. "I'm sorry, honey. I have so many things on my mind. My brain is scrambled. Where did Father Gregory invite you to go with him?"

"He and Sister Eva want to take a few of the boys and one girl in our Sunday school class to a Hawks game Friday night. Can I go with them, please? I promise to behave in school and do well on all of my assignments. I'll do every one of my chores around here without complaining if you'll let me go."

"You may go to the basketball game, Tyler, but I'm going to hold you to your word. And you can't hang around those bad boys at school anymore. They're nothing but trouble, and I don't want you to be involved in their foolishness. Do you understand?"

"Yes, ma'am."

Royce hung up the phone after her brief conversation with Brandon, and she turned on the television. As she surfed through the channels with the remote control, snatches of their last date ran through her memory. No fireworks. Not even a tiny spark. The guy just did not do it for her. He was handsome enough, and he definitely knew how to show a girl a good time. Attorney Brandon Hartwell was also a big spender with an appetite for the finer things in life. More importantly, he had been a perfect gentleman so far. With so many good qualities, Royce couldn't understand why she hadn't melted under his romantic heat yet.

Her sister, Zora, had encouraged her to give the good- looking lawyer one more chance by going out on another date with him. Royce's initial response to that suggestion had been laughter. She had already planned to serve Brandon a pink slip. She figured if he hadn't lit her fire after five dates, he simply lacked the ability to do so.

But now that Royce had lost her mind and started salivating over Father Gregory as if he were a slice of chocolate cake, another date with a gorgeous, rich man seemed like a good idea. Hopefully, it would be the distraction she needed. So, Friday evening while Tyler and his friends would be cheering for the Atlanta Hawks at Philips Arena with the priest, she'd be enjoying spicy Jamaican cuisine and reggae music at the Golden Grove with Brandon.

Chapter Two

Father Gregory placed the sterling silver bookmark in the crease of his open Bible before he closed the leather-bound book. He turned toward the window to take in the spectacular view of the setting sun. As splendid as God's handiwork was on that fine, cold January evening, it wasn't enough to distract him from his thoughts of Royce Phillips. She was an extraordinarily beautiful woman. Everything about her physical appearance was pleasing to the eye. For the first time in many years, Father Gregory had actually experienced an erection at the sight of a woman. And it troubled him.

At the early and impressionable age of seven, he accepted his calling to serve God and the Roman Catholic Church. Through his many years as an altar boy and later as a scholar of divinity in college and seminary, he had maintained his sacred vow of celibacy to God and the church. But he was human and he, like any other warm-blooded heterosexual male, appreciated the presence of an attractive female. However, there was one significant difference between Father Gregory and most men his age. He had never partaken of the intimate pleasures of a woman's body before. He was a virgin. Sure, he had toiled with curiosity, temptation, and lust countless times over his twenty-nine years, but the Holy Spirit had always sustained his flesh. Miraculously, the devoted priest had remained free of sexual sin his entire life without ever coming close to crossing the line.

Father Gregory wasn't perfect by any means, but he strived to live righteously through prayer before God, his spiritual superiors, and the parishioners he served. Some sins were easier to avoid than others, and according to Scripture, no temptation was common to man. In fact, Royce Phillips had presented him with a unique form of enticement. Her beauty, although a blessing from God, had the potential to be a curse for a celibate man. The silky and unblemished texture of her cocoa brown skin and her long, flowing braids blended perfectly together. Such fine features reminded him of a centuries-old portrait of an elegant African queen. Ms. Phillips's svelte hourglass figure had more curves than a winding road. Her body had been magnificently created. She was absolutely gorgeous, yet she didn't seem to realize it as she'd stood in his office earlier dressed in a coral two-piece exercise ensemble that hugged her shapely form just right. The combination of her good looks and the distinct vanilla scent of her perfume had ignited an unfamiliar flame of desire within Father Gregory so powerful that he had committed most of his time to fervent prayer and meditation after Tyler left the church.

There was something fascinating about Royce Phillips. She was different, special even. And it wasn't just her outer appearance. She had a big heart and kind spirit. According to Tyler, she had willingly agreed to care for him in the absence of his parents—a doctor and his nurse-practitioner wife—who had traveled to the West African nation of Sierra Leone on a medical mission. The recent outbreak of the Ebola virus had weighed heavily on Dr. and Mrs. Benson's hearts, influencing them to travel with a group of Christian doctors on an assignment of mercy. Their goal was to provide lifesaving medical care to the victims of the deadly disease. After careful consideration, one week before the trip, the Bensons made the decision not to take Tyler, their only child, to Africa with them. They felt that withdrawing him from school in the middle of the term to travel to a country plagued by disease wouldn't be in his best interest. So, they'd left him in the care of his favorite aunt, his only aunt, who happened to also be his godmother.

Royce was a bachelorette with no children by choice. At least that was how Tyler had summed up her carefree lifestyle. He'd bragged about how successful a businesswoman she was, owning two full-service health and fitness centers that catered to dozens of celebrities and hundreds of other clients. In Tyler's impressionable eyes, his auntie was loaded. Her knowledge and expertise in all things pertaining to physical health and nutrition had earned her an extremely comfortable standard of living.

Royce traveled extensively and was the owner of an impressive African American art collection that filled her lavish suburban-Atlanta home. Her all-white living room, which housed a baby grand piano of the same color, had always been off-limits to Tyler and any other child. It and all of the other spacious rooms in the home belonged on the pages of a décor magazine in the youngster's opinion. That was, with the exception of his room.

Auntie Royce had allowed her darling nephew to decorate his walls with posters of basketball greats, past and present, and hip-hop music icons. Tyler had every electronic gadget and video game imaginable in his private quarters along with a humongous flat-screen television, a touch-screen computer, and a state-of-the-art stereo system. He swore that the lovely Royce Phillips was better than Santa Claus any day of the week.

Aunt and nephew were very attached to each other. Tyler had said they had a special relationship, but in recent weeks he had begun to miss his parents terribly. That's the reason he had started acting out at school and hanging with the wrong crowd, he'd explained to Father Gregory. He just wanted to have fun and be considered one of the "cool kids." Skipping classes and participating in food fights in the cafeteria hadn't earned Tyler any cool points with his aunt, though. His misbehavior had caused her major grief and concern. Turning her wayward nephew over to Father McGreevy was the only solution she could come up with at the time. But now that the elder priest had moved away, the responsibility of getting Tyler back in good standing with his aunt and his school's officials had fallen into Father Gregory's hands. He was sure he could successfully handle the task. His only concern was his keen attraction to Royce. It was a potential distraction. Yes, Father Gregory would keep his distance from her by any means, but he was fully committed to ministering to Tyler's spiritual and emotional needs.

"I had a wonderful time with you, babe. You know, the night doesn't have to end." Brandon closed the small gap between him and Royce and encircled her waist with both arms. "I'd love to come inside for a nightcap."

"That's not a good idea. As I told you before, my nephew is living with me right now, and he'll be here for the next several months. I don't want to give him the wrong impression."

"You're an adult. Kids don't have the right to interfere in the lives of grownups. He's old enough to understand that men and women get together from time to time to indulge in grown folks' activities."

Brandon leaned in for what was meant to be a surprise kiss, but Royce had sensed it coming. She reacted quickly to thwart his efforts by turning her head to the side. His lips made contact with her long braids dangling against her cheek. Brandon opened his eyes, lifted his head, and gave Royce a puzzled look. She was about to address the issue of the kiss when a pair of bright headlights pulled her away from the moment.

The car stopped directly in front of her house. The sleek, red sports car was a two-seater. Sister Eva didn't drive anything that stylish or fast. *Father Gregory,* a still, small voice within whispered. Royce's body responded with a slight shiver to the name and became warm when an image of the man it belonged to suddenly appeared inside her head. She immediately took a step backward, freeing her body from Brandon's unwanted embrace.

"Hey, sweetie," she called out to Tyler the moment he exited the car. She watched him walk slowly up the long walkway in her direction. "How was the game? Did the Hawks win?"

"Who's he?" Tyler's eyes narrowed.

Embarrassed and slightly annoyed by the whole scene, Royce looked toward the sports car still parked in front of her house. The engine was purring, and the headlights were shining ever so brightly. She turned to face Brandon, intentionally ignoring her nephew's question. "I think you should leave now. Tyler and I need to talk."

Without protesting, Brandon descended the three brick, half-circle steps and left Royce standing alone on her stoop. She watched as he slowed down his pace and greeted Tyler, but he got no response from him. The obviously upset boy glared at him before turning cold eyes on his aunt. Royce braced herself for a confrontation.

Father Gregory honked his horn twice and sped away seconds after Tyler turned and waved good night to him. He couldn't explain it, even if his life depended on it, and the reality of it all disturbed him beyond insanity: he was jealous. The sight of Royce Phillips in another man's arms enraged him.

He rounded a curve leading to I-75 North, clutching the steering wheel tight with pure anger churning inside. Father Gregory couldn't recall a single time in his life when he had felt so helplessly flustered over a woman. He had a mother whom he adored and two amazing sisters. He had never been jealous of their relationships with others. He didn't even know Royce. They had no emotional ties whatsoever. He was her priest, her spiritual leader. And she was a member of his congregation. They weren't lovers, and they never would be. But Father Gregory's attraction to Royce had taken wings, and he lacked the power to control it. He hated to admit it, even to himself, but he wanted her. He craved her like the forbidden fruit that had caused Adam's fall from grace in the Garden of Eden. Royce, a woman, was the one thing he, a Catholic priest, was sworn and avowed to never have. Yet she was the single thing he desired more than anything else under the heavens.

"Peace be unto you."

"And also unto you," the congregation responded in unison to Father Gregory.

He raised both hands high toward heaven. "Let us depart from this place with a spirit of peace and goodwill in the name of Jesus Christ, our Lord and Savior. Amen."

The priest left the altar and made his way up the center aisle. He marched slowly behind the servers bearing the cross, candles, and the book of the Gospels. Hands folded in front of him, he focused straight ahead as the organist played, filling the sanctuary with "For the Beauty of the Earth," the recessional hymn.

It had been a glorious mass, and Father Gregory's sermon titled "Triumph Over Temptation" couldn't have come at a better time for Royce. She had battled lust and other impure thoughts the previous week. She couldn't rid her body or mind of her mounting magnetism toward Father Gregory no matter how hard she'd tried. And for that, she felt like a heathen.

It was a blessing to be able to come into the house of the Lord to pray to God for forgiveness and to partake of Holy Communion for the cleansing of her sinful soul. But even as she'd sat in a pew close to the back of the church in the right wing, she struggled with desires of her flesh. At one point during the sermon, Royce had expected God to strike her with lightning for allowing her imagination to creep underneath Father Gregory's white and gold chasuble. She could've sworn she was able to make out his firm pectoral and abdominal muscles through the fabric. No priest had any business with a body that damn fine.

Thank God for the Scripture reading about Jesus' temptation by Satan in the wilderness. Royce drew strength from what she'd heard. The words had enabled her to abandon her immoral thoughts and focus on the sermon being given by Father Gregory, her priest, instead of yearning for him as a delicious male specimen. She'd felt empowered and ready to fight all forms of temptation in the coming week. But now, watching Father Gregory's towering, toned frame make its way up the center aisle, Royce's forbidden fantasies had returned to her psyche for another visit. She was perplexed because she had never responded mentally or physically to a man the way she did to the new priest. It was just a silly crush, a brief phase, she'd told herself. But her heart and flesh mocked those words and struck her with the truth.

As shepherd over the flock of Lord of the Harvest Roman Catholic Church, Father Gregory's divine order was to nurture Royce's soul. But if she were able to wish upon a star and be granted her most-desired wish, he would no longer be her priest. He would be her *lover*.

Chapter Three

"I read your next move. You're too predictable." Father Gregory shot the basketball he'd just stolen from Tyler straight through the hoop.

"I'm left-handed. It's hard for me to go to my right when I'm coming down the court."

"You'll have to work hard and master it if you want to make the basketball team at your school." Father Gregory threw a bounce pass, returning the ball to Tyler. "Now, let's try it again."

For an hour, with very few breaks in between, they went at it up and down the court. Each time Tyler tried to drive to the basket, Father Gregory put great defensive pressure on the left side of his body, forcing him to maneuver to his right. Sixth-grade boys' basketball tryouts at Saint Xavier's Preparatory Academy were coming up next week. Father Gregory had promised Tyler and Royce that he would spend as much time as he could spare helping Tyler improve his skills on the court. After all, Father Gregory was a decent baller, having played from middle school all the way through high school. Two private colleges had offered him scholarships to play for them, but athletics was not a part of his life's calling. His commitment to serve God and the church took precedence over everything else, including his personal life.

Up until recently, Father Gregory had never questioned or given a second thought to the path he'd chosen. The idea of living a life outside the priesthood was inconceivable once upon a time. Serving God and the church under the sacred vow of celibacy was his destiny, or so he'd thought. Until he met Royce a few weeks ago, he was 100 percent certain that he had been created to become a priest. Now, he was confused and unsure about everything. His faith was shaken, and he had a troubled soul. Royce's sudden entrance into his life was similar to a powerful tornado unexpectedly touching down on land in a small city. His world had been turned upside down.

The kinds of dreams he'd once dreamed at night had changed. Gone were the visions of him preaching to the masses in the West Indies or feeding the starving children of Kenya. His heavenly vision of meeting and spending quality time with Pope Francis had vanished, too. Royce's beautiful face and shapely body continuously invaded his dreams now. Every night she came to him in an erotic fantasy filled with a sizzling sexual encounter that snatched him from his sleep with a full erection and his body drenched with perspiration. Each dream was vivid and so lifelike. Father Gregory could actually feel Royce's soft hands exploring his body, stroking his hard penis, giving him pleasure. Her moans of fulfillment caressed his ears as his body thrust in and out of hers during their steamy lovemaking. He was convinced that he could taste Royce's chocolate nipples and smell the savory scent of her liquid desire in the air. As real as the dreams all seemed, they were sinful and shameful yet passionate and gratifying to his body and mind. The conflicting feelings of enjoying the nighttime fantasies while loathing the guilt and disgrace they caused left him torn.

Daybreak wasn't much kinder to Father Gregory. The sunlight did nothing to erase thoughts of Royce from his mind. Constantly throughout the day, he had to remind himself that he was in the Lord's house, where visions about making love were unacceptable. He would immerse himself into his work at the church, trying his best to recapture some semblance of his once calm and uneventful life as a priest. His days of tranquility, unwavering faith, and a strong commitment to his vow of celibacy seemed like a part of his past. It had all been replaced by fear, uncertainty, and the question of why the Roman Catholic Church would forbid a priest to take a wife.

Marriage was honorable in the sight of God. It was a holy ordinance. Eve had been created for the sole purpose of fulfilling Adam's needs. The Almighty knew it was not good for man to walk the earth alone without a mate. If the Creator sanctioned marriage, who was Man to disallow it for others? Father Gregory never in the past had questioned his church's policy against a priest's right to marry. He had simply accepted it as a sacred law that strengthened a man of the cloth's commitment to God and the church. Today he wasn't so sure about his belief in the marriage of a priest to his bride, the church. It no longer seemed sensible. And he was certain it wasn't natural.

Father Gregory took his eyes off the road for a few seconds to sneak a peek at Tyler. The child was sweating profusely after their basketball training session. His head was thrown back as he gulped down a sports beverage from a huge bottle.

Like many times before, the priest wanted to ask Tyler about the man he'd seen embracing Royce on her stoop that night of the Hawks game. Was he her boyfriend? He wasn't her fiancé. Father Gregory knew that for sure. There was no ring on Royce's left ring finger. Any man in his right mind who'd been blessed with a woman like her for a fiancée would have marked his territory with the biggest and most expensive diamond money could buy. No, the mystery man on Royce's stoop that evening was not her fiancé, but he could be one day. He wasn't a priest bound by a manmade tradition that prohibited him from ever marrying a beautiful woman or filling her womb with his seed to bear his children. The thought was unsettling in his spirit, and he didn't care to dwell on it.

"Will your aunt be home by the time we get there?"

"I think so. Why?"

The question, although totally innocent, made Father Gregory squirm uncomfortably in his seat. He tightened his grip on the steering wheel and smiled at Tyler. "I feel better whenever I leave your house knowing you're under the supervision of your aunt. That's why."

"I feel you. Hey, Auntie Royce said if I make the basketball team, she'll let me have a sleepover so I can celebrate with a few of my friends. I can only invite five guys over, though. Rico, my best friend, is coming for sure."

"You should make the team, Tyler. Your game has improved. We'll practice again Friday after we deliver commodities to the elderly in the Wilshire Retirement Village. That is, if your aunt approves. Ask her and let me know."

"Oh, she'll approve. Auntie Royce isn't mad at me anymore for the way I acted when I saw her with that dude. She said I was very rude and disrespectful. But I didn't mean to be. I just don't want her to have a boyfriend."

"So, was the guy your aunt's boyfriend?"

"No!" Tyler snapped. "He's just a friend. They hang out sometimes while our cousin, Andra, watches me, but I had never met him before. I guess I was surprised to see him, and it made me mad."

"Why are you so protective of your aunt?" Father Gregory probed with deep curiosity and concern.

"I'm responsible for her while my mom and dad are away. My grandparents down in Thomasville said I'm the man of the house while I'm living there or until she finds a husband." Tyler turned to his priest. "I don't want Auntie Royce to get married. Some men aren't nice to women."

"There are lots of good men out there who would treat your aunt like a queen if given the opportunity. Maybe she hasn't met the right one yet."

"If you weren't a priest, you could date her. I would like that because you're cool and I like you. I know you would never hurt Auntie Royce like that loser, Marlon, did."

"Who is Marlon, Tyler, and what did he do to your aunt?"

The boy turned to stare out the window. "I don't want to talk about it."

Royce self-consciously pulled the hem of her lavender T-shirt down over her hips and leggings. She stepped aside to allow Tyler and Father Gregory into the house. "I wasn't expecting company. Please excuse the way I'm dressed." She gave Tyler a kiss on the cheek as he crossed over the threshold. Then she quickly moved backward, careful not to touch Father Gregory. Royce didn't trust herself not to do something totally unladylike. The front door closed with a light thud.

"I just wanted to deliver your nephew safely to your doorstep. I'm sure he's famished. He burned a lot of energy on the basketball court today."

"Well, lucky for him, I left work early this afternoon so I could come home and prepare his favorite meal."

"Did you really, Auntie?" Tyler's eyes grew wide with excitement.

Royce couldn't help but laugh. "I sure did, sweetie. Go and wash up while I fix your plate."

"I'll leave you two to eat and enjoy each other's company."

"No, Father Gregory, you should stay. You've got to taste Auntie Royce's famous shrimp scampi and scallop linguine. It's the best."

"I'm sure Father Gregory has other plans for the evening. You know how busy priests are, honey," Royce said, running her fingers through her nephew's curly hair. She held her breath, hoping she was right about Father Gregory's schedule. She didn't want him in her private domain any longer than necessary. He was an invited guest in her dreams every night. She enjoyed him in her bedtime fantasies. But she didn't see a need for the physical torture his presence at her dinner table would inflict on her sex-deprived body.

"Come on, Father Gregory. You have to eat something, so you might as well eat the best seafood pasta in the world right here with us."

Royce noticed conflict straining the priest's countenance. He wanted to stay and have dinner with them, but something was holding him back from accepting the invitation. What was up with him?

"It does smell good," he finally said with a sexy smile on his face. "My mouth is watering. How can I refuse such delicious-smelling food?"

"Yes!" Tyler pumped his fist in the air. "I'll be right back. I'm going to wash my face and hands."

Chapter Four

"Tyler, it's time to take a shower, honey. You have school tomorrow. And I'll bet Father Gregory has something more important to do tonight than play video games with you. Lots of people depend on him. Who knows when a church emergency might require his attention?"

"We've got to play one more game to break the tie, Auntie Royce. I promise just one more game."

Royce folded her arms across her chest and leaned against the doorjamb, watching her nephew and their priest battle it out in a game of *NBA 2K17*. Dinner had been a smooth and pleasant experience. The food was exceptional, she had to humbly admit. Tyler had dominated the mealtime conversation, mostly talking about school and basketball. A few times during dinner, Royce had caught Father Gregory staring at her from across the table. She had only noticed him checking her out because she'd taken frequent peeks at him as well. His penetrating gaze caused her body to shudder with nervousness and rise in temperature. It could've very well been Royce's imagination, but she thought she'd detected a hint of something in the depths of his ebony orbs that was akin to desire.

No one had ever accused her of having an inflated ego or being arrogant because of her good looks before. But she could usually tell when a man had the hots for her. She was seldom wrong when it came to reading a male admirer's vibe. Then again, it was Father Gregory, her priest. He could've been praying for God to bless her home because of the hospitality she'd extended to him. Or he may have been in deep meditation. Royce had no idea, but something in his eyes, smile, and body language had pushed all of her feminine heat buttons whether he'd intended to or not. Tonight's dream would be hotter than all of the ones before it. The priest's invasion of her home, and him sporting a navy and white jogging suit that displayed more of his magnificent physique than she'd been prepared to see, would no doubt take her nighttime fantasies to a brand-new level of heat.

Waterloo, Sierra Leone
West Africa

"Once again, you're allowing your overactive imagination to get you all riled up."

"No, I'm not, Eric. You didn't hear Royce's voice. She sounded bubbly, almost animated. You wouldn't have thought she was talking about her priest. She was raving on and on like she was talking about a *man*."

Dr. Eric Benson reached over and took his wife's hand as they walked side by side down the hall of the small medical clinic. He stopped in his stride and held her in place. "Royce is a sensible chick. She would never make a move on a holy man, and if he were to ever make a pass at her, she would shut him down immediately. So, stop worrying about nothing, okay?"

"I have a funny feeling in the pit of my stomach. Something ain't quite right. I understand why the new priest is spending time with Tyler. We agreed he needed counseling. But why is the man eating dinner at Royce's kitchen table and washing her car?"

"He ate dinner with them twice. Both times were after basketball drills. Father Gregory helped Tyler wash Royce's car when he arrived early to pick him up for the youth dance at the church. What's the big deal?" Eric removed his keys from the pocket of his white lab coat and unlocked the door to his office.

Zora rushed inside the office ahead of her husband. She turned and narrowed her eyes at him after he closed the door behind them. "The big deal is my little sister sounded like a teenage girl with a crush on the cutest male teacher in the whole damn school! She was giggling and babbling about how deep he is into fitness. Did you know he drives a red sports car? What kind of priest shoots basketball, pumps iron, and whips around town in a two-seater?"

"He's the same priest who tutors our son, trains him for basketball tryouts, and keeps him out of trouble at school."

Eric took a seat behind his desk and busied himself making notes in a stack of charts. Zora stood in place above the desk as her mind replayed the conversation she'd had with Royce early that morning. She was convinced she wasn't imagining anything. There was something strange going on between her little sister and the new priest at Lord of the Harvest Roman Catholic Church.

From the pictures Tyler had emailed to her a few days ago, Zora had learned that Father Gregory was a tall, fit, and fine-looking man. Any woman could find herself drawn to him, but not Royce. She was supposed to know better. After the fiasco with Marlon Burrell, her need for caution when dealing with members of the opposite sex should've been heightened to the highest degree. Stylish-dressing hunks who talked fast and dreamed over-the-top dreams had been banned from her life forever. Married men and good-looking gold diggers didn't stand a chance either. But priests were absolutely off-limits. They were considered taboo for any devout Catholic woman, the ultimate no-no. A million Hail Marys couldn't save Royce from the consuming flames of hell if she were to lay a finger on Father Gregory. It didn't matter how handsome his face looked or how chiseled his body was. Royce had better hang a cross around her neck and invest in a chastity belt. No matter what measures were necessary, under no circumstances should she fall for a priest. Ever.

***

"Whoa!" Royce yelled after Tyler burst into her home office out of breath. He almost knocked the chair over with her sitting in it. "What's going on?"

"I made the team! I made the team, Auntie Royce! The coach posted the names this afternoon."

"Congratulations! I'm so proud of you, Tyler." She wrapped her arms around his lanky body and squeezed. "Let's order pizza from Romano's Italian Kitchen to celebrate."

"Cool! But I've got to call Father Gregory first. Can I invite him over to eat with us? I never would've made the cut without his help."

Royce wanted to see Father Gregory. God and Satan alike knew she truly did. But she'd made a promise to herself that she would stay clear of him at any cost. As much as she hated to disappoint Tyler, she had to do the right thing. "You may call him and tell him your good news, but I think we should celebrate alone this evening. I've had a long and busy day. I don't have the energy to play host to anyone except you, sweetie."

"But you won't have to do anything. I'll set the table and wash the plates. I can—"

"I'm sorry, Tyler," Royce apologized, shaking her head. "It'll be just you and me this evening."

"Congratulations again, buddy. I'm very proud of you. I'll see you at mass Sunday morning."

Father Gregory hung up the phone and swiveled around in his chair a few times in deep thought. He was happy Tyler had earned a spot on the basketball team at Saint Xavier's. The boy was so excited that he'd talked nonstop for twenty minutes on the phone. The priest smiled, reflecting on the sound of his raspy voice filled with enthusiasm over his accomplishment. Tyler had worked tirelessly to earn a spot on the team. No one knew that better than Father Gregory. That's why nothing would've pleased him more than to have been able to celebrate with Tyler and Royce this evening. But for some unknown reason, she had balked at the idea. Her claim that she was exhausted from work made sense to Tyler, and he'd accepted it as the gospel truth. But Father Gregory had a hard time believing it. He wondered if Royce had other plans. Maybe her friend was coming over later after Tyler had gone to sleep. It was a possibility. Royce had probably planned a romantic evening with the guy. Father Gregory couldn't help but wonder if the man would spend the night and share Royce's bed with her.

He stood from his seat and began to pace the floor inside his spacious office. It was not his business how Royce conducted her life. His duty as her priest was to pray for her and offer her spiritual guidance on her Christian journey whenever she sought his counsel. Even so, Father Gregory's feelings for Royce, outside of the sanctity of the priesthood, were genuine. He didn't want her heart to be broken again by a man undeserving of her affections. He didn't know the details about her relationship with the Marlon character Tyler had spoken of, but he sensed the man had caused Royce undue pain. He was the reason the boy was so overprotective of his aunt and distrustful of any man who expressed the slightest interest in her. It was humorous, because the only man Tyler approved of spending time with his aunt was one who was forbidden by his religion to have any personal dealings with her. But Tyler had no authority over his aunt's personal life, and neither did Father Gregory.

The reality of the situation was clear and could not be changed. Royce was a modern-day woman with no husband. There were no restraints on her social life, from a religious aspect or otherwise, that prohibited her from dating. It was not a spiritual offense for single men and women to court one another in the Catholic Church. However, fornication was indeed a sin in the sight of God. But so was lust of the flesh. It was a transgression that Father Gregory fought to overcome every day. Thus far, he was losing the battle, but he wanted desperately to rise above his fault and please God. That had always been his desire. His heart for ministry had not changed. His circumstances had. Just like King David's ungodly craving for Bathsheba, Father Gregory was in a constant struggle with his desire for Royce. But he was determined not to fall. Maybe it was best that he hadn't been invited to the Phillips home for the pizza celebration. As always, God had protected him from temptation.

Chapter Five

Tyler released air from his cheeks and shot the ball and missed. He closed his eyes as sweat poured down his face, and he frowned at the laughter and heckling that exploded throughout the gym.

Damien, the center and tallest guy on the team, retrieved the basketball. "You're a loser. How did you make the team?"

"Maybe he should be playing for the girls!" yelled Romello, the team captain and starting point guard. He gave a couple of his amused teammates a high five.

"That's enough! No one has the right to criticize anyone else's skills or lack thereof on the court until you all have mastered the plays. Now, quit your yapping and let's take it from half court." Coach Yarborough looked at Tyler head-on. "You can make this shot, Benson. I know you can. You've got to believe in yourself. Don't let your teammates get inside your head."

The Saint Xavier Bobcats ran the same play five more times before Tyler finally made the shot. By then, his teammates were frustrated and didn't care to join in the celebration with him and Coach Yarborough. They all left the court and headed for the locker room with major attitudes.

"They don't like me, Coach," Tyler mumbled, tilting his head toward the other guys on the team. "Damien and Romello said I'm not good enough to play with them. Maybe they're right. It did take me a while to nail that shot."

"Forget about them. I chose you because you're a team player and you know how to follow instructions. The fundamentals of basketball are second nature to you. The other coaches and I can tell you've been trained well."

"I practice every day except Sundays. On Tuesdays and Thursdays, Father Gregory drills me for hours. He's taught me a lot."

"It's evident. Besides that, your grade point average is higher than every other boy's on the squad. You may be the only kid on the court if Damien, Romello, and their crew don't start cracking the books."

Tyler gave Coach Yarborough a half smile before he walked away feeling much better. With more practice, his game would improve and build his confidence. Father Gregory would help him.

***

"I'll serve the food and drinks as soon as your last guest arrives."

"Okay. He'll be here soon!" Tyler yelled over the noise in the room. His eyes never left the television screen as his hands shifted fast and wildly, maneuvering the video game remote.

Royce smiled and shook her head. She must've lost her mind, allowing Tyler to invite five sixth-grade boys over for an entire weekend. The noise level had spiked off the chart. Jokes and trash talk could be heard all the way in the kitchen, where Tyler's favorite party treats were being prepared by Ms. Essie, Royce's housekeeper. The boys had cluttered the den terribly with paper cups, candy wrappers, and smelly tennis shoes. It was expected to get a lot worse after the food had been served. Boys were just plain old messy, and it wasn't a secret. But Royce didn't care this weekend. It was all about Tyler. His behavior at school had improved and so had his grades. And to put the icing on the cake, he was now a member of the Saint Xavier's Bobcats basketball team.

The doorbell rang, announcing the arrival of Tyler's fifth and final overnight guest. Royce stepped over a few duffel bags and a pile of sleeping bags scattered about the floor. Neither Tyler nor his rowdy group of visitors responded to the chime rippling through the house. They were too busy laughing and yelling over the competitive video game in progress. Royce's den reminded her of a boy's college dorm room. She hurried to the door barefoot to welcome the last boy to the slumber party. Smiling, she pulled the door handle and was immediately struck by something with more crackle than lightning.

"Ms. Phillips, how are you this evening?"

Sound and time paused as Royce took in the raw masculinity of the chocolate god standing tall on her stoop. Her eyes undressed him shamelessly before her proper Southern upbringing snatched her back to decency, dousing her flame of lust.

"Come in, Father Gregory. I'm surprised to see you."

He entered the house. Then he stuffed his hands inside the pockets of his jeans and smiled. Royce almost fainted. The simple motion drew attention to his thighs and the manly member nestled between them. Royce lifted her eyes back to Father Gregory's handsome face.

"I promised Tyler I would stop by for a couple of hours if I finished up at the church in time. I hope it's okay with you that I'm here."

Royce filed a mental memo to lock Tyler in the basement for thirty days with no food or water for inviting the priest to his get-together without asking her permission. "It's fine," she lied. "I told him he could invite whomever he wanted to as long as I was familiar with the boy and his parents. You're not exactly a boy, though, Father Gregory. I haven't met your parents either."

"I can call my mother right now." He grinned and reached inside the pocket of his black leather bomber as if he were searching for his cell phone. "She and my stepfather will gladly tell you how great a guy I am."

Royce returned his infectious smile, deciding to play his little game of dare. "Or maybe your parents will tell me all of your secrets."

"I don't have any secrets. Honestly, I was a good kid. Mom, Max, and my sisters can confirm it. They knew I was going to be a priest even way back when I was in elementary school. Hopefully, they'll all visit me some time this coming spring. I'll invite you and Tyler over so you can meet them. You'll hear all kinds of stories about my years as an altar boy who loved basketball and church. What were you like as a young girl?"

Royce attempted to hide her shock, but she was totally caught off guard by Father Gregory's question. She regained her composure. "You'll have to follow me into the kitchen if you want to know about my misbehaviors as a child growing up in South Georgia. Essie probably thinks I ran off and left her to serve the food to the boys all by herself. Come with me."

Fascinating. No other word could better describe Royce Phillips as far as Father Gregory was concerned. She was like a human magnet. Her bubbly and spicy personality pulled you in and made you want to be in her presence forever. She was quite entertaining, too.

Tyler and his friends were enjoying her wild sense of humor and her playful nature. Royce had accepted every challenge they'd set before her. They hadn't expected her to shoot hoops with them outside on the court situated in her sprawling backyard. Then there was the water balloon fight that her team had won hands down against Tyler's team. Father Gregory was amazed by Royce's energy level and ability to out-strategize a group of youngsters without much effort at all. And she was a skillful dancer. Rico, Tyler's best friend, had pumped up some music from his digital recording device, which he'd connected to a pair of large stereo speakers in the corner of the den. Royce rushed into the room and started wiggling and gyrating to the beat like a teenager.

The boys went crazy over her impromptu performance. Two of them responded with some hip-hop moves made popular by singers and rappers on the music video channels. Father Gregory hadn't danced since his high school senior prom eleven years ago, but he was tempted to join in on the action the instant he saw Royce's hips swaying and thrusting rhythmically to the music. His better judgment kicked in, and he stayed put in his corner of the den, where he watched her in awe until the song ended. Royce then returned to the kitchen to prepare movie-time snacks for the boys. Gory horror movies were next on their agenda. The requests for popcorn, chili dogs, and soda seemed only natural.

Father Gregory wandered mindlessly into the kitchen a few minutes after Royce had left the den. Her back was to him as she prepared platters of food for Tyler and his guests at the stainless-steel center island. Ms. Essie had gone home for the evening, leaving all of the kitchen duties to Royce until tomorrow morning.

"Do you need any help?"

Royce's high-pitched shriek bounced off the kitchen's four walls. She spun around quickly, clutching her chest. She was visibly startled. "Oh, my God! You scared me."

"Forgive me," Father Gregory apologized, rushing to her side. He sincerely hadn't meant to frighten her. He rubbed the center of Royce's back in a circular motion. The gesture had been intended to soothe her, but touching her singed his palm and caused it to tremble. Her skin was soft, and the scent of vanilla rising from her pores teased him into an aroused state. He withdrew his hand and backed away. "Are you okay?"

"I'm fine." Royce smiled and turned around to lift a platter from the island. "And yes, I could use some help. You can serve the boys these chili dogs while I gather the rest of the snacks."

Chapter Six

Royce collapsed forward on the island and rested her head after Father Gregory left the kitchen. Her nerves were completely frazzled and her body engulfed with pure lust. The priest had frightened her within seconds of a heart attack it seemed, but that wasn't the most troubling effect his surprise visit to the kitchen had caused. His closeness, the rich tone of his voice, and his God-given good looks had combined and launched a terrible attack against Royce. It had left her fever-ish with feminine need. She wanted the man in the worst way, and she was afraid she would offer herself to him if he didn't leave her home soon.

Royce hurried to the refrigerator to find something cool to drink. Her body temperature had shot through the roof. Anything wet and cold would perhaps help bring it down. There was half a bottle of Riesling tucked between several jugs of the assorted organic fruit juices Royce usually drank. She actually preferred a beverage a hell of a lot stronger than the German white wine, but it would have to do for now. Royce uncorked the bottle and took a long swig like a Saturday-night wino. She swallowed hard and immediately felt a relieving buzz, but it did nothing to quench her thirst for a certain sexy priest roaming around in her den.

Sighing in frustration, Royce put the wine back in the refrigerator and returned to the island. She grabbed the huge bowl of popcorn and a handful of napkins and made dreaded steps in the direction of the den. The silence she met at the entrance was kind of eerie. It was dark in the room with the exception of the light from the big-screen television. Five pairs of preadolescent male eyes were glued to the drama unfolding as the surround-sound speakers blasted screams of horror throughout the room. Father Gregory was just as absorbed in the scary movie as the boys.

Royce wasn't a fan of ghosts, vampires, or psychotic mass murderers, but she wanted to hang out with Tyler and his friends for as long as her energy level would allow her to. She placed the popcorn and napkins on the coffee table and searched for an available space to sit. God must've been playing a cruel joke on her, because there was only one vacant seat in the entire room and it was right beside Father Gregory. Royce felt trapped. She looked at the empty cushion and then at Father Gregory. In that instant, his eyes left the television screen and locked with hers. Even through the darkness, Royce saw a twinkle in their depths. And when he smiled, air swooshed from her lungs. The sight took her breath away, literally.

"There's enough room for you right here," Father Gregory offered in a tone deep enough to make James Earl Jones insane with jealousy. He patted the vacant spot to his right on the loveseat.

Royce now had an idea of how Daniel must've felt walking into the lion's den against his will. The fear of being devoured by something or someone greater and more powerful was paralyzing. And Father Gregory, although clueless to the fact, most definitely had the ability to melt Royce with just one touch. Thank God they were in a room with five preteen boys or otherwise . . .

"Thank you," Royce finally said softly and took the seat next to the man who gave her reason to pause yet tempted her to throw caution to the wind at the same time.

Moments later, there was a scene in the movie where a gross and badly decomposed corpse emerged from a lake armed with an ax. The creepy male character hopped inside a rowboat occupied by a group of six unassuming teenagers.

His shell of a body was covered with blood and swamp slime. Growling and spitting, the ax man went into a chopping fit, swinging and slashing his deadly weapon. Royce screamed and buried her face in Father Gregory's rock-solid chest when she saw the head belonging to one of the teenage girls disconnect from her neck and splash into the lake. The unattached head caused the water to turn a deep shade of red with her blood.

Tyler and his friends thought the gruesome murder scene was cool and thrilling. They laughed and cheered their approval, totally entertained. The sound of loud, desperate cries and a dramatic shift in the movie's background music told Royce the ax-wielding creature from the lake was not done with his fatal assault. She trembled against Father Gregory's body and pressed her face closer to his chest. He draped his long arm around her shoulders, and it felt damn good. Royce was wrong for feeling the way she was feeling, but she was a woman, and for the moment, Father Gregory was just a man.

Royce turned off the television and tiptoed around the sleeping bodies sprawled out on the floor in the den. Father Gregory was a few steps behind her, admiring the view of her backside. It was tight, round, and the ideal size. He imagined it would fit perfectly between his palms as he rubbed and squeezed it while kissing her into delirium. Father Gregory hadn't meant to moan, but the thought of holding Royce in his arms and tasting her lips and tongue had a powerful effect on his body. It was sensually explosive.

"Did you say something, Father Gregory?" She stopped and turned around to face him.

"No."

He followed Royce into the kitchen. It was way past midnight. Father Gregory had stayed at the party much longer than he'd planned to, but he still wasn't ready to leave yet. He was torn between doing the right thing, the godly thing, and following his heart.

"I have a nightly ritual," Royce announced and smiled as if she were about to reveal something classified top secret. "There have been very few nights over the past three years that I've gone to bed without a cup of cinnamon and brown sugar tea. It's an herbal blend that helps me relax. I definitely need a cup tonight after watching that awful movie. Would you like to try some?"

Father Gregory smiled and took a seat at the table. "I'll have some tea. Thank you. I must admit I enjoyed the movie. It's not the type of flick I would've selected, though. You see, I'm more of an action and adventure fan, but the horror movie did hold my attention. I'm sorry it traumatized you."

"I'm fine," Royce assured him, placing the tea kettle on the stove. "I missed most of the more graphic scenes. You should know that. My face was basically plastered to your sweater. I hope I didn't wrinkle it or stretch it out of shape too bad."

"I don't think you did any damage at all."

Truthfully, Royce hadn't spoiled Father Gregory's sweater one bit, but she had tortured his body. Every time her hands touched his chest and she buried her face against it, his belly flip-flopped. Her innocent movements caused tightening in his groin. The vanilla scent of her skin and her warm breath fanning over his sensitive pectoral muscles as she pressed her face closer to his chest intensified his erection. His rigid, engorged shaft had pressed painfully against the zipper of his jeans for the duration of the movie.

Father Gregory had been uncomfortable with his body's compromised state, but he'd found pleasure in being so close to Royce. How could he have not? It wasn't every day a man in his position could spend time and share space with a woman he was attracted to. Every moment in Royce's presence was magical. She was the object of Father Gregory's desire and his greatest temptation. Even as he watched her reach for the teacups in the cabinet, he wrestled with his flesh. He wanted to take her in his arms, kiss her deeply, and explore her body with his fingertips. But he wouldn't be able to stop there. It wasn't possible. His desire for her was too powerful.

Royce turned around with a cup of steaming hot tea in each hand. She walked slowly over to the table and carefully set one on the placemat in front of Father Gregory and the other one to his right. He watched her as she walked around the kitchen gathering teaspoons, sugar, and honey. She was a vision of loveliness, wearing a red velour jogging suit and matching red and white sneakers. Her braids had been pulled back and secured neatly in a red elastic band at her nape. When Royce returned to the table, Father Gregory immediately got up and pulled out her chair like his stepfather had taught him. He retook his seat and smiled at Royce.

"Thank you."

"You're welcome."

"Tyler told me you want to go on a Christian mission to Africa. What countries are you considering?"

"I would love to travel the entire continent if I could. However, I've narrowed my choices down to Kenya, South Sudan, and Ethiopia."

"Why are you only interested in East African nations?"

Father Gregory took a sip of his tea and chuckled lightly. "Good question."

It *was* a good question. But it was only the first of many to come. Royce and Father Gregory sipped tea and questioned one another on several topics as hours ticked by. They laughed, talked, and even debated a few issues. And they held nothing back. Each indulged the other on subjects that were serious and thought-provoking. There were funny moments as well. Royce had a great sense of humor, and she was very smart, too. The more she opened up to Father Gregory, the stronger his magnetism toward her grew. He ignored his need for sleep and the fact that he had an early morning meeting with the deacons at the church. Unknowingly, the extraordinary Royce Phillips had cast a spell on him, and he was defenseless against it. With every passing hour, he knew he should've left her, but he couldn't. He was mesmerized, planted in his chair. It wasn't until the dark sky began its transformation into dawn, with the stars giving way to the sun, that Father Gregory snapped out of his trance.

"It's morning. I didn't mean to spend the night."

"You were invited to a *sleepover*," Royce reminded him with laughter in her voice.

"I was, wasn't I?"

She nodded.

"Yet neither one of us slept at all. As a matter of fact, I cheated you out of some beauty rest, although you don't need any. I mean, of course you need to rest. You just don't have to worry about the beauty part."

Father Gregory drew in a deep breath when Royce lowered her eyes and blushed. Her humility regarding her stunning good looks was remarkable. If any woman had a right to be vain, Royce certainly did, but she chose to be meek instead. That made her even more beautiful. Her predawn glow made her look angelic yet sinfully irresistible at the same time.

"Thank you," Royce mumbled in a soft voice seasoned with shyness.

"I only spoke the truth." He stood from his seat. "I'll walk you to the door."

Chapter Seven

"Thank you for coming to hang out with Tyler and his crew. I could tell he was happy you showed up."

Father Gregory smiled, and for the first time, Royce noticed a deep dimple in his left cheek. It was a total turn-on. Every woman appreciated a good-looking man with a great smile and dimples. The new discovery caused the imaginary butterflies in her belly to flutter.

With his hands tucked inside of the pockets of his black leather bomber, Father Gregory stared at the ecru marble floor in the foyer briefly before he looked into Royce's eyes. "I had fun."

"I'm glad you did."

He snapped his fingers as if he'd suddenly remembered something important. "Make sure you remind Tyler and his friends about the trip to the Blue Ridge Mountains next month. They'll all need to come to the meeting on Wednesday at the church along with their parents to sign up."

"I'll tell them."

They fell silent as seconds passed. A longing, the likes of which Royce had never experienced before, swept her away and into another world. The man standing an arm's length away from her was no longer a priest, the forbidden recipient of her affections. In Royce's dream-filled eyes, he was the antidote for her ailment of an aching and abstinent heart. Her desire for him instantly upgraded to a necessity.

Before rational and sound judgment could deter her actions, Royce threw her arms around Father Gregory's neck and covered his lips with her hungry ones. She whimpered and moaned when she felt his strong arms encircle her waist and pull her body fully against his. Her tongue twirled, tasted, and teased his, and he became aroused. His penis, large and harder than steel, pressing against Royce's lower body near her feminine spot caused hot liquid desire to pool in the crotch of her panties. She instinctively ground her vagina against his erection as his tongue twisted and tantalized hers. The spark that began with a kiss elevated to an inferno, threatening to burn out of control the moment Father Gregory lowered his hands from Royce's waist to squeeze her bottom. She became weak and wanton. Her nipples hardened and tingled. She caressed his back and neck and reached up to run her fingers through his hair. The feel of his hands rubbing and gripping her backside was pushing her closer and closer to the edge. Royce was feverish with need. Her body and soul were on fire. The blaze was satisfying and sweet.

The boys' voices and the sound of the television in the den coming to life interrupted the kiss. Royce quickly stepped away from Father Gregory, trying to catch her breath. Her mind left the fifth dimension and returned to sanity. Royce felt ashamed. She avoided eye contact with Father Gregory.

"Royce," he whispered and extended his hand to her.

She shook her head and backed away with tears in her eyes. "I am so sorry. I . . . I don't know what came over me. I had no right to kiss you. I feel like such a fool."

"No. It was my fault. I could have stopped it from happening. I should've stopped it, but I didn't."

"You should leave now." Royce rushed to the door and unlocked it. "Tyler and his friends are awake. If they see you—"

"I understand, but we need to talk about this."

"I don't think so. Let's just forget about it. Okay?" Royce lowered her head in shame. Tears spilled from her eyes.

Father Gregory reached out and cupped her chin and gently lifted her face. Their eyes met. "I can't forget about it and neither can you. We *will* discuss what happened here. I'll call you. Goodbye, Royce."

"Your sermon this morning was very moving, Father Gregory."

The priest smiled and shook the older woman's hand. "God bless you, Mrs. Nottingham."

Once she hobbled away with the support of a cane, he reached for the hand of the next person in the long line of parishioners waiting to greet him. Careful to maintain his smile despite the inward turmoil raging within, Father Gregory greeted a young couple and their infant daughter. The hand shaking and the exchanging of pleasantries continued as church members made their way toward the priest.

His eyes drifted to the back of the line, where he noticed Tyler standing. Royce wasn't with him, and Father Gregory knew exactly why. She was avoiding him, as she had been since the kiss they'd shared. He had called her several times over the past twenty-four hours so they could talk about what had happened between them, but she hadn't answered her cell phone. He then attempted to reach her on her land line, but both times Tyler had claimed she was busy cooking and hosting his guests.

Father Gregory was sure she was having a difficult time sorting through her emotions over the kiss. He too was still trying to wrap his mind around it. Their passionate display of feelings they obviously had for each other would forever be embedded in his memory. He had relived the moment over and over again, recalling how amazing it'd felt to hold Royce in his arms and kiss her like he'd done a thousand times in his dreams. The pleasure far exceeded anything he'd ever envisioned. Her soft and supple body meshing with his as their lips and tongues mated was the most physically satisfying experience of his life. But it could never happen again, even though Father Gregory believed he would dwindle away and die if it didn't.

Tyler was now a few feet away. He smiled and waved at Father Gregory, and he nodded to acknowledge the boy. The next several parishioners filed past him in a blur. Their words and comments about the morning mass went unheard. Father Gregory didn't even see their faces. Royce occupied every corner of his mind.

"What's up, Father Gregory? You did your thing this morning. I think King Solomon was a real cool cat the way he built that fly temple and all."

"So, you didn't fall asleep during the sermon this morning?" He folded his arms across his chest and smiled.

"Oh, no, sir. I was really feeling it."

Father Gregory hesitated, a little uneasy about asking the question that had nagged him all during the mass. But he needed to know, and Tyler was the only person who could give him an answer. "Where is your aunt this morning?"

"She was tired, so she stayed home to catch up on her rest."

"How did you get to church?"

"I hitched a ride with Mrs. Tennyson. That's Rico's mom. He was the last guy to leave the sleepover. I asked them to drop me off here on their way home. I was hoping that you would give me a ride back if you're not too busy."

"No problem. I'll drive you home, but you'll have to wait for me to finish talking to the rest of the church members."

"Cool. I'll see you outside."

"Auntie Royce, I'm home!" He turned to Father Gregory. "I smell food cooking. She must be in the kitchen. Come on."

Tyler led the priest into the kitchen where they found Royce standing at the stove, stirring something in a saucepot. She was humming. There was another pot, a much bigger one, filled with simmering contents on another burner.

"It smells good in here, Auntie. What're you cooking?"

Royce spun around with a wooden spoon in her hand, slightly startled. Then she flinched with embarrassment when she noticed Father Gregory standing a couple of feet behind Tyler. "I didn't hear you come in, sweetie." She approached her nephew and planted a soft kiss on his forehead. "How are you, Father Gregory?"

"I'm fine. I missed you at church this morning."

"I was exhausted, so I slept in. Thank you for bringing Tyler home. It was very nice of you."

"It wasn't a problem. Anyway, I thought it would give me an opportunity to talk to you about something."

Time was officially up. Royce hadn't really expected that she could avoid forever Father Gregory and the conversation they were destined to have. It was inevitable. The air between them most definitely needed to be cleared so her world could return to normal, whatever that meant. Even after they set boundaries in place, and Royce was sure that they would, her life would never be the same again. She had experienced a gratifying release of passion in the arms of Father Gregory, and there was no way in hell she would be able to look at him as just her priest anymore. He was a sexy, desirable, virile man. She knew that now without a doubt. Royce had imagined what his tongue would taste like and how his body would feel under her fingertips. The memory of the pressure of his erect shaft grinding into her core caused a streak of heat to shoot up her spine.

Royce swallowed hard. "Lunch is almost ready. You might as well stay and eat with us. You and I can talk afterward."

Chapter Eight

"I'm sorry," Royce and Father Gregory blurted out in unison as soon as Tyler left them alone in the kitchen.

"I apologize for allowing the situation to spiral out of control, Royce, but I have no regrets."

"Do you mean you wanted me to kiss you?"

"I must confess that I'd thought about it, wondering how it would feel. How could I not have? You are a very beautiful woman with a charming personality, and I'm attracted to you."

Royce sighed, looking into Father Gregory's eyes. "I'm attracted to you too. What do you suggest we do about the chemistry between us? We couldn't possibly enter into an affair, could we?"

"Of course not." He reached across the table, took Royce's hand into his, and returned her gaze. There was nothing he desired more than a romantic relationship with her, but it wasn't possible. Life seemed so unfair at the moment. "I'm a priest. It would be a sin for me to become involved with you. My vow to God and the church won't allow it. I took an oath of celibacy. It's a serious and sacred oath. I'm married to my church, Royce. There can never be anything romantic between us."

"I understand."

"Do you really? I don't want you to think that I'm rejecting you for any reason other than the religious calling on my life. You're extremely desirable, Royce. The hours we spent talking that night were special. And the kiss . . . it was the most amazing experience I've ever shared with anyone. If I weren't a priest, you and I would be together if you would have me."

"Oh, I would," Royce whispered on a soft breath.

"I'm sorry, but it just isn't meant to be. We can't ever be alone together again. The temptation is much too great. We're emotionally and physically attracted to each other, so it wouldn't be wise to test our wills."

"What about Tyler? Are you going to stop spending time with him because of me?"

Father Gregory shook his head. "I'm committed to Tyler. I'll continue tutoring and counseling him. He and I will practice basketball drills on our scheduled days as usual. But you and I," he said, pointing his index finger back and forth between them, "we can only be in each other's presence when others are around. Are we clear?"

"Perfectly."

"Very well. Tyler's first basketball game of the season will be Tuesday. I'll be there to support him. I suppose you'll attend."

"Yeah, I'll be the crazy lady cheering louder than everyone else in the gym."

"Auntie Royce, the telephone is for you." Tyler appeared at the kitchen door with a cell phone in his hand.

"Take a message, honey."

"It's my mom. She says it's important."

Father Gregory stood from his chair. "Thanks again for lunch. I'm going to leave now so you can talk to your sister." He turned to Tyler, remembering what had happened the last time his aunt had walked him to her front door. "Come walk me out, buddy."

Royce took the cell phone from the boy when he walked past her. "Hey, girl."

"What is Father Gregory doing at your house again, Royce?"

"He brought Tyler home from church because I didn't go this morning. I showed my appreciation by inviting him to lunch."

"My son said you guys finished eating lunch over an hour ago. He told me you were in the kitchen talking to Father Gregory. What is going on between you two, Royce?"

"There's nothing going on, Zora. I promise."

"You have a crush on him. I can feel in my gut."

"I'm not in high school anymore. I'm a grown-ass woman. I don't have crushes."

Zora sat down on the bed and crossed her legs. She wanted to believe what Royce was telling her was true, but her strong instincts wouldn't allow her to. "You better not play with fire, Royce Dominique. You will get burned."

"I won't play with fire. How is Eric?"

"Don't try to change the subject," Zora snapped. "I'm warning you. Stay away from Father Gregory. The two of you have gotten a little too chummy for my taste, and it's dangerous."

"You're worrying about nothing, sis."

"Can I assume that you and Brandon have gotten closer?" Zora massaged her temples when she heard Royce pop her lips in what she perceived to be annoyance.

"Brandon is not the man for me, sis. He just doesn't ring my bell. I talk to him on the phone from time to time, but you can uncross your fingers if you're expecting a love connection."

Zora and Royce's conversation didn't last much longer after that revelation. The older sister had actually called to chat with her son anyway, but after he informed her that Father Gregory had joined them for lunch, she demanded to speak to Royce. Zora believed her warning to her sister regarding Father Gregory had fallen on deaf ears, and that disturbed her. She loved Royce, and she didn't want her to experience another broken heart. But if she was fooling around with a priest, she was going to face something a whole lot worse than heartbreak.

"Yes!" Royce bolted from her seat on the bleacher with both hands raised high in the air.

Tyler had just scored his third basket of the game. Father Gregory was excited too, but he wasn't as animated and expressive as Royce. Whenever Tyler touched the ball, she clapped and cheered loudly, encouraging him. Her simple outfit, consisting of a pair of tight, faded jeans and a royal blue and gold Saint Xavier's sweatshirt, made her look as young and jovial as the cheerleaders. She had pulled her braids into a side ponytail to complete her youthful look. She was stunning even in her casual attire. And she smelled lovely.

Royce jumped up again and cupped her mouth with both hands. "Booo! Booo! You need some glasses, ref! That was a clean block!"

Father Gregory tore his eyes away from the foul line, where a member of the opposing team was preparing to shoot a pair of free throws. He smiled at Royce and shook his head in awe. She was quite knowledgeable about the game of basketball, and she didn't mind challenging the referee's calls. By nature, she was high-spirited, which amused Father Gregory.

He tapped Royce gently on her thigh to get her attention and regretted it immediately. It didn't matter that they were in a gym half filled with other spectators. An innocent touch to any part of her body had the same stimulating effect on his that it would have if they were alone in her bedroom. It aroused him.

"Am I embarrassing you?" Royce looked down at Father Gregory and asked.

"I'm not embarrassed. I just don't want you to upset the ref so much that he'll give the game to the other team. He may go blind all of a sudden and start missing some fouls against our boys. Or he might slap them with fouls they don't deserve."

"Okay, I'll sit down and try to chill out for the rest of the game. But I'll have to make a lot of noise whenever Tyler scores. Is that cool?"

"Yes, it's cool," he told her, trying not to laugh.

It didn't matter if Royce sat down and kept as quiet as a church mouse. She was still hard to ignore. Every time she made a sudden shift in position on the bleacher, her thigh would brush against Father Gregory's, driving him crazy. And as usual, the heavenly scent of vanilla clinging to her soft skin stirred his manly sense. Then there was the memory of them kissing in her foyer, which was sketched in his memory.

Father Gregory couldn't undo the spell Royce had cast on him. He longed for the day when he would wake up completely immune to her raw femininity. His daily prayer was for God to deliver him from his lustful attraction to her. He'd also reaffirmed his vow of celibacy to God. The single kiss he and Royce had shared was an awakening call to nature. It made Father Gregory keenly conscious that in addition to being an ordained priest, he was indeed human, and more specifically, a man. His flesh had needs and desires just like his regular male counterparts, but as a clergyman sworn to celibacy, he knew God required much more of him than others. Therefore, it had been necessary for him to repent and recommit his body, soul, and mind to the Lord after his experience with Royce. Father Gregory refused to fall into temptation again.

"You blew the damn game! How did you miss that shot, Benson? You were wide open!'

Tyler slammed his locker shut and glared at Romello. "You missed a lot of shots, ball hog!

Grady and Quan were open plenty of times, but you wouldn't pass them the ball. You wanted to show off, so you kept shooting bricks. That's how we fell behind in the first place."

"I'm the team captain. I have to make important decisions." Romello approached Tyler to stand nose to nose with him. "I did what I thought would help us win. I passed you the ball because I believed you could tie the game. That was a big mistake. You suck!" He shoved Tyler hard into the row of lockers.

"You suck!" Tyler yelled, shoving him back with all his might.

"Hey! What's going on in here?" Coach Yarborough burst into the locker room. He immediately stepped between the two boys and held his arms out, separating them.

"Benson made us lose the game, Coach."

"We're a team! No one person can blow a game. Every player makes mistakes, including you, Johnson. Now get your stuff and get out of here."

Romello slid the straps on his duffel bag over his shoulder and brushed past Tyler. "This ain't over, Benson," he mumbled under his breath.

Chapter Nine

"I wasn't afraid to fight Romello if I had to. I couldn't let him punk me out. But he didn't even want to fight anyway. When I met him on the court before practice today, he said we needed to squash our beef so we could be boys again."

Father Gregory looked up from his computer screen. "So, this kid who once bullied you and constantly humiliated you in front of your peers now wants to be your friend? How do you feel about that?"

"Romello isn't really that bad," Tyler explained. He picked up a statuette of Jesus from the top of the bookshelf, and with a cloth, he wiped dust from the space it'd occupied. "He's cool. And he's the most popular dude in the entire school. He asked me to hang out with him and his friends sometimes."

"Will you?"

"I don't know yet. I'm thinking about it."

"Think long and hard, Tyler. Romello and his friends are the same group of guys you skipped classes with, which led to you receiving five days of in-house suspension. And didn't they start the food fight in the cafeteria and trash the computer lab? They talked you into joining them, and you got in more trouble, didn't you?"

Tyler nodded and dropped his eyes to the floor.

"Well, I don't believe those are the types of fellows your aunt or your parents want you hanging around with."

"But we're all cool now. Romello apologized, and I let it go. Don't you preach about forgiving people who've done us wrong? Isn't that what the Bible says?"

"It does. As Christians, it's important for us to forgive one another as Christ forgave all of us. But the Bible teaches us to be aware of the company we keep. The fifteenth chapter of Second Corinthians admonishes us to avoid deception because bad company corrupts good morals and character."

Tyler twirled the dust cloth in his hand and squinted. "I don't get it."

"Plainly put, it's not wise for a nice and polite young man like you to hang around troublemakers like Romello and his friends. If you do, in time you'll take on their characteristics and start behaving as they do. You will trade the morals that your parents and aunt have instilled in you for rudeness and mischief. Your reputation will be tarnished. Is that your goal, Tyler?"

"No, sir. I just want to be cool with Romello and the rest of the team."

"I suggest that you continue to be cordial to your teammates, but limit your interaction with them to the basketball court. Otherwise, you'll find yourself in a world of trouble."

"I prefer the lemongrass, mango, and grapefruit blend, Stacie. Add a little bit of honey, and it'll be perfect. Make a fresh batch and distribute free samples during the lunch hour and when the evening crowd arrives. Let me know what the clients think. Thank you."

The young lady who managed the smoothie bar inside Royalty Health and Fitness Center and Spa's midtown location smiled at her boss. "You're welcome, Ms. Phillips."

Royce looked at her watch. She was expecting an important call from a potential new vendor. She left the smoothie bar and headed for her office in the opposite direction. It had been a stress-free and productive morning. The sales team had secured eleven new client contracts already, and it wasn't even noon. The marketing team was doing an excellent job promoting the facility. Royce smiled and waved at the senior men's weight-lifting class in the bodybuilding area.

"Ms. Phillips, you're looking fabulous this morning."

Royce froze in her stroll at the sound of the familiar but undesirable voice. She did a swift about-face. "What are you doing here, Brandon?"

"I was in the area on business. I finished earlier than expected, so I decided to swing by to take you out for an early lunch." He smiled and walked toward Royce, closing the distance between them.

"I don't have time to go to lunch today. And you assume too much anyway. What gives you the right to come to my job unannounced, thinking I would jump at the chance to have lunch with you?" Royce planted her fists on her hips and stared angrily at him. "Your overconfidence is borderline cockiness. I don't like it. You're not my man, Brandon. We're just friends. That's it. You shouldn't have come here unannounced."

"I'm sorry, babe. I didn't mean to overstep my boundaries. Forgive me."

"You're forgiven, but don't ever let it happen again."

Brandon rubbed his hands together and nodded with a bright smile on his face. Most women would've found him irresistible and fallen at his feet, but not Royce. Brandon just didn't float her boat. It was too bad, though, because he was a great guy and Royce could tell that he was really into her. However, the one man she wanted had confessed that he wanted her too, but due to his commitment to a higher calling, they could never be together.

Royce smiled and placed an open palm on Brandon's broad chest. "I'm expecting a call from a potential vendor any minute now. I'll call you this evening."

"I hope you'll give me a ring tonight. We haven't talked in a few days. Just now you were quick to point out that I'm not your man, but I'm trying to be, Royce. What is it going to take for me to win your heart, babe?"

Magically transform into Nicholas Gregory, was Royce's honest answer, but she couldn't reveal that particular thought to Brandon or anyone else. She decided to spare his feelings and pacify him with false hope instead. "I don't know, but I'm sure I'll come up with something by this evening. I'll call you around eight-ish. Is that a good time?" she asked as if she were really going to call.

"Anytime is a good time for you, babe."

***

"Yo, Benson, me and my boys are about to head to the mall to play games in the arcade and eat pizza. You wanna roll with us?"

"I don't know, man. I'm supposed to go straight to the church after practice to volunteer."

"It's cool, dude." Romello smirked and rubbed a hand over his freshly braided cornrows. "The Man Upstairs is more important than your friends and teammates. We'll catch you next time." He turned and walked away with his buddies a few steps behind him.

"Wait!" Tyler hurried to Romello's side. "I'm going. I can sort through donated clothes and shoes for a bunch of homeless people tomorrow."

"Are you sure, man? I don't want you to miss a miracle or some blessings because you're gonna hang out with me and my homies."

"Don't worry about it. Let's roll."

"Come on, ladies! You're acting like a bunch of babies! Put some funk in it! We're almost done! And one, two, three, four, and drop it like it's hot! Come on! And one, two, three . . ."

Royce crisscrossed her legs and dropped her body into a low squat to the rhythm of the music.

Sweat poured down her back and the sides of her face as she led the group of ladies into the final segment of a hip-hop cardio routine. She studied the reflections of the women in the wall of mirrors in front of her. It wasn't hard for Royce to sniff out the slackers from those who were determined to go all the way. Those particular women had mastered the proper breathing techniques for high-impact cardio workouts, and their faces bore tense expressions.

The huge mirrors also made it possible for Royce to notice Cassie, her administrative assistant, enter the room. The petite chick with wild sister locks rushed past the rows of sweaty women who were huffing and puffing their way through the strenuous fitness routine. Something important had brought Cassie to the room. She would never interrupt Royce in the middle of a class otherwise, especially the class that Rain, the mega pop star, attended religiously.

"I'm sorry to bust in here like this, boss lady, but you have a very important phone call."

Pumping her arms and rolling her hips without missing a beat, Royce frowned at Cassie. "Who the hell is it? It better be Barack or Michelle."

"He said—"

"He? Is it Tyler? If it is, I'm going to thump his knucklehead when I get to the church."

"It's not Tyler. It's your priest, Father Gregory. He said it's urgent and he needs to speak with you right away."

Royce stopped moving at once and snatched her white hand towel from the hook attached to the wall of mirrors. She turned to the ladies and yelled over the music blasting through the powerful stereo speakers in the front corners of the room. "I'm going to cut you weaklings some slack today! Class dismissed! Don't forget to stretch and ice your muscles if you feel any tenderness!"

Royce power-walked out of the room and broke out into a full sprint when she reached the hallway leading to her office. There was an unsettled feeling in her belly. Something serious was going on. Father Gregory had never called her at work before. According to Cassie, his reason for calling today was of an urgent nature. Only God knew what that meant. Royce rushed inside her office and walked directly to her desk. She snatched the phone's receiver from its cradle and pushed the flashing light.

"Father Gregory, what's going on?"

"Good afternoon, Royce. I'm sorry to bother you at work, but I felt the need to call you. Tyler never showed up to volunteer today. I haven't heard a word from him. I've called his cell phone several times, but he hasn't answered it."

A combination of shock and physical exhaustion from the workout caused Royce to plop down in her chair. "Where in the world could that boy be?"

"I have no idea, but I intend to find out. I'm on my way to his school. I'm going to drive around that area. Maybe he's hanging out in the gym or in the neighborhood with his teammates. I'll call you if I find him."

"Thank you, Father Gregory. I'm going to shower and call Tyler's closest friends before I go home. Maybe he went to Rico's or Gabriel's house. I just hope he's safe, wherever he wandered off to."

Chapter Ten

Father Gregory's cell phone rang seconds after he returned to his car. He'd walked around the neighborhood where Saint Xavier's School was located, looking for Tyler without any luck. He reached inside the pocket of his leather bomber jacket and removed his phone.

"This is Father Gregory." He frowned at the sound of sobs and a panic-stricken voice screaming on the other end. "Royce, please calm down, dear heart. I can't understand what you're saying. Take a deep breath and start over. I'm listening." He unlocked the car door and sat down in the driver's seat and willed his heartbeat to return to its normal rhythm. The pain in Royce's voice troubled him terribly.

"Tyler has been arrested! He . . . he was hanging out at the mall with those hoodlums on the basketball team. I didn't give him permission to go to the mall. He was supposed to have been at the church with you."

"Where are you, Royce? I could come and pick you up later and take you to the youth detention center. Is there a bond? Maybe we could get Tyler out of lockup."

"I'm on my way to Metro YDC now. I'm prepared to do whatever I have to do to bring Tyler home. And once I get him there, I'm going to kill him!"

Father Gregory checked the clock on the dashboard. He had exactly twenty minutes to get to the church for prayer service and biblical exploration. "I would love to meet you at the detention center, but I'm expected at the church in a little while. Will you call me with an update? I want to speak with Tyler before he goes to bed if possible."

"I'll give you a call as soon as I can. But in the meantime, you better pray for your little friend. He's going to need an entire flock of angels to protect him from me."

Father Gregory bit into his bottom lip to keep from shouting out in pain when he tripped over the curl at the end of the Oriental rug. It had caused him to stumble in the darkness and pound his left foot against the end table. The persistent tapping at the door had awakened him from a restless sleep in the parlor of the parsonage. Father Rivera and Father Schmidt were upstairs in their bedrooms, obviously slumbering through the steady knocking.

Luckily for the mystery late-night visitor, the senior priest at Lord of the Harvest parish had not turned in for the night. He was too worried and upset about the arrest of his mentee, Tyler Benson, to sleep. His on-and-off-again dozing on the leather chaise longue while flipping through Scripture was the only snippet of rest Father Gregory had enjoyed over the past few hours. He had intentionally remained in the parlor past his normal bedtime, hoping that Royce Phillips would call again but with good news this time. He didn't want Tyler to spend the night in juvenile detention. He'd prayed and asked God to allow him to be released.

Father Gregory shuffled to the front door with a throbbing foot, and he disengaged the locks. Certain that one of the nuns or deacons from the church was on the other side, he snatched the brass handle, opening the door wide. The next few seconds whizzed by in a blur. A warm and soft body fell into his arms as the scent of vanilla sobered his senses. The sound of pitiful whimpers and rambling words that he couldn't comprehend were sure signs that Tyler's circumstances were more serious than he'd anticipated.

"They . . . they wouldn't even let me see him! I couldn't see him! He's in . . . in that awful place overnight!"

"Hush now," Father Gregory said, attempting to console Royce. He enfolded her in his arms. "Hush now. Everything is going to work out just fine."

Royce, obviously overwhelmed with emotion, cried continuously as Father Gregory led her into the house. Her trembling body jerked in his arms each time she tried to speak. The sorrow in her stuttered words and whimpers broke Father Gregory's heart. He pulled her body closer to his, and she pressed her face against his chest. He guided Royce down the dark hall in the opposite direction of the parlor. Father Gregory was afraid that her crying would wake the other priests. Mindlessly, he led her into the master suite for privacy. As soon as the door closed behind them, Royce collapsed in his arms. He embraced her and rubbed her back as she wailed out her sadness.

"I told him to stay away from those bad boys. I told him. Why would he go to the mall and shoplift with them? Why?"

"I don't know. You'll have to ask Tyler that. When will you be able to see him?"

"He'll appear before a juvenile judge tomorrow morning at eleven o'clock. My attorney will be there to represent him. Hopefully, the judge will release Tyler since he's never been in trouble before."

"I believe he will."

The room fell silent. The sudden hush caused an acute awareness to strike Father Gregory like lightning. In his arms was the one woman whose heart and body he desired more than anything. She had come to him to be comforted from her emotional pain, and he had done his best to help ease her burden. Now, all he could think about was the pleasure her body was giving his in an innocent embrace. Her soft curves pressing against his rigidness caused his blood to simmer and rush to his penis. Father Gregory swallowed hard and tried to think of a Scripture to help him fight the mounting temptation. His mind went blank.

Royce lifted her head from his chest and stared at his face. Slivers of moonlight peeping through the cracks in the blinds made it possible to see her eyes. They were swollen and red from crying, but Father Gregory noticed something more significant. Royce's deep brown orbs were filled with yearning. She wanted Father Gregory. He saw it clearly.

Without words or forethought, their lips came together in a smoldering, wet kiss with their tongues dancing and devouring each other. Royce tightened her hold around Father Gregory's neck, meshing their bodies closer together. He moaned in delight when she thrust her hips forward and ground against his stiff, enlarged shaft. The feel of Royce's soft hands sliding from his shoulders to caress his chest caused more blood to rush to his penis.

Father Gregory grabbed Royce's round bottom and squeezed it as her hot tongue darted in and out of his mouth. She rocked her hips, stimulating his manhood even more. His erection had become painful, and he needed relief. As if on cue, Royce slid her hands underneath Father Gregory's white T-shirt and explored his pectoral and abdominal muscles. He threw his head back and growled in enjoyment when her fingertips toyed with the hair sprinkled about his chest.

Royce snatched the T-shirt over his head and let it fall to the floor. Then she lowered her hand to his crotch and rubbed the firm bulge. Father Gregory opened his mouth to speak, but no words would flow. Royce kissed and sucked his nipples as she unzipped his jeans. She released the button and maneuvered her hand inside his boxers and started stroking his rock-solid dick.

"Royce, ah, Royce," he mumbled.

"Yeah, baby, this is what you need." She tugged at his boxers and jeans until they fell to his ankles. "Royce is about to give you what you need."

Father Gregory removed his feet from his underwear and pants and stood before Royce as naked as Adam in the Garden of Eden. She kissed him deeply again as she continued to stroke his hardness. He moaned, loving the feel of Royce's hand caressing his manhood.

She pulled back and removed her coat and tossed it on the chair. She unbuttoned her blouse, exposing her black lace bra. Father Gregory watched in awe as Royce did away with her tan slacks. He reached for her, and she took his hand and guided him to the bed. Royce pushed Father Gregory gently, and he landed on his back on the beige duvet comforter. Slowly, she removed her bra and panties while he watched in appreciation. Royce stretched out on top of him and kissed him passionately. He accepted her tongue and rubbed her bare ass. He squeezed and massaged it tenderly as if it were a priceless treasure.

Royce lowered her lips to tease Father Gregory's nipples with the tip of her tongue. She dipped her head lower to kiss his belly button and to slide her tongue in and out of it. Downward, her lips kissed his penis several times before she took it fully into her mouth. Father Gregory's entire body quivered. Royce's wet, warm mouth on his hardened manhood was an introduction to pure ecstasy. She snaked her tongue over the sensitive head repeatedly as she sucked him and massaged his testicles.

"Royce," he called out. "My sweet Royce."

"Yeah, baby, I'm all yours tonight," she answered, lifting her head from his crotch.

Father Gregory pulled Royce up and into his arms before he rolled over on top of her. He fondled both her breasts while kissing the flesh between them. His tongue circled one hard nipple and then the other one. He took one into his mouth and sucked it gently. Royce rubbed the back of his head and arched her back. Father Gregory rubbed her flat belly and whispered her name. He explored her body, caressing her hips and thighs. He reached lower to play with the fine hairs covering her vagina. Royce opened her legs wide to accommodate his trembling hand as his fingers entered her sweet wetness.

"You're so wet," he whispered, sliding two fingers in and out of her dampness, stroking her erect, sensitive bud.

"Mmm, mmm . . ."

The heady aroma of sex lingered in the air as Royce's nectar flowed like a stream under Father Gregory's touch. She hummed appreciatively and spread her legs wider. He liked how her body responded to him. Giving her pleasure pleased him very much.

He removed his hand from Royce's wet, hot vagina and licked his fingers, tasting the moisture of her desire. He loved the flavor of her sex on his tongue. He lowered his face to the junction of her thighs and inhaled its feminine scent. It heightened his arousal to a brand-new altitude. His tongue plunged deep between her folds and stroked her hard clit. It was warm and saturated with her sugary liquid lust. Royce rotated her hips in response to the flicks of Father Gregory's tongue against her stiff, drenched clit. She jerked and hummed as he licked her into oblivion. He felt her beautiful body convulsing. Her soft hums grew into wails. The bed rocked underneath them. The headboard tapped the wall incessantly.

"Yesss!" Royce screamed and gripped the back of Father Gregory's head nestled between her thighs. "Mmm, yesss, baby, yesss!"

The jerking stopped, and Father Gregory lifted his head. He eased his way up Royce's body and looked into her eyes. She panted and smiled. He kissed her lips with a hunger that nearly took his breath away. Royce wiggled her hips until the head of his erect penis was positioned at the opening of her wetness. Their eyes met and locked for what seemed like an eternity. With perfect aim, he entered her body and went completely still.

"Royce," he whispered on a shaky breath.

She didn't answer him with words. Her body took over. She thrust her hips upward as if inviting him in. Instinctively, Father Gregory began to move in and out of Royce slowly. He looked into her pretty brown eyes and got lost. He stroked her long and deeply. Her warmth and wetness fascinated him.

His hardness was buried completely within her feminine walls, sliding in and out with measured thrusts. It felt amazing. He picked up his pace and plunged deeper. A foreign sensation gripped him from head to toe. Making love for the very first time was euphoric. Father Gregory's body had never experienced physical gratification of such a great magnitude. With each powerful thrust, he felt his soul soaring higher and higher to some magical place far, far away.

The edges of Royce's fingernails pressed into the flesh on his back as she cooed, bucked, and rotated her hips in sync with his. She reached up and held his face between her palms and licked his lips. Her hot, wet, open-mouth kisses sent Father Gregory's spirit ascending into the atmosphere, floating above the night's clouds. His inner man defied gravity, looking down at his body as it shuddered madly from an orgasm, satisfying and sweet. He bucked and moaned as warm semen swooshed from his body into Royce's womb.

"Royyyyyce!" He belted out the one word from his soul.

His release must have triggered her second one of the night. She wrapped her legs around his waist and bucked wildly underneath him, purring, "Mmm, Father Gregory . . ."

Hearing those two words, his spiritual title and surname, snatched him from that mystical place and returned him to the real world. It was the world where he was never to lie with a woman, yet there he was.

Chapter Eleven

Royce opened her eyes wide, and instantly visions of making love with Father Gregory the night before replayed in her mind. A lone tear fell from her eye and slid down her cheek. Her heart ached, knowing that she'd had sex with a man of God. She was responsible for his fall from grace and into fornication.

He was asleep, cuddling her affectionately from behind. Royce couldn't move because his hold on her naked body was too tight. She stirred in an attempt to free herself. She wanted to go home so she could pray and cry as loud as she wanted to. She felt sinful, broken, and nasty. Her body was sore, too. She and Father Gregory had made love two more times before they finally fell asleep in each other's arms. Each thrilling episode had been more magical than the one before it. Just thinking about the things they had done to one another caused Royce's nipples and clit to harden.

She pried one of Father Gregory's arms away from her body and rolled out of his reach. He stirred in his sleep but didn't wake up. Royce looked around the bedroom and finally noticed the clock on his dresser. It was almost four o'clock in the morning. She eased off of the bed and began searching the floor through the darkness for her underwear and clothes. She wanted to get out of the parsonage quickly before Father Gregory woke up. She couldn't face him. What the hell was she supposed to say to him anyway?

"Were you planning to leave without saying goodbye?"

Royce closed her eyes and gasped at the sound of his hoarse voice. "I didn't have the heart to wake you." She picked up her panties and put them on with her back to him. "You were resting peacefully. I didn't want to be inconsiderate."

She heard the headboard tap lightly against the wall. He was moving, more than likely getting out of bed. His hands gripped Royce's shoulders. Tears flowed down her face. She wanted to scream. She wished she could escape to unconsciousness.

"We need to discuss what happened here last night. I didn't plan to take you, Royce. It just happened. One minute you were in my arms, and the next thing I knew we were naked in bed, making love."

"It's not your fault. I shouldn't have come here."

"Look at me, Royce."

She stepped away from him and shook her head, refusing to turn around. "I . . . I can't." She grabbed her bra from the floor and put it on. Her blouse and slacks were in the chair. She rushed over and put them on fast. "I'll have Tyler call you this afternoon." She grabbed her coat from the chair.

"I'm going to court. I should be there."

"You don't have to come."

Father Gregory walked over, took Royce by her hand, and gently turned her around to face him. She wiped her tears with her free hand. Her vision was blurred from crying. Father Gregory's body was completely bare. Royce noticed it but dismissed it at the same time. Emotions, raw and jumbled, had overtaken her. She was confused, unable to think clearly.

"I'll be there to support Tyler."

Royce nodded. "Where is my purse?" she asked, pulling her eyes away from his face.

Father Gregory found it on the nightstand. He picked it up and handed it to her.

"Thank you."

"You're welcome." He folded his arms over his chest. "We can't avoid this subject, Royce. We will discuss it tonight. I'll visit you after Tyler has gone to sleep."

Royce blinked as his words settled in her brain. "No! We don't need to be anywhere near each other, especially not alone. I could meet you at a restaurant."

"And who will be home with Tyler?"

"All right, you may come to my house," she agreed reluctantly, realizing her dilemma. "But we—"

"I won't touch you, Royce. I promise."

Father Gregory lifted his head and allowed the pounding spray of hot water to saturate his face. He'd put up a brave front for Royce. His cool and laidback demeanor in her presence had been an act. He was not okay, as he'd pretended to have been. The most sacred vow he'd ever made had been broken. His virginity was gone, completely destroying his commitment to celibacy. The long shower couldn't wash away the guilt, pain, and degradation he felt. Sin was embedded in his skin, seeping into his blood, choking the life out of him.

"Forgive me," he whispered as tears fell from his eyes, mixing in with the water spray. "I have sinned against you and the church. I am so unworthy of your mercy and your grace."

Visions of the passionate experience he'd shared with Royce haunted him. He couldn't escape them. They were too fresh and vivid in his psyche, intensifying his shame. How could something so beautiful and memorable also be immoral and unacceptable? Father Gregory had enjoyed surrendering himself over to the call of nature, although his actions were ungodly. Loving yet loathing the experience tore his heart to pieces. He was a broken man who had engaged in something so fulfilling in the arms of an amazing woman, but it had brought damnation to his soul.

Father Gregory turned off the water and left the shower with mixed thoughts and feelings about the sin he had committed. At the moment he was as close to insanity as he'd ever been. It was a painful burden to bear, and he took full responsibility for what he had done. He would never blame Royce for reaching out to him in her time of need. As a priest, he should've exercised restraint and resisted temptation, but he didn't. He had failed miserably.

He rushed to dry his body and put on casual attire. Dressed in a pair of faded jeans and a sweatshirt, he chose a pair of running shoes and a Chicago White Sox baseball cap to complete his informal look. He hadn't hopped on his Harley-Davidson Iron 883 since relocating to Atlanta. It was time to take his baby out for a spin to clear his head. A long ride before facing Royce and Tyler at court would give him time to talk to God and sort through his emotions.

"I will call you as soon as court is over, sis. I promise."

"I'm so nervous. I don't want my baby to be in jail missing school and church."

"Kirk said Tyler will probably only get probation and be ordered to perform community service, if even that. He's a first-time offender. The worst-case scenario is that he'll be slapped with an accomplice charge. No game discs or other merchandise were found in his possession. Plus he had a pocketful of money. Tyler could've bought anything he wanted from that store. He didn't even run when the security guard chased them. I believe he was clueless about what those thugs were planning to do. They went to the video game store with the intent to steal. Tyler didn't."

"I hope you're right, Royce."

"Trust me. Everything is going to be okay."

"Will Father Gregory be at court?"

"Yes." Royce pushed the single word out as his face appeared in her mind's eye.

"I'm glad to know that. I'll bet he has a mouthful to say to Tyler. Tell him I said there is no need to take it easy on him. I want him to scare the hell out of that boy."

"I'll give him your message. I've got to get dressed now. Kiss my brother-in-law for me. I'll call you later. Bye."

"Father, bless me and be merciful, for I have sinned."

"Tell me. What is your transgression, my son?"

Father Gregory closed his eyes and released a cleansing breath. "I was with a woman who is not my wife. We committed fornication."

"I see. Do you love this woman?"

"I'm not sure. I haven't known her very long. I am extremely fond of her, though."

"Will you continue to court her? Because if you do, your relationship will be strained now that you have crossed the line of intimacy. If you care for this woman and wish to date her, you may sin with her again. Do you think she will make you a fine wife someday in the future?"

I'm just like you. I will never have a wife, his broken heart wanted to confess. Father Gregory rubbed both hands down his face as that thought took on a new and painful meaning for him as a man. He was forbidden to love Royce although he desperately wanted to. She would never be his wife because marriage was not an option for him. "I will have no personal relationship with her from now on. We will never be married."

"Are you sure? I sense that you may be in love with this woman. If you have deep feelings for her, I suggest that you court her in a manner that is pleasing to our Heavenly Father. You should never touch her intimately again. Get to know her better. And when the time is right, take her hand in marriage. Until then, you must pray for your atonement and meditate on Scriptures of restoration. For five days, I want you to recite the Lord's Prayer five times. Then you should recite five prayers of Hail Mary daily in as many days. Read the fifty-first chapter of the Book of Psalms every morning for one week. King David was overtaken by sexual sin just as you were. He wrote the passage as an apology to God and to ask for restoration. You will find healing and comfort in the words. Give thanks to the Lord, for He is good."

Father Gregory folded his hands and responded, "For His mercy endures forever."

"The Lord has freed you from your sins, my son. Go in peace."

"Thanks be to God."

Chapter Twelve

"No, sir, Your Honor, I had no idea that Romello and Damien were going to steal those video games. I swear, sir."

The judge frowned. "Are Mr. Johnson and Mr. Gordon your friends, Mr. Benson?"

"I thought they were, sir. We're on the same basketball team at Saint Xavier's. I really believed they liked me. That's why I went to the mall with them in the first place. I was stupid to trust them. I got arrested because they said I was their lookout man while they were stealing all that stuff, but it's not true."

"It's your lucky day, young man, because I believe you. The case against you is dismissed, but please listen to me very carefully. Be extremely aware of the company you keep. Negative people will cause you to crash and burn very quickly. Do you understand?"

"Yes, sir."

"You are free to leave with your aunt. It's time to deal with your 'friends' now."

Tyler walked up the aisle and straight into Royce's arms. She squeezed him. Father Gregory patted his shoulder and smiled. The three of them exited the courtroom.

"I am so glad this is over, sweetie. Let's go home now and call your parents."

"I hope you've learned your lesson, Tyler."

"I have, Father Gregory. Believe me. You told me Romello and his friends were no good. You were right. I'm sorry I let you down. You probably don't want to hang out with me anymore, huh?"

"Nothing has changed between us. I'll expect you at the church tomorrow after basketball practice."

Tyler hung his head. "I'm not even sure if we still have a team without Romello and Damien. They were our biggest scorers."

"Coach Yarborough will figure it out. You don't have to worry about that."

"Hi," Royce whispered and waved Father Gregory into the house. "I'll take your coat. Let's talk in the kitchen. I made a fresh pot of Jamaican Blue Mountain coffee. Essie baked cinnamon rolls for Tyler's homecoming. They are *delicious*." She hung the jacket on a hook inside the closet in the foyer and headed to the kitchen.

"How long has Tyler been asleep?" Father Gregory asked, following Royce.

"He turned in a little over an hour ago. We had a long talk right before he went to his room. I don't think we'll have any more problems out of him."

"He's a good kid. He just makes poor choices sometimes. It's kind of like what we did last night." Father Gregory took a seat at the dinette.

Royce nodded.

"I messed up."

"*We* messed up." She poured a generous amount of the rich roasted blend into each mug. She placed them both on a tray with spoons, cream, sugar, and a plate of the homemade cinnamon rolls. She left the island to serve Father Gregory before sitting down across from him.

"It can't ever happen again, Royce. Never."

"We've had this conversation before, right here at this same table. We weren't supposed to be alone, kiss, or touch each other again, but—"

"You were distraught last night," he interrupted. "I don't believe you came to me with the intention of us making love. The situation with Tyler had become too much for you to handle alone, so you drove to the parsonage for help. One thing led to another."

"Do you believe in fate or destiny? Aren't some things just meant to happen?"

"Some things do happen naturally, while others are influenced by circumstances. Emotions and lust got the best of us last night. I don't think fate or destiny had anything to do with it. We became weak and helpless. It's strange because that has never happened to me before. I had been celibate all my life, Royce."

Her hand stopped with the coffee mug in it on its way to her lips. She placed it on the table. "Wait a minute. Rewind. Repeat what you just said."

"Before last night, I had never made love to a woman before."

"You were a virgin? Or are you—"

"I was a virgin."

"But Tyler told me you're twenty-nine years old. There is no way . . . I mean, you were so good last night. Forgive me. I am not proud of what we did, but you were incredible. I can't believe you'd never done it before. Wow! I was your first?"

"You were my first, last, and only, Royce. I'll never touch you again. We must use self-control whenever we're in each other's presence. No more dinners or late-night conversations. It's impossible for us to avoid each other forever, though. We'll just have to maintain a safe distance at all times."

Royce laughed and tossed her braids over her shoulder. She laughed again, but louder.

"This is a serious matter, Royce! You shouldn't be laughing."

"It's funny to me how naïve you are. Do you really think it's that simple? Last night was just the beginning. We started a wild fire that is burning out of control. Sure, there'll be some moments when the flames will dwindle to a small flicker. But what are you going to do when the full blaze is reignited?"

"I won't come near you. I'll commit myself to prayer and meditation. By God's power, I won't fall again."

"My heart ached seconds after reality hit me last night. I never meant to make you fall. I didn't want to fall either. But we were too weak. We shared something special. There's undeniable chemistry between us that draws us together. We've tasted each other in the most intimate way known to the human race. Our lives will never be the same. The genie has escaped her bottle, and she ain't ever going back in."

"What are you saying, Royce? Do you believe that temptation and lust are more powerful than God?"

"I'm not saying that at all. It's just that physical desires and the need to be sexual is natural. That's why you were able to love me like crazy last night although it was your first time. Your instincts led you, and they led you very well. You responded to nature, and I could tell that you enjoyed every minute of it. Do you honestly believe that you'll never want me again?"

"I may want you, but I refuse to have you."

Royce nodded, fully understanding that Father Gregory had good intentions, but he was deluding himself. "And when you're being consumed by your own fiery flesh, what will you do for relief?"

"I will pray. The Holy Spirit will sustain me."

"The Holy Spirit is definitely powerful, but it will only deliver from temptation those who truly wish to be delivered."

"I will not be tempted, and I will not make love to you again, Royce. I'll see myself out now. Good night."

Royce kissed Tyler one last time before he boarded the chartered bus on its way to the Blue Ridge Mountains up in Ellijay, Georgia. She waved and blew kisses as the bus pulled out of the church's parking lot. Then she made fast tracks to her SUV.

"Royce, how are you?"

"I'm fine." She unlocked her door and pulled the handle.

"You weren't at church Sunday or the Sunday before. Tyler said you've been busy."

"It's true. I'm taking my businesses in a new direction. The overhaul requires a lot of my time."

Father Gregory nodded and walked closer to her vehicle. "I hope you'll get some rest while Tyler is away."

"Actually, I plan to have a little fun while my nephew is enjoying himself in the mountains. I'm going to let my hair down and explore new social possibilities. Take care, Father Gregory," Royce said, easing into her seat.

"Will I see you at church Sunday?"

"I doubt it." Royce closed the door and started the vehicle's engine. Then she blew the horn, waved, and sped away.

Father Gregory was still standing in the parking lot as other cars departed. Royce watched him through her rearview mirror until he diminished into a tiny speck. Her heart squeezed, reflecting on the emptiness in his eyes when she looked at him. He missed her. She missed him. She wanted him. But she couldn't have him. Royce refused to be responsible for luring the man into temptation even though she'd entertained a naughty thought or two about doing just that over the past few weeks. Somehow, she'd resisted the overwhelming urge to make a midnight visit to the parsonage again on a couple of sleepless nights. It was hard, but she'd been able to talk herself out of it each time. And she did it without the help of her once-trusted vibrator. It didn't do the trick anymore. No sex toy or any other intimate partner could satisfy her like Father Gregory. It was like comparing a hamburger to prime rib. Royce had experienced the best, and she didn't have a taste for anything less.

But the Roman Catholic Church had established the rules centuries ago, and Father Gregory was committed to abiding by those rules. It was his choice, and Royce would not interfere in the life he had chosen to live. She had set him free. The one night they had spent together would forever be cherished in her heart, but the man was lost to her. It hurt like hell, but she was a big girl. She would eventually get over Father Gregory and move on. And she intended to take her first step moving forward tonight.

Chapter Thirteen

"Uh-oh," Royce's cousin, Andra, whispered. "That fine brother who's been smiling and winking at you all night is on his way over here. He's coming to get an 'appreciation dance' for that peach margarita he sent you."

"Ladies, how are you tonight?"

Royce turned around slowly and was immediately blinded by a dazzling smile. "We're fine."

"We certainly are," Andra drawled and tossed her long dreadlocks over her shoulder.

Royce's handsome and stylishly dressed admirer licked his lips as he bobbed his head to the music being performed by the live jazz quintet. He took her by the hand. "Would you like to dance, pretty lady?"

Andra's eyes were glued to Royce. She could feel them crawling all over her face like a pair of pesky ladybugs. Her younger cousin wanted her to dance with the cute guy, but Royce wasn't so sure that she should. He seemed nice enough, and he was delicate on the eyes. A tall and muscular redbone with sandy curls and copper eyes, the dude was a pleasant visual stimulant indeed. The problem was Royce didn't want just any man holding her in his arms. There was only one man whose hands could spark a flame inside of her, but he wasn't on the market. And until she had completely purged him from her system, Royce's heart wasn't free to give to anyone else.

God knew she wanted to be emotionally free. Therefore, she needed to at least make a genuine attempt to get back in the saddle and rejoin the dating race. So, maybe one dance wouldn't hurt.

"Dance with the man," Andra hissed under her breath and rolled her eyes to the ceiling.

Without another thought, Royce allowed the smooth gentleman to escort her out on the dance floor. He lifted her hand and twirled her in a perfect circle before he dipped her body nice and low. The brother was light on his feet, and he moved like a subtle wind.

"What's your name?" he asked, lifting her body from the graceful dip.

"I'm Royce. What do the ladies call you, sir?"

"On the baseball diamond, I'm known as Bullet because I'm fast. Nothing gets past this shortstop.

And when I knock the ball out of the park, it shoots over the wall like a bullet. So, my natural speed earned me the nickname Bullet when I was a kid growing up in West Philly. But my mama named me Chavis Bullard Jr. You should've heard of me. I play for the Atlanta Braves."

"I'm sorry. Your name doesn't ring a bell," Royce lied without stammering. She was familiar with the name, but not the face because she wasn't a baseball fan. However, she, like every woman in America, had at least heard of Chavis Bullard. Just last year he'd been named one of America's most beautiful athletes by *Sports Illustrated* magazine. *Ebony* magazine had hailed him one of its most eligible bachelors of 2016. Royce had lied through her pearly whites just to let a little bit of air out of his balloon-size ego. The shock that creased his handsome face after she'd pretended not to know him tickled her silly. Royce grinned on the inside but kept a straight face as she followed his lead in an easy two-step swing.

"Well, in that case, I'll have to give you complimentary tickets to a seat in a VIP skybox at my first game this coming season. You definitely need to check me out. In the meantime, I'll treat you to candlelight dinners at Atlanta's classiest five-star restaurants and take you on romantic carriage rides downtown. If you like fine jewelry and exotic weekend getaways, I'll gladly oblige you. Money is not an object. I would drop millions a day on a woman as beautiful as you, Ms. Royce."

"I have my own money, Mr. Bullard. I can afford every luxury you just offered me. I don't need a man to lavish me with money, gifts, and expensive vacations. All I want is a brother who can love me and respect me completely for who I am, just the way I am. Royce Phillips is an independent, secure, and very passionate woman in need of a soul mate, not a sugar daddy. I want a commitment, not an arrangement."

Royce dropped her hands from Chavis's broad shoulders and studied his face as the sting of her words finally reached his brain. Obviously, she was the first female to have ever resisted his fame, good looks, and generosity. A million other women would've donated a kidney to a bum on the street for a chance to spend one second with the rich and celebrated baller. But Royce was of a different breed. She wanted the fairy tale. Her heart craved love, passion, and romance. Good girls like her dreamed of happily ever after. She wasn't a gold digger or a female player. Royce was a hopeless romantic, and she desired to be loved. Father Gregory wasn't free to love her, but she was determined to give her heart to someone. Unfortunately, neither Chavis Bullard nor Brandon Hartwell was that special guy. And there would be no settling. Mr. Right was out there somewhere, and Royce prayed that he would find her soon so he could make her forget about Father Gregory.

Before Chavis was able to respond to her tongue-lashing, Royce spun on her high heels and walked away, leaving the baseball superstar in the middle of the dance floor.

Royce, returning home and seeing a form in the shadows, let out a bloodcurdling scream loud enough to wake up every resident in her exclusive gated community. On instinct, she threw a swift left kick that landed hard somewhere on the lower body of her would-be attacker. He yelped and doubled over, no doubt in pain.

"That's what you get, punk! Don't nobody mess with me and walk away without an ass whipping!" She raised the can of pepper spray attached to her key ring and aimed.

"Royce, wait! It's me, Father Gregory."

She turned on the miniature flashlight that was also attached to her keys and shined it on the tall figure dressed in all black. She watched him gradually unfold his body to stand up straight. It was Father Gregory.

"What the hell are you doing hanging around my house this time of night? You were about to get your butt kicked."

"I was out riding my bike to no place in particular. Somehow, I ended up here." He grimaced and reached down to massage his right shin. "Of course, you weren't home. I became concerned because it was late. So I decided to wait here to make sure you got in safely. I didn't mean to frighten you."

"How did you get past the guard shack and through the gate?"

Father Gregory smiled. "I come here often. They know me."

"What if I had been returning home after a date with my man and we were about to turn in for the night?"

"I didn't realize you had a man," he stuttered. "Tyler said—"

"You better stop listening to Tyler so much. He doesn't know everything about me."

Royce turned and walked up the three steps and unlocked her door. She entered the house and deactivated the security system, with the sound of footsteps behind her. It was a chilly night in early March, but Royce was hot. Father Gregory was walking so closely behind her that she could feel his body heat. Completely off her mark, her body jerked when the door slammed shut behind them.

"It's way past midnight. Where were you?"

Royce did a quick twirl with a hand on her hip. "You don't have the right to ask me about my personal life. It's not your business."

"You're right. Forgive me for being intrusive."

"Why are you here anyway?"

Father Gregory looked at Royce head-on, and she nearly melted from the fire she saw in his eyes. No other man on the planet could stare her into submission like he was doing at the moment. Royce was no longer angry with him for almost scaring her to death or prying into her private life. Her body had betrayed her and so had her mind. She closed her eyes and exhaled, trying with all her mental power to recall the words he'd said to her the night of Tyler's release from jail. They were never to be alone again. He would not touch her ever. He would not fall into sexual temptation. Royce suddenly snapped out of her state of horniness and pulled herself together.

"I asked you a question."

"I wanted to see you."

Royce raised both hands and shook her head. "No! No! No! I won't allow you to drag me through an emotional obstacle course. You wanted me. Then you didn't want me. Now, all of a sudden, you want me again? I can't handle this. You laid down the rules, and we're going to abide by them, damn it. Get out of my house!" Royce raced to the door and opened it wide.

"Are you sure you want me to leave?" He reached out and traced her cheek with his index finger.

Royce bristled and backed out of his reach. She wanted Father Gregory to leave, but she also wanted him to stay forever. Her heart and every inch of her flesh yearned for his presence and his fiery touch, but her mind flashed warning signs. A battle of want versus wisdom raged on the inside. If she allowed him to stay, they would make love for sure. And once again, they would tumble through the painful cycle of guilt, shame, and repentance. The talk would come next. *"We can't ever make love again, Royce. I am a priest, and I've made a vow to God and the church."* Royce could hear those words resonating in her ears. They stabbed her heart. She refused to sit through another torturous conversation with Father Gregory about his spiritual dilemma. It wasn't fair for him to make love to her under the moonlight and then, at the break of dawn, lecture her on how sinful what they'd shared had been. Her heart couldn't take it.

The emotional dam broke. Fresh tears flowed down her face. "Leave."

Father Gregory crossed over the threshold into the cold darkness, and Royce moved to push the door shut behind him.

Chapter Fourteen

Before the door slammed shut, Father Gregory turned around quickly and stopped it with his hand. He reentered the house and gave the door a hard shove to close it like a man on a serious mission. He pulled Royce into his arms and kissed her forehead. She pressed her palms against his chest as if she were trying to ward him off, but he used his strength to draw her closer. His lips captured hers in a ravenous kiss. Royce moaned, giving Father Gregory's tongue full access to hers. His hands roamed over her curves, caressing her back, waist, and hips. He gripped her round bottom with both massive hands. She responded by rotating her hips to grind her lower body against his firm penis. He pressed his hardness into the softness between her thighs.

Father Gregory eased his hands downward and gathered the red fabric of Royce's dress. He pulled the short skirt up above her hips. His fingertips skidded over her silk pantyhose and massaged her butt. Their kisses grew hotter and wilder with every twirl of Royce's tongue teasing his. The scent of vanilla on her velvety skin sharpened his manly senses. Father Gregory shifted their bodies until he had pinned Royce's back against the wall. He lowered his lips to lick and suck her neck. He tugged at her pantyhose with both hands, lowering them to her kneecaps. Then he executed the same movement on her thong. His hands trembled slightly and tingled when they made direct contact with her bare flesh. He palmed each firm butt cheek and growled out his need.

He dropped to his knees and buried his face in the wet and hairy spot he'd dreamed about since his first taste of its sweetness. The fabric of Royce's dress fell and covered the top of Father Gregory's head, but he wasn't distracted. He separated the lips of her vagina with his fingers, exposing its stiff, drenched clit. He flicked it with his tongue and immediately felt Royce's hands grab his head. She whimpered and cooed as he licked and suckled her sensitive bud. He snaked his tongue inside of her and curled it gently in and out of her wet walls before he slid it back to her clit, licking it. With each stroke of his tongue, he felt Royce's entire body shiver. As he licked, her body ticked. A tick for a lick continued until Royce's knees seemed to buckle, causing her body to sway. She jerked, seemingly out of control, and showered Father Gregory with verbal appreciation.

"Oooh, baby . . . baby . . . baby!" Royce half sang and half shouted. "Mmm, baby!"

Father Gregory stood and reached behind Royce to unzip her dress. He tugged on the fabric, freeing her arms from the sleeves, and allowed the dress to fall to her ankles. She kicked out of her red pumps as he yanked her stockings and thong from her knees to her ankles. Royce fidgeted her way out of both undergarments. Father Gregory lifted her naked body off its feet, and she wrapped her legs around his waist and rested her head on his shoulder.

"If your room is upstairs, we might not make it," he whispered as he massaged her bare ass.

"We have to go upstairs to my room because that's where the condoms are." Royce kissed his neck. "No more risky business."

Without any further discussion, Father Gregory put his muscles to good use by carrying Royce across the foyer to the bottom of the spiral staircase. She released her legs from his waist and slid to her feet. She started up the steps, but Father Gregory picked her up again and carried her.

"Which way?" he asked when they reached the top.

Royce chuckled and pointed to their left. Father Gregory hurried down the hall and entered the dark master suite. He placed Royce in the middle of the king-sized sleigh bed. She rolled over, reaching toward the nightstand. She opened the drawer and found a row of condoms.

"Come here."

Father Gregory tossed the jacket and sweatshirt he'd just taken off on the bench at the foot of the bed. He licked his lips and smiled. Royce was impatient, and amazingly it intensified his erection. He removed his sweatpants and boxers and joined her on the bed. They embraced. He ran his fingers through her braids and sucked her bottom lip, and she rubbed her soft hand up and down his stiff penis.

"Royce . . . Royce, ah . . . Royce . . ." he mumbled, tossing his head from side to side on the stack of pillows.

Royce lowered her head to Father Gregory's crotch and licked the head of his penis in slow motion. Her tongue traced the perimeter of the sensitive tip nice and slow as she continued stroking the rigid length of him. His heart pounded in his chest like a jackhammer as air swooshed from his lungs. He squealed out Royce's name in a pitch that was too high to be his, he thought. It was unrecognizable to his ears. He was caught up in sexual euphoria, beyond bliss.

Royce lifted her head. She straddled Father Gregory. "Sit up, baby," she ordered, reaching over to place extra pillows behind his back.

She picked up the row of condoms from the bed, removed a single packet, and ripped it open with her teeth. By the light of the moon, Father Gregory watched her roll the condom over his solid manhood. He was pleasantly surprised when she raised her hips and eased her hot, wet vagina down on his penis, taking him in completely. Royce began to roll and bounce her hips up and down unhurriedly at first. Then she picked up her pace, very much to Father Gregory's delight. He matched her motions with powerful upward thrusts. He grabbed her hips and pulled her down onto his lap with force as he pushed deeper into her walls. Royce cursed and bounced. Father Gregory bucked and hummed. The tempo increased, rocking the bed. The headboard tapped against the wall like an African drum beat. Their joint ride to the stars and beyond was exhilarating.

Royce threw her head back, causing her long braids to spill down her back and graze her bottom. "I love you."

Father Gregory's body stiffened when her walls began to contract around his hardness. They clenched and released him repeatedly as Royce's body convulsed. She whispered her declaration of love again. He rolled over on the bed without breaking the connection, reversing the position of their bodies. The stack of pillows toppled. He looked down into Royce's face and smiled. He kissed her tenderly as he slid in and out of her body. She gripped his butt, pulling him in deeper. He continued pumping in and out of her, grunting with every stroke. Royce tightened her inner muscles around his penis and rotated her hips. At last, a climax more explosive than dynamite ripped through every muscle in his anatomy. Father Gregory gritted his teeth against the breathtaking spasms and panted for air. His body gave way to the wonderful sensations. He lowered his full weight on Royce's body while he struggled to catch his breath. Seconds later, he rolled over, a satisfied man with the woman who loved him in his arms.

Chapter Fifteen

The empty spot in Royce's bed caused a dull ache in her chest. She rolled over and inhaled the deserted pillow. The masculine scent lingering on the Egyptian cotton brought back vivid memories of last night. Her and Father Gregory's lovemaking marathon had been quite an experience. They'd carried on like a pair of dogs in heat. At one point Royce became overly exhausted and was in need of something cool to drink. Father Gregory, a self-proclaimed Windy City gentleman, didn't hesitate to run downstairs in his birthday suit to get her a bottle of guava juice. A vision of his naked body floated through her memory. Royce appreciated the vibrant image, but it reminded her that he had left her bed and her home without saying goodbye.

She closed her eyes and pressed her face deeper into the pillow, taking in the scent that was uniquely his. Royce loved him, and she had told him as much. It hadn't been a planned confession. It just kind of slipped out at a time when Father Gregory was hitting her spot so good that her brain took a snooze. Her mental filter had gotten clogged up, and she couldn't hold the words inside another second. The feelings she'd been nurturing secretly in her heart had spilled out in her actions as well as her words. Now, Royce was vulnerable and sad, but she had no regrets. If last night was the final time she'd ever share her body and soul with Father Gregory, she would cherish it for life. At least he knew how she truly felt about him. She had blessed him with a special gift that he was never supposed to have had: the love of a woman.

Royce hugged the pillow tighter, wishing it were Father Gregory. No man had ever made her feel as special as he had. They hadn't known each other long at all, and there were so many things they still didn't know about one another, but he had touched her heart. Royce felt like crying for the life she would never have with Father Gregory, but she smiled instead for the snatches of passion they'd shared.

"I hope you're hungry."

Royce opened her eyes and sat straight up in the bed at the sound of his voice. Father Gregory walked into the bedroom, looking refreshed and

sinfully handsome wearing only his black boxers. There was a tray of food in his hands. Two
coffee mugs of what Royce hoped was tea sat
steaming on the tray as well. It was a scene out
of a dream. After an incredible night of the best
sex she'd ever experienced in her life, the man
she adored was now serving her breakfast in bed.
A girl couldn't ask for anything better than that.

"I'm starving," she said after a few seconds of
silent shock.

"Great." Father Gregory placed the tray on the
nightstand and picked up one of the mugs. He
handed it to Royce. "I ransacked your kitchen
until I found the teabags. You're out of honey. I
used the last of it in your cup. You're not a fan of
sugar. I took notice the night of Tyler's sleepover."

Royce chanced a sip of her tea. "It's perfect.
Thank you."

"You're welcome. I hope you like hash brown
potatoes with bell peppers and onions. I scrambled a few eggs and sprinkled some shredded
cheddar cheese over them."

"It smells good." Royce took the plate of food
and the fork he offered her. She eyed her meal. "I
see you found my turkey sausage links, too. I don't
usually share them, but I'll be nice today." She
sampled the potatoes and scooped up a forkful of

eggs and tasted them. "Mmm, it's delicious. Who taught you how to cook like this?"

Father Gregory folded his arms over his bare chest and stared down at Royce. "When you're single, living away from home with very few friends and none of them are female, you learn certain survival skills. Cooking and washing my own clothes were the first two chores I experimented with. I didn't get either one right the first couple of times, but I eventually learned how to rattle the pots and separate white clothes from colored ones in time with much practice."

"Well, I'm enjoying my breakfast. But you better not think about washing my clothes." Royce pointed the fork in his direction for emphasis. "Essie takes care of my laundry just fine."

"Don't worry. I won't try to send your house-keeper to the unemployment line."

"Aren't you going to eat?"

"I ate two slices of wheat toast and an apple. Breakfast is my least favorite meal of the day. I can take it or leave it." He picked up the other cup of tea and took a sip. "I wanted to feed you before I showered and returned home."

Relief washed over Royce. Father Gregory's thoughtfulness warmed her heart, but she didn't want to read too much into it. He wasn't moving in or even asking her to go steady. It was just breakfast. He was being considerate. However, she expected any minute for him to go into his regular post-sex spiel about the priesthood and his vow to God and the Roman Catholic Church. Royce knew it by heart. She braced herself for the throbbing jab.

"You said you were out riding your bike last night. What kind of bike is it?"

"It's a Harley."

"I didn't see it. Where did you park it?"

"It's on the side of your house in the bushes."

"You hid it," Royce said flatly, slightly annoyed that she suddenly felt like a closet whore.

"I respect your privacy," Father Gregory explained. "Caution was my utmost concern. No one except the guard at the gate knows who I am around here. This is your neighborhood. I'm sure your reputation in the community is favorable. I'd like it to remain that way."

Royce nodded and placed her half-eaten plate of food on the tray. She understood Father Gregory's way of thinking. She even appreciated his concern. It seemed authentic enough. But a fly kept buzzing in her ear, telling her it was his reputation he was worried about and not so much hers. Either way, their affair or whatever was happening between them was top secret for understandable reasons, even though they were two consenting adults acting of their own free will.

"Don't let me keep you here. It's Saturday. I'm sure you have a million things to do in preparation for the noonday mass tomorrow. I think I'm going to relax today. I don't work on weekends unless there's an emergency. Tabatha, my company's executive manager, is very efficient in my absence."

"I feel like I'm being dismissed."

"I would never dismiss you. It's just that I'm a big girl and I know the drill. You don't need to sing me the same song twice."

Father Gregory placed his mug on the night-stand and sat down on the bed next to Royce. He draped his arm around her shoulders. "If there were any way we could be together as a couple in a meaningful relationship, there would be no reason for discretion. Surely, you must know that, Royce."

"What I know is I'm in love with my priest! And we are having a sexual affair. Both times we made love, I lost a piece of my soul to you! When you leave me here alone today, I'll go through withdrawal just like a drug addict does after coming down from a high. You, on the other hand, have mastered the technique of emotionally detaching yourself from me whenever you're wearing your clergy collar and listening to confessions of other people's sins. I can't do that!" Royce patted her chest and broke down in tears. "I can't hide my feelings. They're real."

"It's not easy for me either, sweetheart. Whenever I look at you, no matter where we are or who's around, I want to take you in my arms and show you affection. It bothers me that I can't take you out to dinner or for a walk in the park or a movie out of fear that someone from the church will see us. We would be judged harshly."

"It's not okay for us to date because a priest shouldn't be in the company of a woman unless it's for her spiritual edification. Yet last night you made love to this woman," she reminded him through tears with her hand still on her chest. "God saw you. He saw us, Father Gregory. Is it better to sin in the dark away from the accusing eyes of man while under the all-seeing eyes of God than it is to sin openly before man and God?"

"Sin is sin whether we're making love in secrecy or committing murder in broad daylight. God sees it all. However, because I'm a priest, I have a higher calling. I'm responsible for the souls of hundreds of other people, Royce. God requires much more of me than He does of you because of that. Of course, I'm not expected to be perfect, but there are certain things I should never indulge in. That's why our situation is unique and complicated. There's no solution or compromise for us. I'm sorry."

"There *is* a solution," Royce whispered with tears in her eyes.

"Are you asking me to choose? Is that what you want me to do, Royce? You expect me to choose between you and God and the church?"

"No. I would never ask you to do that. But what if by some fluke or miraculous act, you were granted the power and right to choose? Would you remain a priest or would you free yourself to have a life with me?"

"I refuse to answer that ridiculous question, Royce. It's sacrilegious."

Father Gregory got up from the bed and gathered his clothes. Royce watched him dress in silence. She was physically and emotionally numb, yet her tears kept falling. The words she needed to say were on the edge of her teeth, but her heart wouldn't allow her to speak. She was dying a slow emotional death, but she wanted to live.

"Get some rest, Royce. I'll call you later."

She held her breath as she heard his footsteps descending the stairs. When the front door opened and quickly closed, Royce allowed herself to breathe again. It was the sound of his motorcycle roaring, putting distance between them, that caused the wall of emotions to topple completely. Royce felt like her heart had been shredded into a million pieces. She buried her face into the pillow and cried as if she were in mourning.

Chapter Sixteen

"Father, you have another confession. He's in the sanctuary praying."

"He?" Father Kyle asked, lifting his bushy, gray eyebrows.

"Yes, sir. It's a young man. He's dressed in all black and wearing a hoodie," the nun whispered. "I suppose he wishes to conceal his identity. Nevertheless, he lit a candle and is now kneeling in prayer. I can send him to the confessional whenever you're ready."

Father Kyle closed his Bible. "Send him back," he said and stood. "Are there any others, Sister Amelia?"

"No, Father. He appears to be your last one."

The priest left his office through the back door that that led him down a narrow, private passageway to the confessional. He took his seat on the bench in the closet-like compartment and waited. In Father Kyle's three and half decades in the priesthood, he had heard thousands of men and women acknowledge all types of sin. Each had expressed remorse to some degree, while others attempted to justify their offenses, but they all wanted God's forgiveness in the end.

Confession was definitely good for all souls, and it was a spiritual necessity. It was the first step to redemption, and it often helped to bring closure to the repentant transgressor. Father Kyle stroked the sides of his chin with his thumb and index finger as he waited for the young man who was about to pour out his heart to him to take his place. It was honorable of him to come seeking the Sacrament of Penance and Reconciliation. More young men and women alike would fare better by his example. Footsteps and movement on the other side of the wooden lattice screen alerted Father Kyle that his candidate for confession had arrived. He waited, giving the young man time to kneel in humility before he spoke.

"What brings you here today, my son?"

The sniffles on the other side of the confessional caught the priest totally off guard. There was no light in the small space where the young man kneeled in preparation for the sacrament, so his features were completely hidden by darkness. But Father Kyle knew beyond a shadow of a doubt that he was crying. Whatever sin the fellow had committed, it had bound him with grief. The priest waited patiently for him to speak.

"Once again, I have been with a woman who I am not married to. I am filthy and unworthy, Father. Have mercy on me." He sniffled.

The hairs on Father Kyle's nape bristled. He had heard the young man's voice only once before today, but he was certain that he was the same person he'd ministered to a few weeks ago. "Were you overtaken by lust again or did you resist the Holy Spirit's power to sustain you, my son?"

"I went to her of my own free will, Father. I tried to stay away from this woman. I prayed and I prayed and I prayed for God to save me from myself, but I was too weak. I had to have her."

"You love this woman, don't you?"

"I believe I do."

"Does she not love you as well?"

"She loves me."

"Good. My advice to you is to take this woman as your wife immediately. It is apparent that you cannot resist her. Through Scripture, the Apostle Paul encourages those of us who are feeble in spirit and are unable to abstain from sexual sin to marry. Otherwise, you will be consumed by flames of lust. Certainly, that is not your desire."

"I want to please God, but I can't because of my attraction and need for her. I'm powerless. Forgive me."

"That is why you must make her your bride. It is better to marry than to burn."

"I can't marry her!"

Father Kyle paused, confused by the young man's perplexing circumstances. He couldn't understand why a man who was in love with a woman and intimately involved with her would not make her his wife. "Why can't you and this woman be joined in matrimony? You've professed your love for her and assured me that she loves you. What is the problem?"

"It's complicated, Father."

"Is she the wife of another man, my son?"

"No, sir."

"Are you married to someone else?"

"No, I am not."

"I don't understand. Please enlighten me," the priest pleaded.

"Circumstances beyond my control forbid me to take a bride." Father Gregory sighed. "Look, Father, what must I do to be forgiven?"

"The blood of Jesus has already cleansed you from all unrighteousness, my son. But are you repenting today only to fornicate with your beloved again and again? Surely, this is not the kind of life you wish to live."

"I want to live a life that honors God, but I also want a life with the woman I love. Unfortunately, it is impossible for me to have both."

"I cannot give you proper guidance unless you confide in me completely, my son. What are you withholding from me?"

"I've told you everything you need to know."

Father Kyle heard movement on the other side of the screen. He assumed the young man had stood from the kneeling bench. He didn't want him to leave. The Holy Spirit told him that he was deeply troubled and in need of spiritual counseling. Father Kyle didn't want their session to end before he could help him. "Do not leave. Please let me help you, child of God."

"You can't. Thank you for your time, Father. Goodbye."

Father Kyle bowed his head in defeat when the door on the other side of the confessional closed. His heart went out to the young man. He was terribly disturbed and torn. His love for God was sincere. Father Kyle could hear the passion in his voice. But he also very much loved the woman he was involved with. It was a peculiar situation, but it was also simple. Marriage was honorable in the sight of God. The Almighty Himself had ordained it in the Garden of Eden for Adam and Eve. It was a holy covenant between God, a man, and his bride. The young man had given Father Kyle the impression that he was forbidden to marry, as if he were a priest.

"Nooo," Father Kyle drawled out and shook his head. He chuckled at the preposterous thought. There was no way that the young man could be a priest. He'd said he couldn't marry his lover, but he didn't offer an explanation. Maybe he did not meet the approval of the woman's father. Or perhaps, their families were involved in some kind of feud. Father Kyle had no idea what the problem was, but he believed it was a serious one. He wanted to guide the repentant soul through his issues, and he planned to do just that the next time the fellow came to confession. And he would come back. Father Kyle didn't doubt it for one moment. The young man would fall into temptation again. It was inevitable because his love for the woman and his sexual attraction to her was much too strong for him to abstain from lying with her. The Holy Spirit was preeminent and could deliver him from fornication, but only if the young man would yield to Its control and authority.

"The body of Christ," Father Gregory said softly, holding the bread before the lips he'd tasted and kissed passionately more times than he should have. He should never have kissed them at all, but it was too late.

"Amen." Royce opened her mouth and extended her tongue to receive the communion bread from her priest and lover.

He placed it on her tongue quickly, cautious not to touch any part of her luscious mouth. That simple mistake would've been hazardous to his mental health. It had been difficult enough maintaining focus during the mass, especially during his sermon. Father Gregory had studied all afternoon and into the evening after returning home from confession. He had been prepared this morning to deliver what he'd considered a thought-provoking homily on charity and sacrificial service. But he'd made the terrible misjudgment of looking at Royce when he mentioned missionaries traveling abroad to third-world countries to minister to the less fortunate. It had reminded him of her sister and her brother-in-law over in Sierra Leone, providing aid to the victims of the Ebola virus. As soon as Father Gregory looked at Royce while making his point, he regretted it. Surely it was Satan who had caused her to appear as naked as a stripper as she sat in the pew, listening to the sermon. His eyes almost shot from their sockets at the erotic figment of his imagination. Father Gregory lost his train of thought and stumbled over the words that he'd memorized. They were fresh in his mind until the devil started playing dirty tricks on him.

He did manage to pull himself together after clamping his eyes shut tight and pleading with God to have mercy on his wayward mind. By divine grace, the attentive congregation of Lord of the Harvest Roman Catholic Church didn't seem to notice their senior priest's pitfall in the pulpit. After he'd fully regained his composure and opened his eyes, bright smiles on faces filled with expectancy seemed to encourage him to continue his sermon. Father Gregory only hoped that his underlying message on charity and servitude had been well received by everyone under the sound of his voice.

He frowned inwardly as he continued serving communion bread to the parishioners. His thoughts had floated back to Royce. Her accusation that it was somehow easy for him to switch his feelings for her on and off on a whim was totally false. But she was upset and emotional at the time she made the charge against him. If only she knew the truth. Her very presence was a major distraction to him regardless of the setting. She caused his brain to go completely blank with her smile. And his body never ceased to betray him whenever he inhaled her signature scent of vanilla wafting from her skin. Her sassiness and sense of humor only added to her overall appeal. Any man with good sense would be drawn to such a rare jewel.

Father Gregory had confessed his love for Royce to the priest at Divine Trinity Roman Catholic Church, but he hadn't shared his feelings with her. While they were making love into the wee hours of the morning, she had opened her heart and whispered the three special words to him. He was too shocked and mentally off-balance to respond to her declaration. It still hadn't settled into his brain. Royce loved him. It was an awesome feeling to be loved, yet it was bittersweet. Even though they were in love, there was no future under the heavens for them because of his life's calling to ministry.

As the last few souls approached Father Gregory to receive the Lord's Supper, he sneaked a peek in Royce's direction. Her seat in the pew was now empty. She had left the mass before the dismissal prayer.

Chapter Seventeen

"Did you enjoy the Blue Ridge Mountains, Tyler?" asked Father Gregory.

"Yeah. We had a blast."

"What did you guys do up there?"

"Deacon Moreland and Deacon Barkley built a huge bonfire Friday night. We roasted hot dogs and marshmallows while some of the other older dudes told scary stories. It was cool. We went hiking Saturday morning and horseback riding that afternoon. What did you do over the weekend, Father Gregory?"

"I, um, I was pretty busy. I studied a lot, preparing for my sermon. I visited another Catholic church on the other side of town Saturday after the noonday mass here. Basically, I did nothing exciting at all," he lied.

Tyler opened another box filled with children's books. He handed a short stack to Father Gregory. "Auntie Royce stayed busy too. This morning I heard her telling my mom she went out for drinks and dancing at a nightclub. She met a man, a major-league baseball player, but she wasn't impressed by him. He plays for the Atlanta Braves. You've heard of Bullet Bullard, right?"

"I have," the rattled priest confirmed. "Why?"

"He's the dude who put the moves on Auntie Royce at the club Friday night. Bullet is rich and famous! I don't understand why she dissed him. He offered her VIP tickets to a skybox at his first game. And he invited her to fly away with him to some tropical island. Can you believe she turned him down?"

"Imagine that." Father Gregory placed a row of Bibles on the bookshelf.

"I don't know what's wrong with my auntie. She should've given Bullet a chance. I would've approved of him."

"You would have? Why, Tyler? Because of his millions and his fame?"

"Yeah. But maybe he's a cool cat like you, except he's free to marry Auntie Royce and become my rich uncle." The boy laughed and picked up a box of hymn books and carried them to the other side of the church's small library.

Father Gregory's hands were itching and on fire. He was a few hot seconds away from snatching up his cell phone and calling Royce to interrogate her about her night out on the town. But what could he possibly say to her? They weren't exactly in a relationship, per se. And she had rejected Bullet Bullard's advances. Very few women, if any, would have walked away from a star athlete. However, Royce had, and she'd returned home unmoved by his money and stardom.

A streak of heat crept up Father Gregory's loins as he reflected on how Royce had spent the duration of the night after she'd arrived at her house from the club. The memorable scenes of the kiss they'd shared in her foyer and their steamy bedroom escapade well into the predawn hours paid his brain a visit. He would never forget the sound of Royce's voice when she confessed her love for him. If there was a more pleasing verbal expression to a man's ears, Father Gregory had never heard it before.

He suddenly broke out in a cold sweat when he realized he would never hear those precious words again. How could a man live without a woman after knowing her body, tasting it, and having her scent buried in his skin? The fact that he'd fallen madly in love with Royce would make it even more difficult to walk away. His life would be incomplete without her, but damned to hell with her. The Apostle Paul believed that a priest should not marry because the duties of a husband would hinder his ability to effectively serve God and the church. He would be torn between Christ and his bride.

"I am not the Apostle Paul."

"What did you say?" Tyler shot Father Gregory a puzzled look.

"Um, nothing. Just thinking out loud."

Paul's personal commitment to bachelorhood and celibacy with no scriptural base at all had somehow unleashed a curse on every Roman Catholic priest who dared to serve after him. It was so unfair.

"Oh, well, I'm done," the boy announced, pointing to the eye-catching media display he'd constructed with CDs, DVDs, and Blu-ray discs.

"You did a good job, buddy. I better get you home so you can eat dinner. I want you to be well rested for tomorrow's game."

"It won't matter. We're going to lose no matter what. We suck without Romello and Damien. Everybody blames me for them being expelled from Saint Xavier's."

"Those two were thrown out of school because they were sentenced to sixty days in juvenile detention for theft by taking. How is that your fault? You should be angry with them. They tried to throw you under the bus after they got caught shoplifting. Next season there'll be a new group of players at your school, and the team will be much better."

"I hope so, because if not, we'll have another losing season."

Royce looked past Tyler's slim and tall frame as he entered the house. The front door was still open, giving her a perfect view of the candy-apple red two-seater and its driver. Father Gregory waved before he honked his horn twice and sped away.

Royce slammed the door. She felt her blood pressure rising. She was ticked off. How dare Father Gregory not walk Tyler inside the house as had become his custom? She would've behaved and kept her hands to herself. It was a promise they'd made to each other in their secret phone conversation the night before. They'd vowed to conduct themselves as friends from now on. There would be no more kisses and definitely no more lovemaking. It was impossible for them to pretend that they were just priest and parishioner, so they had agreed to be friends.

But Royce knew better. There was no way in hell that she and Father Gregory could be just friends. They had experienced too much passion and intimacy, intensifying the sexual chemistry between them. Their hearts had a strong connection that couldn't be ignored. Royce was hooked on his love, and she didn't want to be cured. She wanted Father Gregory in her life forever, but she also wanted him to honor his vow to God and remain a priest. She loved him too much to force him to choose between her and his faith. But she wasn't satisfied with just being his friend. She was willing to give it a try, though. She had no other choice. Father Gregory had made it perfectly clear that their sexual relationship had come to an end and would never be rekindled. Royce didn't think it was possible, but she didn't bother to tell him. He would have to make the discovery on his own.

"I am so proud of you, Tyler." Royce grabbed her nephew in a bear hug and kissed his cheek. "I'm going to do something special for you this week. You were balling out there, Mr. MVP," she said, releasing him from her hold.

"Thanks. I still can't believe I hit thirteen points. I've got to call my dad in the morning to tell him that we won our final game of the season."

"I'm sure he'll be proud. I am." Father Gregory extended his hand for a fist bump.

Tyler tapped his fist with his. "Yeah, he'll be proud, and so will my mom."

"We better get going, sweetie. You need to do your homework. I'll swing by the Burger Zone and buy you the usual."

"Can I have hot wings instead?"

"Of course you can. Let's go."

Tyler turned to Father Gregory before they headed for the gym's exit. "I'll see you tomorrow."

"Sure thing, buddy. I'll see you later, Royce."

She smiled and waved quickly and followed Tyler out of the gym.

Father Gregory felt an icy chill when Royce walked past him. She hadn't fully acknowledged his presence all evening. Their eyes had met as soon as she arrived at the gym for the game, but she quickly looked away. Normally, they would sit together and cheer for Tyler as he played. Today she'd sat in another section on the opposite side of the gym. Father Gregory couldn't blame Royce, though. She was simply following the rules he had set regarding their friendship. It was the most difficult decision he'd ever made in his life, but it was for the best. At his request, they were keeping a safe distance from each other, but they would always be cordial whenever they ended up in the same room. Tyler was their link to one another, although they did speak on the phone from time to time. But talking wasn't enough.

There were nights when Father Gregory would lie in bed unable to sleep, wishing that Royce

would pay him a secret visit at the parsonage.
He didn't necessarily want to be intimate with
her. He just wanted to be in her presence. She
was a joy to be around. Her smile and sense of
humor brought out the best in him. The silent
moments when he would lie with her in his
arms were priceless. However, his relationship
with God was more important to him. It was the
reason Father Gregory had ended his brief affair
with Royce. As a priest, he had chosen God over
the woman he loved, and she had accepted his
decision. Because of their resolution, he expected
peace and blessings in his future and in Royce's
as well.

Chapter Eighteen

The slow pitter-patter of unexpected rain woke Royce from a restless sleep. The light taps against her windowpane reminded her of a sluggish jazz drummer playing off the beat. It was an on-and-off-again sprinkle that she hoped would soon end. Royce closed her eyes and rolled over onto her back, willing her brain to return to subconsciousness.

"Royce!"

Her heart did a somersault when she heard a male voice call her name. A soft tap on her windowpane followed the faint shout. There was another strike against the glass and then a third one. Royce heard her name again. The rich timbre was louder this time. She wanted to attribute the voice outside her window and the tapping to her imagination or sleep deprivation, but her heart told her the truth. Father Gregory was outside.

He wanted to see her. Royce's pulse accelerated from the thrill of being wanted.

She reached over and turned on the lamp on her nightstand, but she didn't sit up in bed. Seconds passed as she lay flat on her back with her heart racing, waiting to hear his voice and the sound of rocks hitting her window again. The light from the lamp was her signal to acknowledge his presence outside. It was his turn to respond.

"Royce, it's me, Nicholas. Come to the door."

Nicholas? Royce repeated the name silently. A smile crept across her face. She'd never addressed him by his first name, not even while they were in the throes of passion. During those steamy moments, his actions were anything but priestly, yet she still called him Father Gregory. Another rock or some unknown object pounded against the windowpane. Royce snatched the covers from her body and left the bed. She tiptoed to the window and turned the wand to open the Venetian blinds. There, below on the ground directly beneath her bedroom window stood the finest man in the universe. He was dressed in black from crown to sole. Royce released a breath she'd been holding in anticipation of the visual treat her eyes were now beholding.

"Please come to the door," he pleaded. "I have something I want to give you."

Royce hesitated, unsure of the purpose of Father Gregory's late-night visit. They were just friends, so why couldn't he visit her during the daytime or at least before nightfall? Real friends didn't have to hide out and spend time together behind the shadows of darkness. But Royce and Father Gregory's relationship had long since passed the purity of friendship, regardless of the unrealistic agreement they'd made. They were lovers in every way that truly mattered. No vow to God or the Roman Catholic Church could erase the bonding of their souls. Even if they never made love again, they would never, ever be just friends.

The love in her heart yanked her from the window and down the stairs. Dressed in a pink, sheer nightgown that was mid-thigh in length, Royce floated lightly over each step. Fortunately, Tyler was a sound sleeper. He was probably more tired than usual because of all the energy he'd exerted in his game-winning performance on the basketball court the prior evening. Royce wasn't concerned about him waking up before six o'clock, his normal stirring time. In fact, it was hard to wake the boy most mornings. No, he wasn't going to get up anytime soon.

Royce stopped when she reached her front door. She was nervous, excited, and horny, but she didn't want to reveal her impure feelings to Father Gregory right away. Desperation wasn't sexy at all. She raked her fingers through her braids and exhaled. After a quick count to ten, she deactivated the security system and opened the door.

Royce would never develop immunity to his good looks or raw sex appeal no matter how many times he graced her with his presence. Father Gregory was the total male package dressed in a black turtleneck sweater, a pair of black jeans, and his signature black leather bomber. The outfit hung on his exquisite physique perfectly. His handsome face, chiseled body, and charm were more lethal than an arsenal of high-powered weapons. One touch from him could cause Royce's pink thong to magically drop to her ankles. And there would be no turning back after that. The late-night visit would end with a sexual explosion if they weren't careful.

"May I come in?"

Royce nodded mindlessly and stepped aside.

Father Gregory entered the warm foyer with a beautiful bouquet of white long-stem roses in one hand. In the other, there was a small, flat gift wrapped in bright red paper and shiny gold ribbon. "These are for you," he whispered, handing Royce the roses. "This is too."

Royce raised the flowers to her nose and inhaled the heavenly scent. "Thank you. They're very pretty." She took the offered gift and smiled. "Thanks."

"You're welcome." Father Gregory looked toward the staircase. "Tyler is asleep, I hope."

"You weren't concerned about my nephew when you were tossing rocks at my window and yelling like a maniac."

"I guess I acted sort of silly, huh?"

"You sure did."

"I tried to call you, but you didn't answer your cell phone. I would've awakened Tyler for sure if I had called the house phone."

"My phone is in my purse. I'll bet my battery needs charging by now."

"Can we sit down? I'd like you to open your gift."

"To what do I owe the flowers and a surprise gift, sir?"

Father Gregory took Royce by the wrist. "Let's sit down, so I can tell you."

The unexpected visit, the roses, and the present had already knocked Royce off of her game. His take-charge attitude only stoked the fire. There was nothing sexier than a charming man in control and bearing gifts. Royce's womanly senses peaked to red-hot alert. Something serious was about to go down. On a whim, she decided that her all-white formal living room was the ideal spot for them to talk and do anything else that was on Father Gregory's agenda. She led him to the double glass doors and stopped.

Royce faced him in the dark hallway and handed him the roses and unopened gift. "Take off your shoes before you go inside. I'll be right back."

She padded away on bare feet to the kitchen before Father Gregory had a chance to respond. Royce gathered a pair of candles and a lighter and then walked straight to the den. In the closet, she found a huge blue chenille blanket. With everything she needed, she returned to the living room where the love of her life sat on one of the white sofas waiting for her. Royce placed a candle in each of the crystal holders at the ends of the mantle and lit both of them.

From his slouch on the sofa, Father Gregory reached out his hand to her. "Come and sit down."

"I will, but I want to serve you something to drink first. Let me get you a glass of mango juice. I'll have a glass of wine if that's okay with you." Royce paused, cocking her head to the side. She smiled. "I can sip wine in your presence, can't I?"

"Of course you can. As a matter of fact, forget about the mango juice. Just bring the bottle of wine. We'll share it."

Royce hurried to the kitchen to remove the bottle of Riesling from the refrigerator. She made haste uncorking it, and she selected a pair of crystal wineglasses from her stemware collection. Her mind was spinning in every direction, and her body was vibrating with anticipation. Wine, flowers, and a gift could lead to only one thing. But there was something missing. *Mood music!* If added, some smooth jazz would spice up the atmosphere, making it just right for romance. Royce returned to the living room, clutching the bottle of wine in one hand and the pair of wineglasses in the other. She was surprised that Father Gregory was no longer sitting on the sofa. He had spread the blanket over the thick white carpet and sprawled out on top of it. He looked irresistible lying on his side with his elbow pressing into the blanket while the side of his face rested on his fist.

"I see you've made yourself at home," Royce said, offering him the wine and the glasses.

Father Gregory gave her a lazy smile and sat up. He removed the wine and glasses from her hands. "I hope you don't mind." He placed everything on the coffee table.

"Not at all." Royce picked up a remote control from an end table and pushed a button. The smooth sound of jazz legend John Coltrane making love to his saxophone filled the air. "You're a jazz lover, I hope."

"It's my favorite. Coltrane, Miles, Monk, and Parker were some serious cats. I like Ella Fitzgerald, Dinah Washington, and Billie Holiday, too. Max, my stepdad, has a vinyl collection of all the late greats. I grew up listening to jazz because of him. He used to sit in the den on Saturday nights, puffing on his pipe and sipping brandy while Lena Horne sang him to sleep. Every now and then my mama would join him, and before the night was over, they'd dance. My sisters and I would twirl around them like we were at a jazz club."

"It sounds sweet." Royce sat on the blanket and tucked her feet under her bottom. "My parents loved jazz when they were younger. They still do, although they don't listen to it as much as they used to. Mama likes the blues, too. Daddy doesn't care for it. He says it's too depressing."

Father Gregory removed the wine and one of the glasses from the coffee table. He poured a moderate amount in one glass and offered it to Royce. Then he filled the other halfway for himself. "Cheers," he said, touching her glass with his before he took a sip. "Mmm, this is good."

"How often do you drink alcohol?"

"Seldom. The last time I had a drink was Christmas Eve. I sipped on the same glass of merlot all evening at my parents' house." He looked at the unopened gift he'd placed on the coffee table.

Royce followed his line of vision. "I guess I should open that now." She placed her wineglass on the coffee table.

Father Gregory nodded.

"It was very nice of you to bring me flowers and a gift. What's the occasion?"

"I've never had the pleasure of courting a woman before. I thought it'd be nice to be a gentleman and bring you something nice. You're special to me, Royce."

"How special?"

"Until I met you, I had no desire to date any woman or make love to one. Now, I want it all, but unfortunately, it's not possible. Of course, our circumstances are screwed up, but it doesn't change how I feel about you. I love you, Royce. I know that I shouldn't, and God knows I've tried not to, but I'm powerless. If there were any possibility for us to be together, you would be mine in every way that counts." He lifted the gift from the table and gave it to her.

He loves me. The three words brought tears to Royce's eyes. She let them fall freely as she opened the gift. She tried to control her hands and keep them from shaking, but she was too emotional. She felt special in the magic of the moment. Underneath the pretty red wrapping paper was a velvet jewelry box of the same color. Royce's heart palpitated. She paused as her eyes fluttered shut.

"Go ahead, sweetheart. Open it."

Royce did as she was told and was surprised beyond her fondest fairy tale. The lovely diamond-encrusted, heart-shaped pendant on a white gold herringbone chain blew her mind. A fresh flow of tears pooled in her eyes. She was helpless to stop them from falling.

"It's beautiful. Thank you very much."

Father Gregory wiped Royce's tears away with the back of his hand. "I'm glad you like it. As soon as I spotted it at the jewelry store, I knew it belonged around your neck."

"What do you mean?"

"I can't marry you or even have a normal relationship with you because of the priesthood. But I can't stop loving you. I would give you the world if I could, Royce. You deserve it and so much more. Since I can't give you the one thing you want more than anything else, which is my hand in marriage, I plan to give you all that I can."

Chapter Nineteen

"Auntie Royce! Where are you? I need extra money today. Auntie!"

Royce stirred from her sleep when she heard Tyler bouncing down the stairs and yelling through the house. She suddenly remembered where she was and that she wasn't alone. Father Gregory was sleeping and snoring lightly on the blanket beside her. Thank God he was fully dressed. They'd chosen not to make love the night before. Instead, they'd sipped wine and talked until sleep overtook them. In a way, a night of sharing their feelings, desires, and ideas had been more intimate than sex.

Royce hurried to the mantle and blew out the candles. Darkness swallowed the room. She returned to the blanket and knelt down. Pressing her lips to Father Gregory's ear, she whispered, "Tyler is awake. Stay here and don't make a sound. I'll be right back."

He reached up and stroked the side of her face and nodded.

Royce stepped outside the double glass doors and stumbled over Father Gregory's black running shoes. She snatched them up quickly and tossed them inside the living room and shut the doors. Tyler was in the kitchen. She could hear him opening and closing cabinets. Royce composed herself and walked down the hall.

"What's up, Auntie?"

"Good morning, sweetie. How did you sleep last night?"

"I was tired. My body and my brain went on strike as soon as my head hit the pillow. What about you? How did you sleep, Auntie?"

"I slept like a baby, sweet pea. Come upstairs when you finish eating your cereal. I'll give you the extra money you were screaming your head off about."

"That was close, Royce." Father Gregory embraced her from behind and kissed the back of her neck seconds after she closed the front door.

"It would've been a disaster if Tyler had caught you here. Thank God I was able to think fast. Let's go to the kitchen so I can feed you before you leave to start your day."

"I'm sorry, but I don't have time. I have a nine o'clock appointment at the church."

Royce turned around in his arms to face him. "When will I see you again?"

"I could come here tonight."

"I would like that."

He lifted the diamond-filled pendant from her chest. "I'll call you when I'm five minutes away."

"I'll be waiting."

Father Gregory leaned in, placed a chaste kiss on Royce's lips, and left.

"Father, I did not come today to confess any sin. I want you to know that I have spent time with my lover, but we did not yield to temptation. God is good."

"Indeed He is," Father Kyle agreed. However, he was a bit worried about the young man on the other side of the confessional. He sounded as if he truly believed his troubles with fornication were behind him. Unfortunately, he was sadly mistaken. There would be temptation as long as he loved the woman he was involved with and they still had not married. "I am happy that you were not consumed by your flesh. But what do you suppose will happen the next time you are in the presence of your beloved? Are you now immune to your attraction to her? Has your sexual appetite for her miraculously disappeared?"

"No, it hasn't, but we've made an agreement. We can love each other without having a physical relationship. Although I'm not proud to confess this, we slept together last night. But nothing happened. We held each other and talked, but we did not fornicate."

"Did you desire to be intimate with her?"

"Of course, but I didn't have sex with her. We abstained. Isn't that wonderful?"

"I must admit that was a great spiritual accomplishment, but it was also very foolish of you, my son. You tempted yourself. Only an unwise man would place himself in the path of lust and destruction. God had mercy on you, but He will not rescue you the next time you take fire into your bosom. If you walk upon hot coals, your feet will be burned. If you wish to be free of sexual sin, my advice to you is to do away with this woman once and for all or marry her."

"I can't live without her. I won't live without her."

"Then marry her or perish."

Father Gregory left the confessional abruptly, slamming the door behind him. He was very angry with Father Kyle and shocked by his straightforwardness. Deep in his heart, he knew that the older priest was right, but he didn't want to receive his spiritual wisdom or advice on the matter. Looking back on the time he'd spent with Royce last night, he now realized that he had acted foolishly. Yet he was very much pleased with himself for not making love to her like he'd so desperately wanted to. He was certain that God was happy with him for practicing self-control. So, why had Father Kyle been so cynical?

Father Gregory hopped on his Harley and sped away from the church. He didn't want to think about Father Kyle and his warnings. What did he know about women anyway? He was just some miserable, old dude bound by the traditions of the Roman Catholic Church to live an empty and boring life without the love of a woman. It wasn't fair or natural, and it wasn't the kind of life he wanted to live. Father Gregory wanted Royce, and it pained him to imagine living without her.

"God help me," he whispered as the wind blew in his face. He whipped around a curve with visions of Royce's smiling face flashing in his memory.

She was so beautiful and kind. He loved her, and that was all there was to it.

"Are you sure you don't want me to come? I'll be extra careful and quiet. We won't get caught."

"It's not a good idea. I just don't feel comfortable with you visiting while Rico is here. He's like a nephew to me. He roams around the house freely just like Tyler. Can you imagine what would happen if he got up in the middle of the night to go to the kitchen to get something to drink and found you here?"

Father Gregory tossed the scene around in his head a few times. "We would have a lot of explaining to do."

"Correct. That's why we can't risk it. We can hook up this weekend. Glenda will return from her business trip Thursday night. She wants Tyler to come over after school Friday. He'll be there until Sunday evening."

There was a knock at Father Gregory's office door. He covered the mouthpiece of the phone with his hand. "Come in."

Sister Ellen Marie walked in smiling and carrying a stack of mail in her hands. She stood in the middle of the floor, facing his desk.

"I need to take care of something right now. I'll call you as soon as I get home."

"Have a good weekend, Tabatha. And please don't call me unless there's an emergency."

"I won't, boss lady. I'll have everything under control."

Royce strolled out into the parking lot with pep in her step and a smile on her face. Tyler was spending the weekend with Rico and his mother, and she would have the house to herself. Last night during their pillow-time phone chat, Father Gregory had promised to visit her at eight o'clock sharp. The thought of spending time with him alone gave Royce an adrenaline rush. By the time she reached her designated parking space, she was humming an oldie but goodie R&B hit by the O'Jays. It was a love ballad that her Uncle Duke used to play on the stereo and sing loud and off-key whenever he'd drunk too much whiskey back in the day. The song perfectly described Royce's situation with Father Gregory. He definitely had his hooks in her.

He'd promised her an unforgettable weekend, and she was looking forward to every minute of it. Royce got inside her luxury SUV and peeled out of the parking lot, humming and counting down the hours until her date. That morning before leaving the house for the office, she'd selected the perfect outfit to wear and decided to order Caribbean cuisine from Masai's on Peachtree. All of their delivery guys knew her well. One of the gentlemen would arrive at her house within an hour after she'd placed her order, and the food would be piping hot.

The only item Royce needed to pick up on her way home was a bottle of wine. She and Father

Gregory had finished the entire bottle the other night while they talked about their families, friends, and futures. Royce had enjoyed their conversation, but she'd wanted him to make love to her. Strangely, he didn't put the moves on her, though. He'd kissed her lips often and embraced her, but nothing else. His actions or lack thereof had surprised her. She had agreed that they would practice abstinence, but she never expected them to really discontinue their sexual relationship. It wasn't possible as far as she was concerned. By some miracle, they had stuck to the plan the other night, but Royce wasn't interested in a repeat performance tonight at all. She wanted to be loved, and she refused to be denied.

Chapter Twenty

"I'm coming!" Royce ran to the door with the cordless phone in her hand. She grabbed the brass handle and pulled.

"You look beautiful." Father Gregory leaned in and kissed her forehead. He looked down at her sock-covered feet. "You need to put some boots on." He handed her a motorcycle helmet and entered the house.

"What's this?"

"It's protection for your head. You can't ride a motorcycle without wearing a helmet. It's against the law in the state of Georgia."

"I don't want to ride your bike. It's too cold out there. I was about to order Caribbean food. And I have a bottle of Riesling in the refrigerator. The fire is blazing in the living room. Let's stay in."

He shook his head and smiled. "We stayed in the other night. I want to take you out. Get your coat, a hat, and some gloves. I'm sure you have some boots. Put them on. Go on now. Your chariot awaits." He swatted Royce playfully on her backside when she walked past him, rolling her eyes.

Father Gregory laughed out loud and took the helmet and telephone Royce had shoved in his chest on her way to the staircase. He sat at the bottom of the steps to wait for her. It was chilly outside, but in his opinion, it was never too cold to go for a motorcycle ride. There was nothing more invigorating than the wind blowing in your face as you took in the sounds and sights of nature from the seat of a Harley. The speed and thrill of it all was an adventure.

"I'm ready," Royce announced from the landing above a few minutes later.

Father Gregory turned and looked over his shoulder in time to see Royce stomping down the stairs like a spoiled brat. He smiled at her defiant body language and the scowl on her pretty face. She was covered in winter gear more suitable for a blizzard than a simple ride on a motorcycle in mid-March. She had tucked her long braids underneath a colorful toboggan and put on a pair of thigh-high riding boots over the legs of her jeans. Her full-length black leather coat made her look mysterious and sexy. Father Gregory watched her descend the steps at a snail's pace. Her bottom lip was poked out like a pouting toddler on the verge of tears.

"We're going to have fun, sweetheart. I promise. Let me take you for a ride and out to dinner, please."

Royce shot him a suspicious glare. "How far do you plan to take me on that motorcycle of yours? There's no restaurant around here where you can wine and dine me without running the risk of us being seen together."

"Don't worry about that. Trust me," he insisted, taking her by the hand. He kissed the back of it. "I promise to show you a good time."

They left the house, and twenty minutes later they were cruising south down Interstate 75. Royce rested the side of her head against Father Gregory's back to shield her face from the sting of oncoming wind. She was holding him around his waist with her fingers interlocked together. He relished the feel of her soft body pressing against him as the night's cool air wrapped all around them. Stolen moments like this particular one tempted him to question God, his religious beliefs, and the vocation he'd chosen. But the night was young and promising, and he didn't want to think about any of that. The woman he loved was with him, and nothing else mattered.

As planned, he guided the Harley off the interstate, taking exit 185 into the small town of Forsyth, Georgia. And as he'd expected, Royce raised her head to check out their surroundings. He couldn't help but wonder what she was thinking as he coasted along. He was from the big city of Chicago. He didn't know a lot about Georgia and even less about cities outside of Atlanta. But there they were in Forsyth.

It was a tiny city with a small population his internet search had led him to. Father Gregory's intention was to spend time with Royce in a safe setting without interruption and away from the eyes of anyone who knew either of them. It was a date, the first one for him since his senior prom. The excitement over that memorable formal event couldn't compare to what he felt at the moment. A simple dinner at a quaint restaurant in a small town with the woman who had captured his heart meant the world to him.

"Where are we?" Royce shouted over the motorcycle's roar.

"We're in Forsyth, Georgia. It's a little town I discovered online."

Father Gregory guided the bike into the parking lot of Shoney's, a popular down-home eatery in the small community. He could only imagine the look on Royce's face. It was a long way from five-star dining, but it would have to do. He whipped the motorcycle into a parking space and killed the engine.

Royce threw her heard back and laughed. "I ate at a Shoney's restaurant in South Carolina once."

"So, you approve?"

"I would've preferred takeout from Masai's and a bottle of wine in front of the fireplace, but I guess this is okay. I like the company I'm with."

They took off their helmets and dismounted the bike. Father Gregory laced his fingers through Royce's and escorted her into the restaurant. A hostess seated them in a corner booth right away. Less than a minute later, the server, a heavyset chick with bright red hair, approached their table and took their drink orders. When she returned with two glasses of lemonade and straws, she took their dinner orders.

"Are you going to be able to eat a triple-decker bacon cheeseburger?"

Royce grinned. "Watch me. I'm going to try your steak and shrimp, too. I'm starving. I don't eat beef often, but whenever I do, I go all out."

"Don't overdo it. I don't want you to get sick."

"I'll be fine."

"I wanted to take you to one of those fancy restaurants downtown Atlanta where there's live music, elegant décor, and gourmet entrées that have names I can't even pronounce. That's what you deserve, but I can't do that."

"I deserve *you*, and I'll take you anywhere and anyway I can. If we have to sneak away to a hick town and eat dinner at a not-so-fancy restaurant for privacy, I don't mind."

"Thanks for understanding. Most women wouldn't put up with me and my complicated life."

"I'm not like other women. I would never place unfair demands and expectations on you. I didn't walk into this situation blindfolded. I made a decision of my own free will to become your special friend, and I accept whatever you can offer in this relationship."

"And I love you for loving me in spite of my circumstances. But I feel so selfish and inconsiderate. A woman like you is worthy of being loved and cherished openly for the whole world to see. Look at us. We're hiding and sneaking around like a pair of runaway teenagers."

"I don't care. I just want us to be together as often as we can. If that means we'll have to hook up at my place after dark or leave the city every once in a while, I'm cool with it."

"You're cool with it for now." He reached across the table and took Royce's hand. "What about on special occasions and holidays or other times when people who're in love usually come together? Will you be fine then?"

"I'll cross that bridge when we get there."

"Sweetheart, there will come a time when you'll no longer be satisfied with the way things are between us today. You'll grow tired of the secret visits and phone calls. They won't be enough anymore. You're going to want more from me, and I won't be able to give it to you."

"I will take whatever you have to offer me because I love you and there is no other man anywhere in the world for me. I'd rather have a piece of you than ten other men at my beck and call."

"What about the celibacy? How long do you think you'll be able to handle that?"

Royce removed her hand from his and looked out the restaurant's window and into the sparsely filled parking lot. "For you, I'll be as chaste as a nun."

"A triple bacon cheeseburger and fries for the lady," the server announced in her deep Southern drawl as she placed a plate on the table in front of Royce. "And I have a medium-well T-bone steak, fried shrimp, and a loaded baked potato for the gentleman. Can I get either of y'all anything else?"

"We're fine."

"No, thank you," Royce said, nibbling on a French fry.

"Enjoy your meal."

Father Gregory looked into Royce's eyes. "Promise me something."

"Anything."

"Promise me that you'll let me know when you become unable to deal with me and our friendship. I want you to be honest with me, Royce. I love you, and I want you to be happy. But if I can't make you happy, I want you to be with a man who can. I'll die an old and lonely heartbroken man, but I'll be at peace knowing you've found love and happiness.

Royce didn't respond. She took a long sip of her lemonade and looked out the window again.

Chapter Twenty-one

A much lower temperature and chilling winds greeted Royce and Father Gregory when they stepped outside of the restaurant. He wrapped his arm around her shoulders and pulled her body snuggly against his side as they walked to his motorcycle.

"I'm freezing."

"I know. The temperature dropped drastically while we were eating and talking. The wind picked up, too. I don't think we can ride back to Atlanta in this kind of weather. We'll turn into a pair of icicles before we ride half a mile."

"What are we going to do?"

"We'll find a motel or maybe a hotel and check in for the night."

Royce smiled on the inside, and her body began to tingle. Mother Nature had done her a huge favor without her even making a request. She was smart enough to know that God would never have put her and Father Gregory in a compromising situation. Some things just happened. In this particular case, the weather had become too severe to handle, and because of it, she had an opportunity she otherwise might not have had.

They got on the motorcycle and rode to a convenience store across the street. Fortunately, the kind cashier directed them to a hotel less than five minutes away in the opposite direction. Royce's teeth chattered as they sped toward the hotel. Her leather gloves did nothing to shield her hands from the icy weather. She pressed the side of her head against Father Gregory's back and closed her eyes. She was grateful when he turned a curve and slowed the motorcycle down. He parked and killed the engine.

"Come on, baby. Let me get you inside so you can get warm."

They dismounted the bike and removed their helmets. Hand in hand they walked into the lobby of the Holiday Inn Express. Royce took a seat in a big, comfortable chair and watched CNN while Father Gregory registered for a room. She sneaked a quick peek at him, and the back view of his body was sweet on her brown eyes.

Dressed in his usual all black, his firm butt looked good in a pair of loose-fitting jeans. Royce thought about how she had palmed it each time he'd made love to her. She hoped she would get a feel of it tonight. He no doubt had every intention of keeping his jewels to himself, but she had another plan. She was already a sinner anyway, sleeping with a priest of all men. Both times had been a mutual decision on their parts, but tonight would probably be different. If Father Gregory did not come on to her, Royce would be forced to seduce him.

"Your room is on the third floor, ma'am." He turned and smiled, waving the key card as he walked in her direction. "I'll ride up with you and check it out to make sure it's okay before I leave you."

"What do you mean?"

He smiled. "I have my own room, sweetheart. I'll be a few doors down the hall from you."

"Why?"

"There were no double rooms available, so I got us a room apiece. We both have a king-sized bed and premium television channels."

They walked into the elevator in complete silence. Royce was livid. How could she make him melt under her seductive heat if they weren't sharing a room? He was taking the abstinence issue a little too seriously for her liking. She knew that fornication was a sin, especially for a priest, but it wasn't like they hadn't already done it before. One more time wasn't going to overflow their sin cups.

Father Gregory opened the door to Royce's room and allowed her to enter first. She tossed her motorcycle helmet on the bed. He flipped on the light and walked around, inspecting the cozy space a few steps behind her. She could feel his body heat. He was torturing her, and she didn't appreciate it. Maybe he thought he could go cold turkey, but she was going to teach him a very valuable lesson in human sexuality.

"I'm tired. I'm going to shower and turn in. Good night." Royce turned around and removed the key card from his hand. She walked past him and went to the door. She opened it wide.

"Well, um, I'm about to brave the weather one more time and go back to that convenience store. I need a razor, a toothbrush, and toothpaste. I'll get deodorant, too. Can I buy anything for you? I used to shop for my sisters all the time. I'm quite familiar with all the girlie stuff."

"I'll be fine. I just want to go to sleep. Good night."

Father Gregory stood quietly in place for a few seconds. Royce had just thrown him a curveball. He was more than likely confused, but she didn't give a damn. She was playing by his rules, but it appeared that he wasn't so sure if he wanted her to. It was too bad, because he would be thinking about her in the middle of the night now that she had flipped the script on him.

"Good night, Royce." He reached out to hug her.

She did a smooth side step out of his reach while still holding on to the doorknob. "That's not a good idea. Remember, we're in love, but we're celibate. Hugging in a room with a bed in it could tempt us to do something we both will regret in the morning."

Father Gregory looked at the condoms one more time, inwardly debating with his conscience over whether he should buy them. The items he had gone to the store to buy were in his hand-basket already. All he needed to do was make his purchases and leave, but his feet wouldn't move, no matter how many times his brain ordered them to. He was torn between pleasing God and satisfying his flesh. Royce was probably asleep by now, but he couldn't get her off of his mind. She was freshly showered in her room, lying in that great big bed all alone. He wondered what she was wearing, since she didn't have a nightgown or any other loungewear.

"Self-control, Nicholas," he reminded himself, closing his eyes. "You've got to be strong and yield not to temptation."

Father Gregory walked away from the condoms and headed for the checkout, feeling empowered. He would deliver the toothbrush, toothpaste, and deodorant he was about to purchase for Royce to her door and leave. He could resist her just like he had the other night. All he had to do was stay in the hallway and not touch her. God would give him the strength to do just that.

"It serves him right." Royce laughed softly and pulled the covers up to her chin. She rolled over onto her belly, very much amused.

Father Gregory had been pounding on her door for five minutes now. He'd called the phone in her room several times, and she'd allowed it to ring off the hook without answering it. Her cell phone battery had died over an hour ago, but it didn't matter. She wouldn't have taken his call anyway. It was his idea for them to have separate rooms, and the celibacy rule was all his too. She was giving him just what he wanted: love minus sex. It was kind of weird, but clearly the nature of men. As long as they were doing the rejecting, it wasn't such a big deal. But now that he was on the receiving end of a snub, he couldn't handle it.

The pounding stopped. Royce got up and tiptoed to the door. She looked through the peephole and giggled softly with her hand covering her mouth. Father Gregory was standing in the hallway, staring at the door. He looked frustrated. There was a bag in his hand. He had gone to the convenience store and bought her some personal items after all. Royce had known he would. He was such a gentleman, but he was also a tease. He wanted his cake, but he wanted to eat it, too. Royce wouldn't allow it.

It wasn't that she wanted him to abandon the priesthood and enter into a full-fledged affair with her. She simply wanted him to be fair and realistic about their relationship. Plainly put, she wanted him to continue being a priest while giving himself completely to her at the same time. He wouldn't be the first Catholic priest to live a secret double life. People all over the world were aware of the countless scandals involving the sexual misconduct of priests. Those cases had brought shame to the Roman Catholic Church. Millions of dollars had been paid in legal settlements to the alleged victims, and the church had lost thousands of members as a result.

No embarrassing scandal would ever arise from a long-term affair between her and Father Gregory. Royce would do everything within her power to keep that from happening. They would practice the utmost discretion at all times. No one, not even Tyler, would have any knowledge of their romance. It wasn't anyone else's business. Besides, God was the only one who could judge their sins, and Royce knew He would. But she was willing to put her soul in jeopardy for the man she loved, even if he wasn't ready to do the same for her just yet.

Sudden movement got Royce's attention as she continued watching Father Gregory through the peephole. He searched through one pocket of his bomber and reached into the other. He pulled out a key card and was about to insert it in the scanner.

Royce turned and ran fast to the bed. She dove on the mattress as the door opened and covered her naked body, head and all. The beat of her heart was out of control. She could hear it thumping in her ears. She held her breath as Father Gregory approached the bed. He stood above her for several seconds, breathing so deeply that she could hear his every intake of air. Royce lay perfectly still, determined to wait him out even if it meant she would have to pretend to be asleep until sunrise.

Chapter Twenty-two

As soon as the door slammed shut, Royce sat up in the bed.

"I knew you weren't asleep," Father Gregory rumbled dryly, glaring at her through the darkness. She could tell that he was upset. "What kind of game are you playing, Royce? Did it ever occur to you that I'd become worried after you didn't answer either phone or come to the door? I knocked on the damn door a million times! What is wrong with you?"

"I'm sorry."

He flung the bag onto the bed. "You should be. I bought some toiletries I thought you would need. I came to give them to you, but you were too busy playing hide and seek. I don't have time for your childishness. A thirty-one-year-old woman should know better than to pretend to be asleep in a hotel room in some strange city when her . . . her, um . . ."

"Say it! Who the hell are you to me? Are you my man? Do you consider yourself my boyfriend?" Royce yanked the sheet from the bed and wrapped it around her body. She jumped up and stormed toward Father Gregory with tears streaming down her face. "You can't introduce me to your family and friends as anyone other than one of your parishioners, so don't you dare get salty with me!"

"Wait a minute, Royce. You said you understood my dilemma and that you could handle it. What happened between dinner at Shoney's and now, huh? Are you having second thoughts?"

"I'm not a light switch, Nicholas! You can't turn me on and off at your convenience! Either you're with me, or you're not. I can handle the secrecy, the infrequent meetings, and you ignoring me in public, but the mixed signals are driving me crazy!"

"What mixed signals are you talking about, Royce?"

"You can't kiss me or touch me and expect my body not to respond. I'm human. I have feelings and desires. I'm committed to living my life on your terms without sex, but it won't be easy."

"I'm sorry, sweetheart." He reached out to take her in his arms.

Royce backed away from him, shaking her head. "I'm wife material, but marriage is an abandoned dream. My father will never walk me down a church aisle in front of my family and friends to exchange vows with you or any other man. I will never carry a baby in my womb and give birth to him or her. No little boy or girl will ever call me Nana or Granny. I'm giving all of that up for you!"

"What do you want from me, Royce? Please tell me exactly what you want me to do."

"Give me you." She sniffled and wiped her tears. "I want your heart. You can still be a priest, but I need you to love me and be committed to me too. You don't have to choose. You can love me, God, and the Catholic Church."

This time Royce allowed Father Gregory to take her in his arms and hold her. He was glad she didn't resist his affection. He loved her more than he thought was possible. His feelings for her ran deep. It was the kind of love she deserved minus the commitment that should've come along with it, but it was the best he could offer.

"Royce, I love you so much," he whispered softly before he kissed her lips.

"Make love to me. I need you to love me tonight." She wiggled free from the bedsheet, allowing it to fall to the floor.

Father Gregory pulled her soft, naked body closer to his. He caressed her back and waist as he sucked her tongue. He massaged her butt and pulled her even closer into his muscular frame. His spiritual conscience spoke to him as clear as day, warning him against the sin he was about to commit, but his body would not submit. It was on fire and hard, especially his penis. The feel of Royce's gentle touches on his shoulders and back made him weaker than Sampson after Delilah had cut off his long locks of hair. Her tongue tasted so sweet, and her passionate moans of pleasure stimulated him, blowing his mind. His erection grew stiffer and bigger. The pain in his loins became unbearable. Warm blood swooshing through his veins made his entire body overly sensitive. He inhaled the womanly scent of her desire, and it pushed him to the point of no return.

Royce's hands underneath his sweater and T-shirt teased his nipples. Her tongue mingled with his, twirling and tasting it. Father Gregory was horny and helpless, drowning in a sea of sizzling seduction without a lifeline. He hummed when he felt Royce's hand ease inside of his boxers, stroking his hard penis with the perfect amount of pressure and in a tempo that matched his ragged breathing. She had unfastened the button and zipper on his jeans so quickly and smoothly that he didn't notice her handiwork until he felt her stimulating his sensitive penis, caressing the rigid length of it. She ended the kiss abruptly but only long enough to pull his sweater and T-shirt over his head and drop them to the floor. Then they were at it again, sharing hot and juicy kisses with their tongues mating feverishly.

Royce started walking backward toward the bed, pulling Father Gregory along with her. She tugged his jeans and boxers lower to his knees and continued sliding her closed palm up and down his penis until they fell back on the bed. On instinct, she spread her legs apart. Father Gregory was still holding and kissing her and moaning in her mouth. He was wedged between her thighs with his hardness at the opening of her warm wetness. Royce rolled her hips and lifted them, welcoming him in. Seconds passed as his body lay perfectly still on top of hers. His breathing was choppy and labored. He was conscious but with limitation. His body had impaired his brain's ability to think clearly. Father Kyle's warning got lost somewhere between the aroma of sex floating in the air and the sparkle of desire in Royce's eyes slashing through the darkness. To love her or not to love her was the question that hung over him like a cloud.

Royce reached up, framed his face with her palms, and pulled it down to meet hers. "I love you," she whispered on a faint breath.

"I love you too."

Their mutual affirmation of love was the reintroduction to the beautiful harmony of two bodies joining together as one. It was an easy entry and a flawless fit. Father Gregory filled Royce's snug, wet walls to capacity. The reunion was gratifying just like returning to home sweet home. Each of his powerful strokes was met with a strong thrust. Royce rotated her hips and gripped his butt, pulling him in deeper. Father Gregory moaned and whispered a promise to love her forever each time his firm shaft slid in and out of her hot, drenched vagina. Royce tightened her inner muscles around his hardness, taking all of him in to the hilt. His eyes rolled to the back of his head, and he gritted his teeth.

"That's my spot, baby! Wooo, baby, that's my spot. Stay right there."

Father Gregory willed his body to slow down. He wanted Royce to climax first, but he felt a wave of sensations stirring within. He threw his head back and belted out her name. She rocked her hips fast and pressed her fingertips deep into the flesh on his butt. The bed squeaked and jolted back and forth. If there was an occupant on the other side of the wall, he or she was receiving more than an earful.

Royce purred and screamed her appreciation for all the good loving she was enjoying seconds before she fell apart. Her body writhed and wiggled underneath Father Gregory's. She clasped her fingers together at the back of his neck and met his gaze. The love he saw in her eyes for him and the way she worked her body catapulted him into an explosive orgasm that made him see bright stars and hear sweet music.

Waterloo, Sierra Leone
West Africa

"Where the hell could she be this time of morning?" Zora slammed the outdated cordless phone into its cradle on her desk.

"Is there something wrong, Mrs. Benson?"

Zora plastered a fake smile on her face and turned to stare at Fataba, her medical assistant. "I'm a little annoyed because I can't reach my sister. I've been calling her since last night, but she hasn't answered either of her phones. My son doesn't even know where she is."

"Is your sister married, ma'am?"

"No. Royce is very much single."

Fataba smiled, displaying the wide gap between her two front teeth. "Maybe she is with a man."

That's exactly what I'm afraid of. Zora shivered at the thought. According to Royce, she was no longer seeing Brandon, the cute lawyer. And she hadn't mentioned meeting anyone other than the pro baseball player she had all but dismissed at a nightclub a few weeks ago. If she was with a man and they had spent the entire night together, he was someone new. Or maybe not.

Zora picked up the phone again and dialed Royce's cell phone first. Her unanswered call rolled over to voicemail after the first ring, but she wasn't able to leave a message. The fifteen-plus messages she had left last night and this morning had jammed up the recording space. Royce's house phone rang several times without an answer before her outgoing message filled Zora's ear. She ended the call and mentally replayed her last conversation with Tyler. He'd specifically said that Royce would be home all weekend reading and relaxing with a couple of bottles of wine. That's what she had told the boy. She'd never mentioned the possibility of going out or having a guest over.

"Something strange is going on with my sister, Fataba."

"What do you mean by strange, ma'am?"

"I think she has a secret lover, and I have an idea who he is."

"I hope he is a very nice man who loves her. Maybe they will marry and live happily ever after with lots and lots of beautiful babies."

Zora shook her head and sucked her teeth. "It will never happen with this man."

"Oh, no! Is he a playboy? That is what we call a man who beds many women with no intention of marrying any of them. Is the man you believe your sister is involved with a playboy, Mrs. Benson?"

"No. He's a hell of a lot worse. He's a *priest*."

Chapter Twenty-three

"Let me help you."

"Thanks," Royce said softly and allowed Father Gregory to remove the towel from her hands. She closed her eyes as he dried the back of her body.

His hands were magical. Royce savored the moment. She could definitely get used to showering with Father Gregory and having him dry her back in the morning after a night of Olympic-style lovemaking. Every muscle in her body had been stretched, twisted, and flexed to the max last night. She was sore, but she had no regrets. And she hoped Father Gregory felt the same way.

He tossed the towel on the bed. "You're dry. We'll eat breakfast here before we head back. Do you have a taste for anything in particular?"

It was a loaded question, but Royce decided to behave. "We could go back to Shoney's. They have a breakfast buffet."

"Shoney's it is."

Father Gregory untied the towel covering his lower body and walked across the room to the chair in the corner that he'd draped his clothes over. He began to get dressed. "What's on your agenda once we return to Atlanta?"

"Nothing. What do you have to do other than preach at the noonday mass?"

"I need to study and polish up my sermon right away. I don't want to fumble in the pulpit. I could drop by and check on you later tonight. I'm sure that wine is good and cold now. I would love a glass or two."

"Okay, it's a date."

"Hurry up and get dressed. I need to be back at the parsonage by ten."

"Like I said, sir, Ms. Phillips doesn't work at either location on the weekends unless there's a special event or an emergency. I'll let her know first thing Monday morning you stopped by, Mr. um . . ." Tabatha stretched her eyes.

"It's Burrell." He licked his lips and flashed a decent smile. "Actually, it's Dr. Burrell. But I want you to tell Ms. Phillips that Marlon paid her a visit. She'll know exactly who you're talking about. Nobody knows me better than my Royce. We've got history. Anyway, please give her these for me, too. They're her favorite." He handed Tabatha a bouquet of fresh assorted flowers in vibrant colors.

She twisted her lips and took the bouquet. The sweet scent of the flowers' petals reminded Tabatha of springtime. They were gorgeous, but they weren't Royce's choice of flowers. She adored roses, red ones in particular. "I'll put them in a vase of water and place them on Ms. Phillips's desk. Is there anything else, sir?"

"That will be all for now, sweetie. I'm sure I'll be seeing more of you in the future."

"How will that be possible, Dr. Burrell? Do you plan to take advantage of one of our membership plans here at Royalty Health and Fitness Center and Spa? Allow me to suggest the Platinum Plus plan. It guarantees you full access to all areas of our fitness facility and a personal trainer as well as a nutrition consultant. You'll be eligible for unlimited spa treatments, including services provided by our team of highly skilled masseuses, estheticians, hairstylists, and nail technicians. Would you like to sign up today?" Tabatha smiled sarcastically and watched the cocky doctor's ego deflate before her very eyes.

His scowl, although meant to insult her, was quite amusing. "Do I look like I need to join a damn gym, girl?" He smoothed his expensive cashmere sweater over his lower body and stuck out his chest.

He wasn't a fat man by most women's standards, but Tabatha could've very well pointed out his love handles and the beginning of a belly bump. However, she was too professional and polite. "It's not up to me to determine that, sir. I think you and your mirror should make that decision. I just assumed you were interested in a membership here based on your statement about seeing me in the future. I'm sorry if I offended you."

"Well, you did, and I'll be sure to tell Royce how you threw shade at me. You better give her my message and those expensive flowers, too. If I don't hear from her by Tuesday, I'll know you tried to sabotage me."

Tabatha motioned for Mr. Jeff, the head janitor at the facility, the moment the infamous Marlon Burrell turned to leave.

"Yes, ma'am," the older gentleman sang in his Jamaican accent. "What kin me do fer ya?"

She shoved the pretty flowers in his direction. "Put these in your trash bin for me, please."

"May I keep tem fer me wife, ma'am, eh? She likes flowers."

"Sure. Take them home to Ms. Della. She'll appreciate them more than Royce ever will."

"Tank ya, ma'am."

Tabatha picked up the phone and dialed her boss's home number.

"So, you're going out *again*, Father?"

Father Gregory eyed Father Schmidt quietly for a few seconds. He slid his arms inside the sleeves of his leather bomber and nodded. "Yes, I'm going for a ride on my bike. It gives me time to think, clear my head, and commune with the Almighty. Do you have a problem with that?"

"Oh, no, Father, there is no problem at all," the middle-aged priest answered, shaking his head. "I just thought the weather was a bit too nippy for a bike ride. Anyway, Father Rivera and I are going to take in a movie tonight and perhaps play pool afterward at a bar in midtown. We were going to invite you to come along with us."

Father Rivera stood under the doorjamb of the parlor, smiling and nodding without saying a word.

"Maybe we can hang out some other time. I've planned to make a couple of stops while I'm out riding. You know, to check on a few of the elderly church members."

"We understand. Enjoy your ride, Father."

"I'm sure I will. You two have fun at the theater and the pool hall. Don't drink too much beer, Father Schmidt." He turned to Father Rivera. "You're driving, right?"

The chubby priest with the bright smile nodded.

"I'm glad." Father Gregory put on his black leather gloves, lifted his helmet from the coffee table, and left the parsonage.

"It's much too cool outside to ride a motorcycle. He won't be back before sunrise. It has become his pattern, you know."

"Why do you suppose he always dresses in all black like a ninja?" Father Rivera snickered at his own question.

"I have no idea. It is strange, isn't it?"

"It is very strange. I heard the housekeeper tell the cook that his clothes often smell like vanilla."

"Vanilla?" Father Schmidt repeated.

"Yes, Father, I distinctly heard Ms. June say vanilla. She and Mrs. Ellison weren't aware that I was standing right outside of the kitchen door. They laughed and started whispering after that, so I walked away."

Father Schmidt sat down on the leather chaise longue, deep in thought about an evening of motorcycle riding in the cold weather, black clothes, and the sweet scent of vanilla.

***

Royce checked the caller ID screen on her cell phone and knew right away it was Zora calling again. The country code and phone number had been committed to her memory. Royce loved her big sister to infinity, but she was getting on her nerves with the constant phone calls. Between both voicemails on her two phones, Zora had left Royce a total of twenty-six messages over the past twenty-four hours. Each had reeked of sarcasm. Her voice was high-pitched and animated in tone. Zora had all but accused Royce of being up to no good and ignoring her calls in order to avoid a heart-to-heart with her.

Royce massaged her left temple and reluctantly pushed the power button on her cell phone. "Hello?"

"Where the hell have you been, and why haven't you answered my calls all weekend? I was worried sick about you."

"Well, how are you, Zora Chanel? Me? I'm well. Thanks for asking. Dang! Z, you sound like Mama."

"I have tried to reach you a thousand times since Friday evening. I've called Tyler and Andra and neither of them knew where you were or who you were with. What's going on with you, Royce?"

"There is nothing going on. I decided to cut off myself from the rest of the world while Tyler was away. I turned off my phones and relaxed with a few romance novels and some good wine."

"You must think I'm a damn fool! I know exactly what you're doing, and I'm afraid for you, sis. Please stop all this nonsense before you get hurt, honey. Nothing good will ever come of it. He's not the man for you."

Royce was stunned to silence by how well Zora knew her. They were five years apart in age and separated by thousands of miles of water and land, yet somehow she had figured out her current situation. Royce cleared her throat. "What are you talking about, Z? Who is 'he' and what are you accusing me of doing with him?"

"I'm not stupid! You have fallen in love with Father Gregory, and I believe you're sleeping with him. There you have it. You forced me to say it. Are you happy now, damn it?"

"No. Actually, I'm sad, Z. How dare you accuse me of something so immoral? I can't believe you think I'm nothing more than a conscienceless slut." Royce jumped up from the loveseat in her bedroom when she heard the familiar roar of Father Gregory's motorcycle drawing near. She looked out the window. "I have to go now. Call me again real soon with more accusations and condemnation, sis. I can hardly wait for it."

"Royce, don't you dare hang up the phone. I'm not done talking to you. Royce! Royce!"

She pushed the power button to end the call just as the doorbell rang. Royce dried her eyes with the tail of her shirt and ran down the stairs to answer the door.

Chapter Twenty-four

Father Gregory stepped inside the warm house out from the cold, dark night and closed the door. He pulled Royce into his arms and hugged her tight. Pulling back, he studied her expression. "What's wrong? You don't look like you're happy to see me."

"I am more than happy to see you," she said honestly, giving him a half smile. "As a matter of fact, I was getting impatient. What took you so long?"

"You don't want to know, sweetheart."

"I need to know if it's bothering you. Let's talk in the den. Go ahead. I'll get the wine and glasses."

Royce padded into the kitchen, trying her best to force the crazy conversation she'd just had with Zora to the back of her mind. Marlon's unexpected visit to her job would have to stay on the back burner as well. Apparently, Father Gregory was dealing with a situation too. Whatever it was, she wanted to help him work through it if she could.

Royce removed the bottle of wine from the refrigerator and uncorked it. The wineglasses she chose were the same pair she and Father Gregory had sipped from the other night. The two pieces of crystal stemware now served as mementos to her. They were special symbols of the love Royce had for the exceptional man who had captured her heart. As complicated as their relationship was, she still loved Father Gregory very much and was willing to go through the fire, risking all to be with him.

Hurrying into the den, Royce felt a combination of fear and anxiety. She found Father Gregory sitting on the loveseat with his head relaxing on the back rest and his eyes closed. "What's up?" She sat down next to him and handed him the wine and one of the glasses.

"I'm being watched."

Royce frowned. "Who's watching you and why?"

"Apparently, the other two priests I share the parsonage with have been monitoring my comings and goings."

"How do you know that? With all the ducking and dodging we've been doing, I'm paranoid sometimes. Maybe you are too."

Father Gregory shook his head and sighed as he poured wine into the glass. He offered it to

Royce, and she accepted it before she handed him the empty glass she'd been holding. "I wish it were a common case of paranoia, but it's not. You should've seen how they were eyeballing me when I was preparing to leave to come here. They were judging me, baby. Father Schmidt had the nerve to tell me it was too cool for me to go out for a bike ride."

"He said what? Who the hell does he think he is?"

"I don't have a clue. I just know I didn't like the tone of his voice when he asked if I was going out again. Then when he mentioned the low temperature, something in my gut told me that my personal life had been the topic of his and Father Rivera's discussions. I believe they're monitoring me."

Royce took a sip of wine and swallowed. "What are you going to do now that they've dropped you a hint?"

"*We* are going to have to watch our backs and practice extreme caution from now on, young lady."

"Maybe you should drive your car over here sometimes and leave your motorcycle at home."

"That's not a good idea. Most of the church members know what kind of car I drive. Priests don't generally cruise around in bright red Corvettes, so my car gets a lot of attention from the parishioners. Only Father Schmidt, Father Rivera, and you know about my motorcycle. I've never even shown it to Tyler. My bike will continue to be my form of transportation here."

Royce nodded silently. Her day was turning out to be a train wreck after such an amazing morning. She had awakened at the crack of dawn in her lover's arms and allowed him to have his way with her. They'd showered together and talked over a delicious country breakfast. The ride back to Atlanta was windy and cold, but she hadn't minded much because she was with the man she loved.

After returning home, Royce's day slowly went up in flames without warning. First, there was the phone call from Tabatha, informing her that Marlon Burrell, of all lowlife losers, had had the nerve to show his smug face at her place of business. The dude had obviously lost his mind over the three years since he'd deceived her. And although Zora's suspicions about her affair with Father Gregory had been correct, Royce didn't appreciate all of the phone calls or her funky attitude.

"I have something I need to tell you too," she whispered after some time. "This day continues to go down the drain."

Father Gregory placed his glass of wine on the coffee table and squeezed Royce's thigh. "What is it, baby?"

"My ex had the boldness to show up out of the blue at Royalty's Marietta location this morning looking for me. Tabatha called me to let me know shortly after you dropped me off."

"Why would he want to see you after all this time, Royce? You told me you broke up with him three years ago and you haven't heard from him since."

Royce swallowed the marble-size lump in her throat and licked her lips. They suddenly felt dry under Father Gregory's unexpected interrogation. "I don't know. Tabatha said he came bearing flowers and that huge ego of his."

"Flowers, huh? It sounds like he wants to reconnect with you romantically."

"I don't want Marlon, baby. I have you. You're the only man I need."

"But he came to give you flowers. The next time he pays you a visit he may offer you the engagement ring the priesthood forbids me from giving you."

Royce shifted her bottom from the loveseat to Father Gregory's lap. She wrapped her arms around his neck and looked into his eyes. "First of all, Marlon better not show his face at either one of my facilities again. Each of them is considered private property by law. I'm the sole owner of both, and I have the right to ban him from my establishments. Security staffs at both sites have already been made aware of it. And that fool could waste his money on a million rings. I wouldn't care. I don't want Marlon, his flowers, his diamonds, or anything else. It's over between us."

"What did that guy do to you, Royce? I know he hurt you, but I don't know how. It must've been awfully bad because Tyler hates him. In fact, because of this Marlon character, he doesn't want you to get involved with any man, except maybe Bullet Bullard." Father Gregory grinned with a mischievous twinkle in his eyes.

Royce pinched him playfully on his shoulder. "How do you know about that?"

"I have my ways of finding out things. But don't change the subject, baby. Tell me about your relationship with Marlon."

"We were introduced by a mutual friend, my financial advisor's wife. It was around the time I was looking for a building to renovate to start my business. I was a young and ambitious healthcare professional. I had money, a master's degree in nursing from Georgia State, and I was a few months shy of receiving my certification in fitness education and instructional training. Marlon was older and charming. He pursued me with the determination of a stalker."

"Didn't you tell me he was a doctor?"

Royce nodded. "He has a Ph.D. in microbiology. At the time, he was teaching at the Emory School of Medicine. I'm not sure if he's still there, and I don't care, either. Zora loved him and thought he was the perfect man for me, so I dove in headfirst. I was constantly at high-society functions, meeting all the right people to help me get the fitness center up and running. We traveled extensively, sometimes with other couples both married and not. We were happy and on our way down the aisle, or so I thought."

"He didn't want to get married."

"He claimed he did, but his actions told me something altogether different. We had just celebrated our one-year anniversary on the island of Tortola. My first facility was open and thriving. The second location was almost finished. Life was good, but I noticed that Marlon was absent more than usual. I was too busy to investigate, so I ignored it until the grand opening of the new facility. My parents and the rest of my family had come up from Thomasville. All of my friends and associates were in place, but Marlon was again MIA."

"Where was that fool, Royce?"

"He was at home with his wife and their sick son."

Father Gregory's jaw dropped, obviously in shock. He wrapped his arms tighter around Royce's body, and she rested her head on his shoulder, still relaxing on his lap.

"You had no idea he was married with a child, did you?"

"Of course not. You see, when Aris Leland first introduced me to Marlon, he had just called off his engagement to his longtime girlfriend. Her name was Jita. Soon after we became a couple, Marlon found out she was pregnant. He chose not to tell me, although the child was conceived before we ever got together. He claimed he was afraid I would leave him if I knew he had a baby on the way with his ex. And on the other end, Jita had threatened to return home to Canada once the baby was born if he didn't end his relationship with me. She wanted him to marry her and help her raise their child. Jita wanted them to be a family. Maybe Marlon was torn, but he could've handled the situation differently in order to save me from the pain and embarrassment."

"How did you find out he had married the mother of his child and was living with her?"

"When he didn't show up for the grand opening and didn't immediately call me with an explanation, I got suspicious. I called in a favor to a guy, a college mate from Georgia State who had once worked as a detective for the Atlanta Police Department. He had a successful investigation and security firm. His name is Edward Colbert. I asked him to investigate Marlon. I gave him the address and phone number to his Buckhead condo along with his cell phone number and other vital information. I held nothing back. Within three days, I was sitting in the living room of his fabulous new home, talking to his wife and watching his sick son struggling to breathe with the help of an oxygen tank. I was devastated but grateful to have found out Marlon was a worthless, cheating snake."

"I'm sorry, baby. You didn't deserve to be deceived. If Marlon didn't appreciate you back then, he's not worthy of you now. How do you feel about him looking for you after all this time?"

"I'm fine. I just don't want to see the bastard. That's why I've taken the necessary actions to keep him away from my job. I heard that his son died before his second birthday and his marriage fell apart shortly afterward. I'm sorry about how things turned out for him and Jita, but it has nothing to do with me."

"You're right. He's a part of your past." Father Gregory kissed Royce on the forehead.

Chapter Twenty-five

Royce calculated her game points quickly for the third time and grinned. "I won!"

"I'm rusty. I haven't played Scrabble since seminary."

"Whatever. All I know is I kicked your butt four games in a row. God gave you a sympathy blessing in the first round. You want to play again?"

Father Gregory stretched and yawned with his palm pressed against his open lips. He admired Royce's competitive spirit. It was appealing, but he had no intention of playing another game of Scrabble with her. He was tired and wanted to go to bed, Royce's bed. "I'm exhausted. Let's turn in." He got up and extended his hand.

Royce stood from her chair on the opposite side of the dinette and placed her hand inside of his. They left the kitchen in silence and headed to the staircase. It was almost midnight. They had consumed a half bottle of Riesling while they talked and played a few hands of twenty-one before finally taking out the Scrabble game. Now, they were going upstairs to make love. Father Gregory knew they shouldn't, but it was inevitable, and he wasn't going to fight the forces of temptation. It was a battle he lacked the fortitude to win. He would deal with the guilt later. Tonight he would love Royce and accept the love she would give him in return.

He flipped on the light and closed the bedroom door behind them as soon as they entered the huge, lavishly decorated space. It was a beautiful suite decorated in soft lavender and cream. Father Gregory felt at home in the room, in the bed that occupied it, and in Royce's arms. He stripped down to his brown and beige checkered boxers, turned back the duvet comforter, and slid underneath the cool, crisp sheets. He sat with his back against the headboard, watching Royce wander slowly around the room opening and closing drawers, gathering her nightclothes. She started toward the bathroom.

"Don't take too long."

"I won't. Just give me a few minutes."

Father Gregory pulled the covers back, revealing the enormous bulge between his thighs. "I want you to come *now*."

"You said you were tired and wanted to go to bed. I assumed you meant you wanted to sleep."

"Does it look like I'm about to go to sleep any-time soon?" He tugged at the waistband of his boxers and raised his hips. He lowered the cotton checkered fabric to his knees, exposing his bare penis, erect and engorged.

"I'll be right back," Royce said with a mysterious smile on her face. Her eyes were sparkling with a hint of spice in their depths. She went into her huge walk-in closet and got a black box. Then she closed herself up in the bathroom.

Father Gregory removed his boxers completely and dropped them to the floor. He placed his hands behind his head and relaxed on two fluffy pillows while he waited patiently for Royce to emerge from the bathroom.

Condoms.

The brief lapse in time had given him the op-portunity to think about protection. The last time they'd made love in the master suite, Royce had taken the condoms from a drawer on the night-stand. Without a second thought, Father Gregory rolled over to the other side of the bed and opened the drawer. Next to a roll of masking tape, lying face up, there was a picture of Royce smiling at him. He picked it up to examine it closely. She was perched on the edge of a big desk, which more than likely was in one of her business offices. The bright orange pantsuit she wore hugged her flawless figure to perfection. The fabric hit all of her curves just right. Her beauty had pulled him into such a deep trance that he didn't even notice that Royce had left the bathroom and was now walking in his direction.

"The head of my marketing team suggested that I sit for a photo shoot for our upcoming new membership campaign," she said softly over his shoulder. "That was his favorite picture of me. Do you like it?"

"You look gorgeous," Father Gregory whispered in awe with his eyes still on the picture. "May I have it?"

"Of course you may, but first you have to play a little game with me."

"No more games, baby. You know what I want to do." He placed the picture on the nightstand and rolled over onto his back and reintroduced Royce to his stiff penis. But she had an eyeful for him too. "Girl, what are you wearing and what are those . . . those *things* in your hands?"

Royce crawled onto the bed wearing a waist-high, black leather vest without buttons. Her firm breasts were in plain view, displaying her hardened nipples, which reminded him of a pair of Hershey's kisses. There were tiny silver spikes splattered about the leather. The ends of the black chiffon scarf neatly tied around her neck swayed with each motion she made. Father Gregory was spellbound by the matching leather thong covered with smaller spikes and secured by a pair of bows, one tied at each of Royce's curvy hips. He sat up and opened his arms to her.

"Get back, naughty boy!" She swung a short-handle whip and struck him on the wrist. "You've been bad, so you'll have to be punished. I'm going to make you my prisoner," Royce announced and grinned, holding up a pair of shiny handcuffs.

Father Gregory was totally oblivious to the type of game Royce had in mind, but the whip, handcuffs, and skimpy leather outfit had piqued his interest. His body went into adrenaline overload. He wanted to play along. "How bad have I been, and how long is my sentence?"

"You've been terrible. I'm going to lock you up for life." Royce snatched the scarf from around her neck and waved it in the air high above her head. She straddled Father Gregory and leaned down to lick the side of his face. "I must blindfold you." And she did with the scarf, securing it tightly over his eyes before dismounting him.

Father Gregory laughed as his heart raced at high speed. "What else are you going to do to me?"

Royce pulled both his hands in front of his body and bound them with the handcuffs. She pushed him, rolling him over onto his belly. She gave him a lash on his butt with the whip.

"Ouch! Royce, not so hard, baby."

"Shut up! You will get no mercy from me. Take your spanking like a man." She swung again and again. "Beg for mercy, you naughty boy."

"I'll be good. I promise, baby. I promise to be a good boy."

Royce gave his body another push, reversing his position on the bed. She straddled him again. She leaned in and covered his lips with hers. He snaked his tongue inside her mouth, and she twirled hers around it. The kiss was hot and moist. It caused Father Gregory's toes to curl and his dick to throb. He wiggled beneath Royce, hoping to maneuver his rigid member close to the opening of her sweet spot. He felt weak and helpless without the use of his hands.

He mumbled against her lips, "Baby, baby, I need you to—"

"No! You're being punished." Royce raised her body to her knees and then stood up on the bed, looking down at Father Gregory's face.

"I'm in pain, baby. Look at me. I'm about to explode. Take the handcuffs off. Untie the blindfold, too."

Royce laughed. She stuck two fingers inside her vagina and kneeled on the side of Father Gregory. "Taste me," she whispered, rubbing her feminine juices over his lips. She dipped her fingers into his mouth, and he sucked them. She rubbed her entire hand between her legs and smeared her womanly moisture all over his face and lips. "Am I sweet?"

"You're sweet, Royce. Now, take off the handcuffs so I can eat you, baby."

"Beg me."

"Please remove the cuffs and the blindfold. I'll be better than good. Please, baby. I promise."

Royce showed mercy to Father Gregory and freed him from the handcuffs. As she was untying the blindfold, he reached up and snatched it off quickly.

"Now, it's my turn. I owe you a spanking."

Royce screamed and giggled like crazy and tried to crawl away from him, but she was too slow. Within seconds, she was on her back, trapped in place. Father Gregory handcuffed her with her hands above her head. Then he took the scarf and secured it over her eyes. He searched the bed and found the whip.

"You've been bad." He swung the whip and landed a light lash on her thigh. "You've been really, really bad."

"Spank me, baby. Spank me."

Father Gregory hadn't expected Royce to encourage him. He'd figured she would beg for mercy like he had. Shocked, he didn't know what to do. This whole handcuff-and-whip drill was foreign to him. While he'd found it to be somewhat of a turn-on at first, it was a little too strange for his taste. He had finally learned the definition of the word "kinky." He now also knew how good it felt to be in control. Power was a damn good thing.

Chapter Twenty-six

Father Gregory leaned down and kissed Royce's soft lips. She purred and offered him her tongue. He sucked it gently before he kissed her chin and neck.

"Aren't you going to spank me?"

"I don't want to spank you, baby."

"But I want you to. Come on. Spank me, Daddy. Spank me."

Maybe at another time and in another place, he would've given Royce a spanking, but Father Gregory didn't want to tonight. He reached over to the nightstand and opened the drawer. He refused to listen to another word about whips and lashes. The handcuffs and the blindfold he could handle, but not so much the spanking routine. He found the masking tape and tore a piece off. Royce continued begging for a spanking, but he silenced her by pressing a strip of masking tape over her mouth. She shook her head and moaned.

The sultry sound was more pleasing to his ears than her kinky spanking nonsense. It had been fun for a while, but at the moment, all he wanted to do was satisfy his appetite for Royce by feasting on her body. And because of the tape covering her mouth, she was unable to protest. She couldn't speak or see, and she wasn't able to touch him in response. Something about her limitations stoked the sexual flames to an immeasurable degree of heat. The atmosphere was hotter than lava.

Father Gregory sucked and slithered his tongue over Royce's chocolate-drop nipples repeatedly until her body went limp and her moans lowered to deep growls. He kissed a path down to her thighs, then on to her knees, and much lower to her toes. He took each of the ten manicured digits into his mouth and sucked them one by one. Royce's quivering body shook the bed violently.

He retraced the wet path up her body and stopped at the leather and spiked triangle between her thighs. Slowly, he pulled the bow strings, one on each side of her hips, and pulled the leather forward as if he were removing wrapping paper from a Christmas gift. To his surprise, Royce had a fresh, custom-designed Brazilian wax. The remaining patch of fine, curly hair was neatly shaped into a diamond at the lips of her vagina.

Father Gregory licked the hair over and over again until Royce spread her legs apart, revealing her love bud, hard and glistening with her feminine honey. His tongue teased the very tip of the stiff and sensitive flesh, causing Royce to jerk and whimper. She writhed and attempted to talk against the tape covering her mouth. Father Gregory inserted two fingers inside of her wet depths, sliding them in and out while he licked her taut clit. He licked and suckled the moist and swollen bud until Royce bucked and hummed through an orgasm that lifted her body two inches off the bed and back.

Father Gregory reached for the row of condoms he'd found earlier in the nightstand drawer. He had never put one on before. Royce had done the honors the last time. He relieved her of the handcuffs, removed the blindfold, and snatched the masking tape from her mouth.

Royce smiled when their eyes met. She took the condoms from his hand. "No more risky business."

Father Gregory relaxed on the bed while Royce opened the condom. He drew in a quick breath of air as her closed palm stroked his stiff dick. "Please don't tease me, baby. I can't take it much longer."

Royce rolled the condom over his penis and flipped over on her hands and knees. "Hit it from the back."

It took a minute for her request to sink in, but the old saying was true: some things were just natural. Father Gregory positioned his body behind Royce's. With his hand, he guided his dick to the entrance of her saturated vagina. He rubbed the tip against her moist lips, teasing her. Then without warning, he pushed deep inside of her and began to ease in and out slowly.

Royce cooed and told him how much she loved him each time he entered and withdrew. He thrust inward, and she backed into his hips in perfect orchestration. Their tempo quickened and intensified. Father Gregory tightened his hold on Royce's hips as he chanted her name rhythmically. He pushed forward with force and pulled back. She backed in and retreated while rolling her hips. Their bodies worked harmoniously as they climbed to higher sexual dimensions. Royce reached her peak first. Her walls squeezed him, pulling him in deeper.

"Ah, Nicholas." His first name escaped from her lips in a smooth contralto note.

He responded with wild and bottomless strokes into her warmth before he collapsed fully on top of her soft, sweat-drenched body.

***

Royce swiped at what felt like a bug crawling across her forehead. She shook her head several times and drifted back to sleep. The crawling sensation returned, annoying the hell out of her. She slapped her forehead with her palm and opened her eyes.

The sun was shining brightly in the sky, casting light through the cracks of the Venetian blinds. Royce sat up in bed and discovered that it wasn't a bug crawling on her after all. The heat vent blowing above her bed was causing the black chiffon scarf hanging from the headboard to wave back and forth over her face. And the rumbling noise that she'd heard throughout the night was snoring from her bed partner, who was still asleep with his mouth wide open.

Royce checked the clock on the nightstand and went into a panic. "Oh, no! Nicholas! Nicholas, wake up! It's ten minutes after six."

"Damn it! I'm going to be late for seven o'clock mass." Father Gregory jumped up and grabbed his boxers from the floor. "There's no way I can make it in time."

"I'm sorry. I should've set my clock."

He ran to the foot of the bed and found his sweater, jeans, and tennis shoes on the floor. He began to dress. "It's not your fault, sweetheart. Don't worry about it. My jacket is in the den. Come downstairs and lock the door behind me. I don't want you to fall asleep with the door unlocked."

Royce nodded and followed Father Gregory down the stairs. She stood naked near the front door and waited for him to get his jacket from the den.

"I'll call you after noonday mass is over," he said, walking toward her. He kissed Royce softly on her lips before he opened the front door. "Get some rest. You need it."

Royce secured the lock. Then she climbed the steps slowly and went straight to her room and returned to her warm bed.

"Here he comes," Father Rivera announced in his thick Spanish accent. He closed the curtains in the parlor's front window and ran to the foyer of the parsonage with his Bible in tow.

Father Schmidt was there waiting for him. He frowned and put his all-weather coat on over his snow-white alb. "He's late! Mass will start in twenty-five minutes. He will never make it in time. Such behavior is unacceptable. God is not pleased."

Father Gregory rushed into the house and came face-to-face with his two fellow priests and housemates. "Good morning."

"Good morning to you. How was your ride, Father?"

"It . . . it was fine, Father Schmidt," he stuttered, removing his jacket. He hung it on the coatrack. "I need to shower and get dressed. Excuse me."

"Will you arrive at the church in time to deliver the homily, Father?"

"I'll be there."

The two priests watched his back as he hurried down the hall to his bedroom. The sound of his door slamming shut boomed throughout the house.

Father Schmidt sucked his teeth in disgust. "He lacks the righteousness and integrity of a priest. The man is a disgrace. Did you smell him?"

"I did," the chubby priest said, grinning and nodding. "But he did not smell like vanilla to me. Tell me, Father Schmidt, what was that scent I smelled on Father Gregory?"

"It has been many, many years since I inhaled a scent of that kind, but I'd recognize it on my deathbed."

"What is it? Please tell me."

"The scent, my dear friend, is that of the most intimate part of a woman's body. The vagina."

***

Father Gregory slammed his office door behind him and unzipped his cassock. He snatched the holy garment from his body and flung it onto his desk. Nervously, he paced the floor in front of the bookshelf. Guilt and shame were gnawing a hole straight through his soul. There was a dull ache in his heart that just wouldn't go away. It had been there since this morning when he looked into Father Schmidt's accusing eyes the moment he returned to the parsonage. The smirk on the man's face and the tone of his voice were clear signs of judgment. It was as if he knew exactly where Father Gregory had spent the night, the person he'd been with, and the sinful acts they'd committed.

He rubbed his hand over his face and immediately smelled Royce's feminine scent on his fingertips. There wasn't enough time for him to shower before he dressed for mass. Time had been his enemy. He'd brushed his teeth, gargled with mouthwash, wiped the crust from the corners of his eyes, and dressed in record time. It was a miracle that he hadn't crashed or gotten pulled over by the police on his high-speed drive to the church. God's merciful angels had protected him indeed. Thankfully, he had delivered a great sermon without blunder or mishap.

He had been his worst critic because of guilt. From the looks on the faces of the members of his congregation, he guessed the homily had fallen on receptive ears. It was a shame that it had come from the lips of a hypocrite. Once again, God had shown him favor. If only he could be as faithful to God as He was to him. Father Gregory wasn't just a filthy fornicator. He was also a liar. And he had become very comfortable and careless in his double life. His love affair with Royce had become his top priority. She now was the center of his universe, not God or the Catholic Church. It had never been his intention to fall in love and enter into a secret relationship, yet there he was.

Father Gregory rounded his desk and plopped down in the chair, troubled and spiritually crushed. There was only one way for him to attain the peace he desired. He needed to confess his sins and ask for forgiveness, but he didn't want to. Stubbornness had settled in his broken spirit, and he was ashamed. Father Kyle had warned him that he would fall into temptation and fornicate with Royce again if he did not leave her, but he had refused to take heed. And because he'd decided not to follow the older priest's spiritual advice, he had sunk deeper into sin.

Chapter Twenty-seven

"My parents are driving up here from Thomasville Friday to pick up Tyler. He's going to spend his entire spring break with them. I hope I'll see you often while he's away. These past few weeks have been torture. I was surprised when you called today and asked me to meet you here."

"I'm sorry we haven't spent very much time together lately, but I felt we had to cool things down for a while. That Sunday morning I overslept and almost missed mass was my wake-up call."

Royce kissed Father Gregory's bare chest and rubbed his flat belly. She lowered her hand to his crotch and gently took hold of his penis. It hardened instantly under her touch. She began to stroke him. "So, now we're hiding out in hotel rooms in the middle of the day. You better be glad I'm the boss at my job. Otherwise, I wouldn't be able to drop everything at once and meet you whenever you call."

"Thank you for being so cooperative and understanding, Royce. My schedule and my situation make it hard for us to hook up sometimes. I'm sorry."

"It's okay. We're together now, and that's all that matters. How much time do we have?"

"Two hours."

"Let's make the most of it."

Father Kyle gave up on completing his sermon. He would start afresh in the morning. He placed his pen on top of his notebook and allowed his thoughts to go adrift. More than a month had passed since his last meeting with the mysterious young man in black. Father Kyle had thought of him often, praying that he had taken the woman he loved as his wife. It was clear that he had no plans of dissolving his relationship with his lover. Therefore, Father Kyle could only hope that they were now living happily together as husband and wife. If that wasn't the case, then the troubled fellow must've given in to his flesh and was deeply involved in a sexual affair. Of course, the elder, very concerned priest had no way of knowing for sure. Only God knew the young man's present circumstances, and He alone had the power to save his soul.

Father Kyle's heart went out to the unidentified man. He felt a strong connection to him because many years ago he had faced a very similar dilemma, but it was much more complicated. Days after completing his studies at Notre Dame Seminary in New Orleans, Louisiana and weeks before his vow of celibacy, Father Kyle met a beautiful woman. Priscilla Lee, a Tulane University graduate student, had declared it her mission to rid the world of hunger. Her chance meeting with the would-be priest took place at a picnic at her school one late spring afternoon. It was instant love for the young aspiring priest. At the time, he was scheduled to begin his first order at a church in Spokane, Washington that upcoming summer. Priscilla's kindness and good looks caused him to question the calling he believed God had on his life. He had begun to have second thoughts about taking the oath of celibacy and joining the priesthood too.

It was a whirlwind love affair, one befitting the pages of a spicy romance novel. Two virgins from Christian families with deep roots in their respective churches who were on the path to become vessels for God in ministry introduced each other to passion. The soon-to-be priest and the future missionary spent every waking moment of the day together. And by night they made love on a lopsided sofa bed inside his modest studio apartment on Burdette Street.

As weeks passed and spring yielded to summer, Priscilla asked her beloved to abandon his orders and the priesthood to spend the rest of his life with her. Together they would spread the love of Jesus and minister to His people through the United Methodist Church, where he could be ordained and become a pastor. More importantly, it would've been permissible for him to marry, eventually becoming her husband and the father of her children.

It was a very difficult decision, the hardest one he'd ever faced. But after two weeks of praying, studying Scripture, and consulting with fellow aspiring men of the cloth, Jacob Anthony Kyle decided to continue on his path to the priesthood. Priscilla was heartbroken, and so was he. He loved her dearly and wanted a life with her, but a man in his position—one with a higher calling—had to deny his desires for God and the Roman Catholic Church.

He and Priscilla made love for the very last time and said their goodbyes the night before he rose early in the morning and boarded a plane to Spokane. They never saw each other or even spoke again. God had yet to send a sunrise that Father Kyle had witnessed without thoughts of his sweet and beautiful Priscilla. It would be totally untruthful of him to say he had no regrets having chosen the priesthood instead of a life with her. However, he believed he had done what was best for him and God. He only hoped that the young man who he prayed for daily would make the right decision and marry his lover and be saved from fornication. After all, he wasn't a priest. He was free to enjoy a bride and father children while living a life pleasing to the Almighty.

"That must be Tyler." Royce left her parents at the dinette and walked out of the kitchen. She was nervous about them meeting Father Gregory. Harold and Estelle Phillips were very perceptive people. And they knew all about chemistry, having been married for forty years. Royce was prepared to put on an award-winning theatrical performance for her mom and dad. She hoped Father Gregory would rise to the occasion as her costar.

Royce rounded the corner and came face to face with her nephew and her man. It made no sense for a priest to look so damn deliciously hot in customary clergy attire. Royce drew in a quick breath as her eyes roamed over the tight muscles under his long-sleeved black shirt and suit jacket. The traditional white collar was crisp. His simple black slacks looked as if they had been designed for only him. She blinked when she imagined what was underneath the dark fabric.

"Are they here yet?" Tyler asked with eyes as bright as a pair of twinkling stars.

"Who are you talking about, sweetie? Were you expecting company today?" Royce teased and rubbed the top of his curl-covered head.

"You know who I'm talking about, Auntie. Did Grandpa and Granny come yet? I don't see their car."

"They're in the kitchen, honey. Grandpa parked his Buick in the garage."

"Yesss!" He broke out in a swift sprint toward the kitchen.

Father Gregory pulled Royce into his arms and kissed her fully on the mouth. She returned his embrace and savored the short kiss. He smiled at her, and it lit her fire, but she mentally put her body on ice for the time being.

"Are you ready to meet my folks, Father Gregory, sir?" Royce smiled at him, but she was fighting a hearty laugh. By the end of the night and no doubt in the nights to come this following week, she wouldn't be calling him by his spiritual title and surname. Nothing but sweet endearments would come from her lips as they made love.

"I'm excited about meeting your parents." He waved his hand. "After you."

Royce led Father Gregory into the kitchen. She was more than nervous. She smiled when she found her parents sitting quietly and listening attentively to Tyler talking nonstop about school and his adventures with his friends.

"Mama and Daddy, meet Father Nicholas Gregory. He's our new priest. He is also your only grandchild's best buddy." She turned around and looked into the most mesmerizing eyes in the world. "Father Gregory, I'd like you to meet my parents, Harold and Estelle Phillips."

He stepped forward with his right hand extended. "Mr. Phillips, it's an honor to meet you, sir. Tyler talks about you all the time."

The older man chuckled and took the proffered hand in a courteous shake. "You're a young priest. I like that. And you're almost as good-looking as me. Thank you for being a role model and mentor for my grandson in his father's absence and mine too. He respects you."

"It's nothing, sir. I'm only fulfilling my spiritual obligation to the youth." His eyes shifted to Mrs.

Phillips. He opened his arms and hugged her. Then he stepped back. "Mrs. Phillips, you're even more gorgeous than Tyler described. He told me Gabrielle Union is going to look just like you in a few years. I had no idea what he meant then, but I definitely know now."

"Oh, hush your mouth now. You and Tyler are good for an old lady's ego, Father. Thank you very much. I'm no Gabrielle Union, but I appreciate the flattery. It may earn you a sweet potato pie next Saturday when we bring Tyler home."

"Did you say *sweet potato* pie? Can I get that in writing, Mrs. Phillips?"

"No need for formalities. My word is my bond, honey. Any priest who's had a positive influence on my one and only grandbaby deserves my great-grandmother's secret sweet potato pie. I'll make sure Royce delivers two freshly baked pies to the parsonage Saturday evening."

Royce stretched her eyes in shock over her mother's words. If the woman knew what had happened the last time her daughter visited the priest at the parsonage, she wouldn't have suggested that she go there again, ever.

"I'll be counting down the days, ma'am. Thank you so much. I love sweet potato pie."

"Are you finished packing, son?" Mr. Phillips redirected everyone's attention to his grandson.

"Not yet, Gramps. Give me fifteen minutes."

Tyler ran out of the kitchen and went upstairs. The adults sat down to get better acquainted while they sipped coffee. Royce was happy that her parents and Father Gregory had finally met. It gave her a sense of satisfaction that he had met their approval as a priest and mentor. She imagined they would feel the same way about him if he had been introduced to them as her special guy or fiancé in another life. Of course, Royce would never have the privilege of presenting Father Gregory to anyone as her man, but wishful thinking had never harmed anyone.

An hour or so later, Royce stood facing her mother in the foyer. Tyler, Mr. Phillips, and Father Gregory were outside loading the car.

"Zora told me you two had a falling out. She said y'all haven't spoken in weeks. I didn't raise you two girls like that. You're all each other has. What could your sister have possibly said to you that was so nasty you won't even take her calls, child?"

"Ask her." Royce folded her arms across her bosom and rolled her neck.

"I did already. That gal wouldn't tell me a thing. She said the grudge is between you and her. But you and Zora are my babies, Royce. I don't like you fussing and ignoring one another. Talk to your sister and forgive her for whatever she said to hurt your feelings. I told her to forgive you too."

"For what? I didn't do anything."

"You can be sassy and mean as a pit bull sometimes, Royce. I'm sure that spicy tongue of yours spat something out that you could've swallowed. Fix this mess. You hear me?"

"Yes, ma'am."

Chapter Twenty-eight

"I put my foot in this." Royce licked the back of the spoon and tossed it in the kitchen sink. Her homemade Alfredo sauce tasted like heaven in a pot. She tossed a handful of fresh baby spinach leaves into the creamy white cheese sauce and grabbed another spoon from the dish draining rack. She stirred slowly, mixing the contents together thoroughly. She reached for the bowl of raw peeled and deveined shrimp just as the phone rang.

Royce wrinkled her nose. She wasn't expecting any callers or visitors except Father Gregory. He wasn't due back to her place for another hour or so. He had gone home to change clothes and to swap his Corvette for his Harley. The early April weather was warm and balmy most nights, making his motorcycle rides comfortable.

Royce walked over to the counter where her cell phone lay charging. She looked at the caller ID screen. "Damn! Why is she calling me tonight?"

Zora was not on Royce's agenda. She had planned to speak with her soon like her mother had requested, but it wouldn't happen tonight. She had more important business to take care of like feeding her man and spending quality time with him. It would be their first full night together in a few weeks. She was glad that Tyler was in Thomasville with her parents. Zora would have to wait until tomorrow for their kiss-and-make-up phone chat. Royce ignored the phone and went back to the stove to add the shrimp to her kick-ass Alfredo sauce.

Waterloo, Sierra Leone
West Africa

"She still won't take my calls, Eric." Zora placed the phone on its receiver and blew her nose with a rumpled tissue. She dabbed her eyes. "I just want to apologize and tell her how wrong I was. I had no right to accuse her of sleeping with her priest. What the hell was I thinking?"

Eric rested on his knees in the bed and massaged his wife's drooping shoulders. "You were being an overprotective big sister as usual, but

this time you took it a little too far, honey. I hope
you've learned your lesson."

"I have. Next time, I'll think before I speak no
matter how strongly I feel about something. I'm
going to keep my mouth closed and stay in my
lane."

"Good girl." Eric kissed the back of Zora's neck
a few times. "You can try to reach Royce again in
the morning. Tonight I want your full attention."

"I'm all yours, Dr. Benson."

"Wait a minute, baby. I left my cell phone in
the kitchen."

Royce ran back down the stairs and went to the
kitchen. She found her cell phone fully charged on
the countertop. She disconnected it from the cord
and hurried upstairs to the master suite. There
was a trail of discarded men's clothing items, all
black in color, on the floor. The trail led to the bed
where Father Gregory was sitting up with his back
supported by a stack of pillows.

"You're not going to need that phone tonight.
You could've left it where it was."

Royce batted her eyelids. "I need it close by just
in case some male suitor calls me to tell me he's
on his way over. I wouldn't want him throwing
rocks at my window and screaming my name for

the entire neighborhood to hear. Some men are so crazy." She laughed.

Father Gregory pressed his lips together and stared at Royce with a stony expression on his handsome face. "I hope you're just kidding."

"Baby, you know I am. You're my heart." Royce sat down on the bed next to him. "I will always be true to you and only you."

"I can't help but wonder sometimes."

"About what?"

"It scares me to think about what's going to happen when some man comes along who can be all that you want him to be and is able to offer you everything I can't. I won't be able to compete with a guy who can give you his hand and heart in marriage and wants you to have his children, Royce. You would be a fool to turn him away."

"I guess I'm a fool, because I wouldn't give him the time of day." She kissed him on the cheek.

Father Gregory took Royce into his arms. "I love you."

"I love you too."

He laid Royce down on the bed and rolled on top of her. She wrapped her arms around his waist, allowing her cell phone to fall to the bed. They started off with soft, gentle kisses and subtle caresses, but soon the heat turned a spark into a full brush fire.

Royce, feverish and brazen, pushed and rolled, reversing their positions on the bed. She sat up on her knees, straddling Father Gregory and relieved him of the only item of clothing he still had on: his black boxers. To return the favor, he lifted the skirt of her simple powder blue baby doll dress up high and pulled it over her head. Royce released the single front clasp on her black lace bra and removed it. She squealed when Father Gregory flipped her over to regain control of the situation. He eased her black thong down her thighs and legs until it was completely off. He tossed it carelessly to the side.

He licked Royce's left nipple a few times and then gently took possession of it with the edges of his teeth. She squirmed and whimpered when he started sucking the taut tip and pinching the other between his thumb and index finger.

"Oh, baby . . ."

"Uh-uh. What's my name, Royce?" he asked between deliberate flicks of his tongue to her sensitive nipples alternately. "Tell me. Say it. Say my name, baby."

"Mmm . . . aaahhh . . . mmm . . ."

"Nah, baby, I want you to say my name."

"Nic . . . Nicholas."

"That's right, baby."

He slid down her body and found her dripping wet, warm, and wide open. He took full advantage of her position by taking hold of her hips to keep her in place as he licked her clit from top to bottom slowly and softly.

Royce panted for air and rotated her hips. "Mmm, mmm, mmm. Oh, yes, baby. Lick me like a lollipop, Nicholas."

"I am, baby. I am."

Waterloo, Sierra Leone
West Africa

Zora looked at the clock on the dresser when the phone rang. She smiled when she thought of her husband and the way he had made love to her the night before. He was an animal, and she had enjoyed every minute of his bedroom performance. The good doctor had kindly given her Saturday morning off so she could rest.

"Good morning, Dr. Benson." Zora's brows furrowed when she didn't get a response from her husband. Instead, she heard heavy breathing and passionate moans on the other end of the call. She sat up in bed when she heard Royce's voice, clear as a bell. She was encouraging some man to lick her and lick her good. Zora clamped her hand over her mouth to keep from screaming. She was spazzing out with shock. Her ears began to ring. Royce must've accidentally called her while she was having sex. The sound of the bedsprings squeaking and the headboard hitting the wall told her so.

"Yeah, baby! Yesss! Yesss! Yesss!" Royce screamed.

Zora wanted to know who the man called "baby" was. She needed Royce to say his name. At the moment, she was moaning and humming and confessing her love for him. Zora was dying to know who he was. Why wouldn't Royce say his name? He apparently was a dynamite lover. He must've been giving it to Royce like a pro, and she was giving it right back to him. All of his groaning and promises to love her to the end of time told her so. There was lots of howling, grunting, and bed shaking going on. The sounds caused Zora's belly to twist in knots. Sweat had begun to trickle down the sides of her face. Her heartbeat tripled with anticipation.

Then suddenly, in the heat of the moment, Royce dropped the bomb. "Oh, Nicholaaas!"

Zora heard the name she'd wanted to hear and instantly regretted it. She wished she had been wrong about her suspicions because it hurt like a

sharp knife in her heart to be right. She pushed
the power button to end the call. She was sorry
and very sad now that she'd learned the truth. But
she was also highly pissed off.

"Marry her or perish."
The last words the older priest had spoken to
Father Gregory haunted him in his sleep. He sat
up, covered with sweat in the bed, and looked
around the room. Memories from last night
floated all around him. He and Royce had made
love on and off all night long. While they were
feeding each other's passions, he hadn't thought
about God, the priesthood, or the church. He'd
been guilty of living in the moment in the worst
way. Nothing and no one else had mattered while
he was holding Royce in his arms, screwing her
into insanity. He was a lost soul, living in two
worlds but not comfortable in either.

"What time is it?"

He looked down at Royce and smiled. "It's
almost four o'clock." He stroked her cheek with
the back of his hand. "Go back to sleep. I'm going
to shower and head home."

"That's a good idea. You should be at the parsonage before the other priests wake up."

Father Gregory nodded and left the bed to prepare for his trip back across town. It was time for him to return to the real world where he was a respected man of the cloth and the shepherd of a flock. But at nightfall, he would once again transform into Royce's secret lover and disgraced sinner. It was a terrible life he was living, one that was torn and tugging his heart in two totally different directions. Father Gregory was emotionally challenged and spiritually unfit. Yet he refused to leave the priesthood, and living without Royce was no longer an option.

Chapter Twenty-nine

Waterloo, Sierra Leone
West Africa

"Hang up the damn phone right now, Zora!"

She continued dialing with her back to her husband.

Eric reached over Zora's shoulder and snatched the outdated cordless phone from her hand. He held it behind his back. She turned around and gave him a lethal glare, but he ignored it. Eric was determined to have his say. "Royce is not a child anymore. She's a grown-ass woman. You are too, so you don't have any business tattling on your sister like you're both back in elementary school."

"Royce may be an adult, but she's not acting very responsibly these days. I'm not home to stop her, so someone else has to." Zora held out her hand. "Give me the phone, Eric. I'm going to call my mother to let her know what's going on. She needs to know what Royce is doing so she can talk some sense into her."

Eric looked down at his high school sweetheart. He knew the first day they met as sophomores that she was the only girl for him. Over the years, Eric had seen Zora's stubborn side more times than anyone else. Whenever she had her mind set on doing something, it was hard to hold her back. But today he was resolute to make her see that she should not make Royce's affair with Father Gregory a family matter.

"If you tell Mother Estelle that Royce is sleeping with her priest, it will break her heart. She'll tell your father, and then all hell will break loose. The family will go up in flames and smoke, and Royce will be the center of everyone's scrutiny and judgment. I guarantee you she'll resent you. Things may never be the same between you two again. Is that what you want, Zora?"

"I want Royce to stop sleeping with Father Gregory! That's what I want. I can't make her end the affair, so I need to talk to the only person who can. I prayed about it all weekend long, and I believe it's what God wants me to do. I have to stop Royce from making a fool of herself."

"You prayed about it?"

Zora folded her arms across her chest defiantly and nodded.

"Well, I think you need to pray some more, because I don't believe God wants you to be a busybody and destroy your sister's life and disrupt our family."

"Royce is ruining her life by acting like a whore with a priest!"

"Honey, Royce is obviously in love. If she weren't, she wouldn't be involved with Father Gregory. You know that better than anyone else in the world. My instincts tell me he loves her too. Why else would he be willfully breaking his celibacy vow and sneaking around to be with Royce?"

"You're either naïve or a typical man." Zora laughed, but it sounded more like an evil cackle from a wicked character in a horror flick. "Just because that good-for-nothing priest is banging my sister's brains out, it doesn't necessarily mean he loves her!"

"I don't know much about Father Gregory, but I've known Royce since she was Tyler's age. I consider her my little sister too. That's why I know she wouldn't be involved with a man unless she truly loved him and she believed he loved her back."

"That may be true, but Royce's history with men isn't all that great. What about Marlon Burrell, Eric? Royce believed he loved her. We all know how that relationship turned out. Don't we? It was a disaster."

"Yeah, that loser fooled Royce and almost caused her to have a nervous breakdown. But if my memory serves me correctly, you were his number one fan," Eric said sharply, pointing his finger at his wife. "It was under your advice that Royce decided to go out on her first date with the man. He was a professional, you said. He was established, you said. He was financially stable," Eric mimicked with a deadly edge in his voice. "The dude was a two-timing bastard!"

"I was wrong back then, but I'm not this time!"

"Honey, it's not about who's wrong or who's right. This situation is all about Royce's right to make her own decisions and for you to stay out of her business. The only thing we can do is pray that she'll be able to live with the consequences. I'll be there for her no matter what like I've always been. I hope you will be too. But as for now, stay the hell out of Royce's business."

Eric placed the phone on his desk. He picked up his stethoscope, hung it around his neck, and left his office.

Cassie stumbled into her boss's office and closed the door. She leaned her back against the wooden slab, trembling with her hands behind her. Her eyes were stretched wide like she'd just witnessed a brutal murder.

Royce looked up from the spreadsheet she'd been reviewing. "Did you forget to knock before entering?"

"Yes, ma'am. I'm so sorry, but we've got a little situation going on in the parking lot."

"What kind of situation, Cassie?"

She pushed away from the door and walked a few feet to stand directly in front of the desk, rubbing her hands together nervously. "It seems like your old friend, that doctor named Marlon Burrell, is braver than any man I know. He's not scared of the security guards, Hard Core, or—"

"Hard Core? You mean the gangster rapper who works out here?"

"Yes, ma'am."

Royce sprang from her chair and rounded her desk. "Is Marlon on the property?"

"Yes, ma'am. Lenny, the security guard, spotted him walking toward the building and he asked him to leave right away. I guess the good doctor didn't appreciate being told what to do, so he started arguing with Lenny and demanded to see you. That's when Hard Core and his crew walked up. You know how crazy that fine-ass rapper is about you. He got in Dr. Burrell's face and shoved him."

"Oh, Lord! Hard Core has a criminal record!" Royce shouted, running toward the door. "I don't want him to kill Marlon because of me and end up in prison for life. His trifling ass ain't worth it."

Cassie ran out of the office behind Royce. They hurried down the main hallway of Royalty's midtown facility and headed for the exit. Through the double glass doors, Royce saw the crowd of people on the east side of the parking lot. Lenny and two other security guards were in the center of the throng of spectators. A group of men was trying to restrain Hard Core, the award-winning rapper, but he was making it difficult. His towering height and muscular build gave him the strength of a dozen men. Marlon was lucky at the moment, but if he kept running his mouth, Hard Core was going to break free and kick his ass. Royce didn't want a murder to go down at her place of business. The negative publicity would ruin Royalty's reputation. Royce pushed the doors, ran outside, and shoved her way through the crowd.

"What the hell is going on here?"

"These play cops tried to throw me off the premises, Royce. They said I'm not welcome here because you've banned me from both of your facilities for life. I want to hear it from you, baby. Is it true?"

Royce walked farther into the crowd of people in Marlon's direction with her hands on her hips. She stopped in front of him and looked up. His eyes used to hypnotize her. Today they caused her stomach to churn. "You need to leave here immediately," she spoke in a calm, soft voice. "This is private property, and the owner has the legal right to practice discretion. If you don't like it, sue me."

"Are you serious?" Marlon smiled bitterly, obviously embarrassed. "Who the hell do you think you are, Royce? I knew you before you had anything to brag about! Now, you think you're too high and mighty for me?"

"Yo, Royce, let me punch this punk's lights out!" Hard Core yelled as he tried to break free from his entourage.

"He's not worth it. Your CD is at the top of the charts, and you just landed a role in John Singleton's upcoming movie. I won't let you ruin your career for him." Royce turned back to Marlon. "I'm about to call the police and have you arrested for trespassing. The dean of your medical school would surely frown upon your incarceration."

"Royce, please don't do that. I just wanted to talk to you, but I got upset when I was told you'd banned me from your businesses. That's all. Give me a break. I just need five minutes of your time. Please."

Royce looked around at the mob of onlookers. She zoomed in on Lenny, her trusted chief security guard, and waved him over.

"Yes, ma'am, Ms. Phillips?"

"I want you, Elroy, and Santana to disperse this crowd for me. Make sure Hard Core and his crew leave pronto. I don't want him to make a pretzel out of Dr. Burrell."

"Got it." Lenny turned around and faced the spectators. "Okay, let's break it up! Move along! Go on about your business!"

"Thanks, Royce. Can we go inside to your office for privacy?"

Royce rolled her eyes to the sky. "Say whatever you need to say right here. And you have exactly five minutes."

"I've missed you."

"Are you serious?"

"Yes, I'm very serious. I know I messed up, but I didn't want to lose you or my son. You and Marlon Jr. meant the world to me. There hasn't been a day since you left me that I haven't thought about you. I was a happy man when we were together. Please forgive me for hurting you. Let me make it up to you. Give me another chance. Give us another chance."

"I've moved on, Marlon. I'm in love with a man who knows the meaning of faithfulness. He's committed to me and only me. I wouldn't leave him for you or any other man."

"I don't see a ring on your finger," he pointed out, inspecting Royce's left hand. "I'll give you a diamond today, the biggest one money can buy. Let me spend the rest of my life making you happy, baby. I want you to be my wife and the mother of my kids. I love you, Royce."

"Your five minutes are up. Goodbye, Marlon."

Royce turned quickly and power walked toward the entrance of the building. Marlon continued shouting, telling her how much he loved her and wanted her in his life. She couldn't return his feelings because she was in love with Father Gregory, but she did want the kind of life he'd offered her. Royce had dreamed of a fairy-tale wedding and a romantic honeymoon on a secluded island, relaxing on a white, sandy beach. She had imagined her protruding belly filled with her husband's child, too. A devoted husband, adorable children, and family holidays in Thomasville had been important components of her life plan. It seemed funny to her how her priorities had changed in a few months. Love made strange things happen for those who dared to dive in.

Chapter Thirty

"I want you to file for a restraining order against him in the morning. I'm serious, Royce."

"That won't be necessary, honey. Marlon is no fool. His job and reputation mean a lot to him. He's not going to risk losing everything for stalking me."

Father Gregory dropped his fork on his nearly empty plate. It landed hard, making a loud crashing sound. "He was brave and determined enough to challenge your security guards and a gangster rapper just so he could talk to you today. He seems like a man on a mission to me. Tell me again why you agreed to speak with him privately."

"He begged me for a few minutes of my time, Nicholas. And I was curious."

"So, you gave your ex-lover an opportunity to declare his love for you and ask for your hand in marriage because you were curious? The man deceived you and broke your heart, Royce! Why on earth would you want to listen to anything he had to say?" he shouted and banged his fist on the table once with force.

Royce flinched and closed her eyes, startled by his anger. "I . . . I don't know. I guess I thought if I allowed him to say his piece, he would leave me alone once and for all. Maybe I was a bit naïve."

"Yes, you were."

"I'm sorry. I didn't mean to upset you, Nicholas. Please forgive me."

The remaining moments of dinner went by slowly and in uncomfortable silence. Royce felt terrible about the Marlon situation, but she wasn't certain why. She hadn't done anything wrong. In her opinion, she had handled the problem quite well. Marlon's marriage proposal had been rejected, and he now knew that Royce was in love with another man and had moved on with her life. He was also aware that he'd been banned from both of her fitness facilities. How much more did Father Gregory think she should've done?

Royce cleared the dinner table, washed the dishes, and put the leftover food away while her obviously disgruntled lover remained in his chair. She felt his eyes all over her as she moved about the kitchen, sweeping the floor. His anger toward her was unsettling and unjustified. There was no reason for him to feel threatened by Marlon or any other man because her heart belonged to him. Their relationship was anything but normal, and its future was uncertain. But Royce loved Father Gregory limitlessly, and she was totally committed to him. Whatever insecurities he had about their relationship had nothing to do with Marlon Burrell. Apparently, he was dealing with some personal issues that he didn't care to share with her.

"Would you like a glass of wine or a cup of tea?"

Father Gregory folded his arms across his chest and shook his head.

"I'm going upstairs to relax. Are you coming?"

"No. I'm going to sleep at the parsonage tonight." He stood from his chair and walked over to Royce. "I'll call you later."

"Nicholas, please talk to me. Why are you so upset?"

"Not now, Royce. I'll call you."

Confused and disappointed, Royce watched Father Gregory exit the kitchen. She stood in place with tears threatening to spill from her eyes, but she refused to cry. Their first serious disagreement as a couple was very painful. Royce was willing to do anything to mend things between them. She loved him so much, and she wanted to make him happy again.

"Damn you, Marlon!"

"He's home early this evening."

"Yes, he is. And he seems to be in a very unpleasant mood. He barely said two words to me
when I asked him about his day."

Father Schmidt moved his chess piece to another position on the game board. "There must be
trouble in paradise. There is no trace of the vanilla
scent on his body, he appears upset, and he's here.
Yes, he and his lover are definitely quarreling."

"Maybe he caught her with another man."
Father Rivera snorted.

"That's possible. Or maybe she wants him to
marry her, and he has refused to do so."

"He can't marry her. He's a priest."

"I know he's a priest, you idiot!" Father Schmidt
snapped. "But he's also a man who is obviously
involved with a woman. He spends lots of time
with her, too. I'm certain that he loves her. Why
else would he put his soul and the priesthood in
jeopardy?"

"I suppose you're right. I am ignorant of such
things. But you once lived a worldly life before
your transformation. You're familiar with the
ways of women." Father Rivera paused and

looked at the older German priest. "Father, what is it like? Being with a woman, I mean."

"If God has created anything more satisfying, He must've kept it only for Himself."

Father Gregory didn't call Royce the previous night as he'd told her he would, and she had lost lots of rest because of it. All kinds of crazy thoughts had kept her awake until the wee hours of the morning. Now, as she sat in a meeting with her marketing team, she was finding it extremely hard to stay awake. She blinked her weary eyes several times and stifled a yawn with the back of her hand. Warren, her chief marketing executive, was addressing the group about the new membership drive, but all Royce could think about was leaving work early so she could hurry home to retire to her bed.

All of a sudden, everyone in the meeting turned to watch Cassie as she tiptoed into the conference room carrying a gorgeous crystal vase filled with red roses. She walked directly to the head of the huge conference table and handed them along with a card to her boss.

"These were just delivered for you," she whispered through a bright smile.

"Thank you, Cassie. Could you please bring me a cup of black coffee? I need a boost."

Cassie nodded and left the room quietly as Warren continued with his presentation. Royce admired the beautiful roses. Deep in her heart, she knew they were from Father Gregory. They were a peace offering. She tore into the card with her pulse racing with anticipation.

> *My love,*
> *I'm sorry. I had no right to take my insecurities and frustration out on you. You handled Marlon like a champion. I should've let it go, but I acted like a jealous fool instead. Please forgive me. I love you with all my heart. I'll see you this evening.*
> *Nick*

Royce wanted to be angry with her sweetheart for the way he'd behaved yesterday and for causing her to lose sleep last night. But the deep and unconditional love she had for him softened her heart. They'd made it through their first lovers' spat, and she couldn't have been happier. Tonight was going to be extra special. Royce would make sure of it. After the meeting, she would leave and go straight to the international market to buy two huge lobster tails and a pair of premium-cut T-bone steaks. Of course, she would pick up a bottle of wine as well. Father Gregory was about to learn how to make up with his woman after a fight.

"Do you miss me?"

"Of course I miss you, sweetie. You're my favorite nephew."

"Auntie Royce, I'm your *only* nephew." The boy's giggle filled the vehicle through the dashboard communication system. "Have you seen Father Gregory?"

Royce's hands tightened around the steering wheel and she bit down on her bottom lip. Her stomach muscles contracted as she envisioned her fine-ass man. "I didn't go to church Sunday."

"So, you haven't seen him?"

"Tyler, where else would I see him besides church?"

"I don't know. Father Gregory does love your cooking. I thought maybe he stopped by for a meal or two."

"The parsonage has a cook who prepares meals daily for him and the other priests there. Father Gregory doesn't need me to feed him."

"I guess not. I'm going to call him this evening to check on him. I miss him. I wonder if he misses me."

"Ask him when you call him."

"I will. I've got to go now. Grandpa and I are going to the lodge to shoot pool and eat junk food. I'll see you Saturday. I love you, Auntie Royce."

"I love you too."

Royce was a bit shaken by Tyler's question about her seeing Father Gregory. Did the boy know something was going on between her and the priest?

"Ain't no way," she mumbled, shaking her head. "It's impossible. No one knows our secret except us."

Waterloo, Sierra Leone
West Africa

"I've decided to call Royce and tell her what I know about her and Father Gregory. You were right. Telling my mother would've caused major problems in the family. Thank you for talking me out of it. I should've known better. Royce is the person I need to have a conversation with."

"Why can't you just leave it alone, Zora? Confronting Royce could backfire in your face. I think you should stay out of your sister's business. I'm against her relationship with Father Gregory too, but it's her life, and she'll have to deal with the consequences. So back off." Eric returned his attention to the soccer game on television.

"I will not! I'm her big sister, and I know she's making a terrible mistake by having an affair with a priest. It's my responsibility to tell her the truth. It's not like I snooped around in her business. Because of her carelessness, the information landed in my lap, so to speak."

"I'm warning you, Zora."

"Don't waste your time, darling. My baby sister and I are due for a little talk about her wild and crazy life."

Chapter Thirty-one

Royce sucked her teeth when her cell phone rang. It was Zora again. It was her pattern to call the landline first and then her cell phone whenever she was attempting to reach Royce. This evening wasn't a good time for them to talk. She had promised her mother that she would reach out to Zora so they could clear the air between them, but it wouldn't be today.

"Aren't you going to answer the phone, baby? Somebody really wants to talk to you."

"I'm busy trying to get dinner on the table. I don't have time to chat. I'm starving. Aren't you?"

Father Gregory walked to the island and stood behind Royce. He wrapped his arms around her waist. "Who are you trying to avoid, Royce?" His kissed the right side of her neck.

"I'm not trying to avoid my sister. I just don't have time to talk to her right now. I'll call her tomorrow."

"I can take over the cooking to give you and Zora some time to catch up. You told me the other day that you two haven't spoken in a while."

"One more day won't hurt us. I'll ring her back early in the morning before I go to work."

"Okay. I spoke with Tyler earlier this evening," he announced, returning to his seat at the dinette. "He said the strangest thing to me."

"What did he say?"

"He told me I should come here to visit you while he's away. He's worried that you're lonely without him. He also said you'd probably be so happy to see me that you would cook for me."

"I knew he'd planned to call you today because he told me so. But I had no idea he was going to ask you to check up on me."

"Tyler is a good kid, and he loves his auntie. He wants you to be happy."

"You make me happy."

"I'm glad. I just hope I can make you happy for a very long time."

Father Gregory's warm, wet mouth left Royce's hardened nipples and moved lower to her flat belly. He kissed and licked her flesh as he inserted two fingers into her dampness. He strummed her clit gently and licked around her belly button. The buzz of his cell phone he'd purposely switched to vibrate mode caused him to freeze in motion.

"Don't answer it, Nicholas. Please, baby, don't answer it."

"I don't have a choice," he whispered with his moist lips still pressed against her belly. He gave her heated flesh one last kiss before he sat up and reached for his phone on the nightstand. "This is Father Gregory."

Royce listened to his side of the conversation in an attempt to guess who the late-night caller was. She covered her face with both hands in frustration. From the sound of Father Gregory's voice, she could tell there was an emergency on the other end of the call. The timing sucked.

"I'll be there in forty-five minutes. I just need to shower and dress first. Then I'll join you and your family at the hospital." He fell silent and glanced down at Royce. "It's not a problem, Mrs. Strozier. I'm your priest, and it's my godly duty to be with you and your family in your time of need. I'll see you soon. Goodbye." He replaced the phone on the nightstand and looked at Royce.

"What is it?"

"The doctors don't expect Mr. Paul Strozier to live through the night. His battle with prostate cancer is coming to a sad end. His wife wants me to come to the hospital and offer his last rites in the presence of the family." He stood from the bed with beads of sweat covering his naked body and made his way to the master bathroom.

Royce released air from her cheeks and rolled over onto her stomach, totally disappointed.

"Tonight will be our last night together for a while. I spoke with my dad this morning. He and Mama will be here with Tyler by noon tomorrow."

Father Gregory swiveled around in his comfortable desk chair a couple of times. "Time sure does fly. How would you like for us to spend our last night together?"

"I'm going to take you out on a date."

"Royce, you know we can't be seen out together in public." He sighed and shook his head. "We've had this conversation a million times. I thought you understood."

"No one will see us. Trust me. You'll see."

Royce paid the attendant inside the glass booth and drove away. She sneaked a peek at Father Gregory and grinned when she pulled her SUV onto the lot of the old drive-in theater. "Surprise!"

"Wow," he said, looking at the monstrous screen. "I haven't been to a drive-in movie since I was a kid. Max used to take the entire family whenever a new Disney flick was released. Those were the good ol' days."

The action thriller had already started. Royce rolled down her window and secured the speaker in it. She turned to her man, who looked irresistible in his signature all-black attire. "Would you like popcorn and a soft drink or are you going to be a cheap date?"

"I'm cheap, but you'll have to treat me to something special when we get home."

"It'll be my pleasure."

Chapter Thirty-two

"Royce, both phones have been ringing all morning long. Maybe you should see who's trying to reach you. It may be important." Father Gregory kissed her lips softly and pulled her naked body closer to his.

"It's Zora. I know it's her. She's the only person inconsiderate enough to call me this time of morning. That chick has no shame. Go back to sleep. We have a few hours before Tyler and my parents will arrive."

The two lovers drifted off to sleep again nestled in each other's arms. They were exhausted after a night of smoldering nonstop lovemaking. Their sex marathon had started at the front door as soon as they returned home from the drive-in movie theater and finally ended at dusk in the master suite. There was a trail of discarded clothes from the foyer to the staircase and beyond. Neither of them had seen the need to gather the garments after the fact.

A few hours later, the sound of the doorbell ringing out of control woke Father Gregory from his sleep again. Royce was lying on top of him as still as a corpse. "Sweetheart, someone is at the door," he whispered and checked the time on the clock. "Sweet Jesus! It's after twelve! We overslept. It's probably your parents and Tyler."

Royce jumped up and ran around the room frantically. She rushed inside the walk-in closet, grabbed a bright orange caftan, and put it on. "Stay here and be quiet. I'll be back as soon as I can."

She rushed from the room and hurried down the stairs, picking up underwear and socks along the way. When she reached the bottom, one of Father Gregory's athletic shoes, his belt, and his jeans were strewn on the floor along with her T-shirt, bra, and sandals. She gathered everything quickly and threw them into the closet near the front door.

"Where is his other shoe? Damn it!" Royce spun around in circles, looking everywhere.

Tyler's voice was growing louder and more impatient on the other side of the door, yelling her name. He was also ringing the doorbell non-stop. "I'm coming, honey!" Royce shouted. "I was asleep." She rushed to the door and deactivated the security system. She took a deep, composing breath and pulled the brass handle. "Hey, you guys. I'm sorry it took so long. I was sleeping like a baby."

"I was about to kick the door in, baby girl." Mr. Phillips pecked his daughter on the cheek and entered the house.

"You always did sleep like a log, child."

"How are you, Mama?"

"I'm fine, sweetie."

"I'm back," Tyler told his aunt and threw his scrawny body into her arms for a quick hug. Then he followed his grandpa into the kitchen.

Mrs. Phillips stood in place with a stony countenance. She stared at the ficus tree in the left corner of the foyer. She walked closer, apparently to get a better look. Leaning over, she lifted a black men's athletic shoe from the ceramic planter. Mrs. Phillips turned to face Royce, who was fidgeting with her fingers nervously and gnawing on her bottom lip.

"Is he still here?" her mother asked, handing her the large sneaker.

Royce hung her head and accepted it. She opened the closet, exposing the other discarded clothing items she'd stuffed inside. She tossed the shoe mindlessly on top of the pile. "Yes, ma'am. He's upstairs in my bedroom. He was supposed to have been gone already, but we overslept."

"Humph, it must've been one hell of a night,"
Mrs. Phillips said with an attitude.

"I'm sorry, Mama."

"Don't be sorry, Royce. Just be careful. I don't
want any hanky-panky going on in this house
while my grandson is here. Send him to Andra
the next time you get the urge. Do you understand
me?"

"Yes, Mama."

"Father Gregory would be happy to spend time
with Tyler while you entertain your male friends."
She snapped her fingers. "Oh, my goodness! I left
his sweet potato pies in a box inside the trunk. I'll
get them and find an excuse for your father to take
Tyler and me to the store. I want that man out of
this house before we return."

"I promise he'll be gone."

Royce ran up the stairs, skipping over them
two at a time. Her mother would have a con-
niption if she knew that Father Gregory was the
male friend she had entertained all night long.
With that in mind, she hurried to her bedroom
to warn him about their sticky situation.

"I'll give you some time to spend with Tyler.
Expect a call from me later." Father Gregory

leaned down and kissed Royce's lips. "It was another close call, baby. We'll have to be more careful in the future. I love you." He pulled her into his arms.

Royce hugged him tightly. "I love you too." She stood under the doorjamb as he descended the three steps.

Father Gregory walked to the side of the house to retrieve his motorcycle from the bushes. He then hopped on the fancy piece of machinery and guided it onto the pavement. He fired the engine and waved to Royce before he sped down the street. His mind immediately went into overdrive, thinking about how close he and Royce had come to getting busted. If Tyler had had his key with him, they would have been exposed for sure. His double life was becoming more difficult to maintain by the day. He would never leave the priesthood or the church, and he wasn't willing to live his life without Royce either. She was his heart and his soul. She completed him. Without her, Father Gregory would not be able to breathe.

"Thanks again for dropping off the pies. Your mother is the master of the sweet potato."

"She does know her way around the kitchen. I'll tell her how much you're enjoying your special treat. Anyway, get some rest, sweetie. You have to deliver three sermons tomorrow. I love you."

"I love you more."

The phone rang again only seconds after Royce had ended her late-night conversation with Father Gregory. She figured he must've forgotten to tell her something. She lifted the receiver from its cradle. "Yes, Nicholas?"

"It's not your priest-slash-bed-buddy. It's your sister, damn it!"

"Zora?" Royce gasped and checked the clock on the nightstand. It was after midnight in Atlanta, which meant it was past five o'clock in the morning in Sierra Leone.

"Yes, it's me. Why haven't you answered any of my calls, Royce? Were you so busy screwing your priest while Tyler was away that you didn't have time to talk to me?"

"What are you talking about? Are you calling me with more crazy accusations about an imaginary affair with Father Gregory, Z?"

"Don't do that, little sister. Please don't insult my intelligence. I know for a fact that you're sleeping with the man. I heard you and him getting busy a few days ago. You must've left your cell phone on the bed while he was serving you his penis. Your naked ass accidentally called me. I heard everything, so you can't deny it."

Silence fell over the phone line after Zora's revelation. Royce fingered her braids nervously. She clearly recalled the night she had insisted on getting her cell phone from the kitchen. She'd lost it somewhere near the bed the moment she and Father Gregory started making love. It was one of the most passionate nights they had ever shared, and Zora had heard it all. Royce and Father Gregory no longer had a secret hidden from the rest of the world. Zora now knew about their affair.

"I love him, Z, and he loves me," she finally confessed as tears poured heavily down her cheeks.

"He's a priest for Christ's sake, Royce! You have no future with him! Nothing good will come out of your bedroom romps with a man of the cloth! When the archdiocese reassigns him to another church somewhere clear across the globe, you will be history!"

Royce had never given any thought to Father Gregory leaving Atlanta to lead another congregation someplace else. They'd never really discussed their future as a couple. He had only promised to love her forever. And that was good enough for Royce for now.

"I'll go with him wherever they send him. It doesn't matter how far away. We love each other, Z. Accept it. We're going to be together no matter what."

Zora laughed hysterically, and it pissed Royce off. "Are you serious? Girl, you are delusional! That man is making a complete fool of you. You're not his first whore, and you definitely won't be his last. You are his Atlanta sex kitten. I'm sure he had one in Barbados, Boston, and in every other city where he's served. Don't be stupid, Royce. Priests have been screwing women and filling their heads with empty promises for centuries. I wish the Vatican would allow them to marry already, so they can stop banging little boys in their butts and having affairs with desperate, naïve women like you!"

"Z, I'm going to hang up now because I love you and I don't want to disrespect you. You have no idea what you're talking about, and I don't have the time or desire to fill you in. But you're wrong, dead wrong," Royce said softly through a fresh flow of tears and ended the call.

Now that Zora knew about her affair with Father Gregory, Royce knew their relationship as sisters and friends would never be the same again. She felt so ashamed. As a young girl, she had admired and looked up to Zora because she was smart, beautiful, and popular. Royce had imitated her big sister and aspired to be just like her. The only reason she had chosen a career in nursing was that Zora had dreamt of becoming a nurse. The

Phillips sisters used to talk about meeting rich and handsome men who would marry them and become the fathers of their children. Zora was the lucky one. She had it all. Royce had fallen short in the romance department. Even now, although she was very much in love with Father Gregory, their relationship was more than complicated. But Royce wasn't willing to give up on what they had. She wouldn't allow Zora to interfere either.

She reached for the phone again to call Father Gregory to tell him about the conversation she'd had with her sister. He had a right to know that their relationship was no longer a secret. Two other people knew now. Surely, Zora had shared her discovery with Eric. They told each other everything.

Royce placed the phone down again suddenly when it occurred to her that telling Father Gregory that her sister and brother-in-law knew they were having an affair may not be wise. What if he became upset and overly concerned? He would probably end their relationship at once. Royce's heart couldn't bear the pain of losing him. She decided he didn't need to know after all.

Chapter Thirty-three

Zora smiled at her mother through the computer screen. She always looked forward to their weekly video chats. It gave them a chance to catch up on all the Thomasville, Georgia gossip. Estelle Phillips always had a mouthful to report. Zora was happy that her mom was technologically savvy at her age. She was so unlike her husband of many years who was still stuck in the Stone Age. Mr. Phillips had invested in a cell phone only last year, and somehow he had lost it at least twice a week every week since he'd brought it home.

"You look pretty in pink today, Mama."

"Thank you. You look like you're dressed for bed. What time is it over there, honey?"

"It's eleven o'clock at night."

"Shouldn't you be asleep already, Zora?"

"No, ma'am. I don't have to work tomorrow. My handsome boss and I are taking the day off to do some sightseeing in Freetown and the city of Bo."

"Where is my son-in-law?"

"He's asleep. He had a long day."

"Eric is such a fine young fellow. I'm so proud of him. I wish your sister could find a good man like him and settle down." Mrs. Phillips looked around the room before she leaned closer to her computer screen. "Royce is seeing someone. I don't know how serious they are, but they're sleeping together. But shush now. You didn't hear that from me."

"Mama!" Zora squealed and pressed her palm to her chest. "How do you know that?"

"Your father, Tyler, and I nearly caught them in the act."

"What? When, Mama?"

"It was the morning we took Tyler back to Atlanta at the end of his spring break. Your sister and her beau must've had a wild night because his shoe ended up in a potted plant. I'm so glad your father didn't see it. He would've taken a switch to Royce. The man had the nerve to still be in the house, upstairs in your sister's bed. She claimed they had overslept, but I think they were too worn out to move."

"That must've been so embarrassing for you. I'm sorry, Mama. If Tyler had found that shoe, Royce Dominique would've had a lot of explaining to do.

Can you imagine how confused my child would've been? My goodness! What was Royce thinking?"

"Like the young folks say, she was getting her freak on. I told her to be careful. I don't want her messing around while my grandson is in the house. She promised me she wouldn't. That's enough about your sister's sex life. I called to tell you about Alberta Dunbar who lives down the street. Can you believe she's about to get married to her fifth husband at the age of sixty-six? She met some retired middle school principal on a cruise ship. I tell you the truth. . . ."

Zora's mind abandoned the video call, but her mother was none the wiser. While Mrs. Phillips was giving her the scoop on Alberta Dunbar's pending nuptials, she was seething about Royce carrying on like a sleazy tramp with Father Gregory. Zora knew beyond a shadow of a doubt that he was the man who had been in her sister's bed the morning her parents had driven Tyler back to Atlanta. She was in love with the priest, and she believed he loved her. Zora closed her eyes and exhaled. She wanted Royce to come to her senses before it was too late. She was playing with fire, and she was going to get burned. The only person who could get Royce to realize how huge a mistake she was making was their mother.

But Zora didn't have the heart to tell her that her baby girl was sleeping with the priest. Such news would cause the poor woman to have a heart attack. Zora would have to come up with some kind of plan to save Royce from herself.

"I have to go home to Chicago next month for my baby sister's wedding, and I'd like you to make the trip with me. I know it's short notice, but she and her boyfriend just decided to get married out of the blue. His army unit is about to be deployed."

Royce rolled over onto her side in the bed, wishing that Father Gregory was lying beside her. "What will your family think about you bringing a woman home?"

"Of course, I won't be able to introduce you to anyone. I just want you to go with me so I can show you around the city. We'll have lots of quality time together in our hotel room, too. It'll be our first romantic getaway."

"I'll go with you," Royce told him, although she didn't like the idea entirely. It pricked her heart that he would never be able to introduce her to his family as the love of his life.

"Great. The wedding is scheduled for Saturday, May the twentieth. But I'd like for us to fly out on the Thursday before. I won't let my folks know I'm in town until Friday evening. It will give us time to hang out and enjoy one another before I have to leave you to celebrate with my family. It's not a perfect setup, but it's the best I can do, baby."

No, it's not perfect. It sucks! I'm your woman, not your closet whore! Royce swallowed those words, but it had taken great restraint to keep her emotions inside. "I understand. We'll have fun. I'll leave Tyler with Glenda Tennyson. Rico will love having him crash at his house for a few days."

"Then it's settled. I'll book two first-class tickets to Chicago in the morning. I believe an executive suite at the Four Seasons will be perfect for us. I'm looking forward to giving you a tour of my hometown. I'll take you to my favorite pizzeria, my high school, and the Sears Tower. We'll even visit my father's grave. I haven't been there in years. I was so young when he passed away. I can't remember very much about him. If we have time, we may go and take pictures of the president's home in Hyde Park."

Royce was amused by Father Gregory's child-like excitement. "I haven't visited Chicago in a very long time. This trip will be special because I'm going there with you."

After a few more minutes of chatting about their travel plans, Royce ended the call. She stared around her dark and empty room. A woman in love wasn't supposed to be lonely. Then again, she wasn't supposed to be in love with a priest either.

"Tell me about your upcoming trip to Chicago." Andra took a sip from her wineglass.

"I'm going there to check out a new fitness facility and meet with the owners. It's supposed to be one of the most modern centers in the country. They have all of the latest equipment and monitoring machinery. I want to get some ideas so I can upgrade both of Royalty's locations."

"What's the name of the facility? I want to look it up online."

"Um . . . um, I can't remember the name. It's a really weird name."

"So, how did you hear about the place?"

"One of my vendors told me about it a few weeks ago."

"Hey, I should go with you. I love Chicago."

"Nooo!" Royce responded louder than she'd intended to. She glanced around and noticed several nearby diners in the popular Buckhead bistro staring at her. She lowered her voice. "It's just that I'll be too busy to hang out with you. I'm going there to work, sweetie. I'll be in and out of meetings all day, pricing equipment, and observing the way the staff operates. You'll be bored to death."

Andra stared at Royce with what appeared to be suspicious eyes, making her feel very uncomfortable. All of the lying and sneaking around she'd been doing recently was causing her to sink deeper into a pool of guilt. She was constantly being dishonest to Tyler and her parents. And she hadn't spoken to Zora since their conversation about her affair with Father Gregory. Royce desperately needed a break from her regular routine of secret rendezvous and calculated lies. The trip to Chicago would give her and Father Gregory the time, freedom, and space to behave like a normal couple without the burden of discretion, until he would have to leave her to be with his family. Even so, she was still counting down the days.

"I made an eight o'clock reservation for us at Alinea. It's one of Chicago's premier restaurants. I hope you don't mind." Father Gregory caressed Royce's thigh tenderly.

"Chi-town is your city. I don't have a problem following your lead."

Father Gregory turned to admire the beauty of the sky from his window seat on the plane.

The soft blue hue scattered with pure white, cottony clouds, illuminated by a brilliant sun, were the magnificent creations of God's handiwork. And the gorgeous woman sitting next to him was the most stunning creature the Almighty had breathed life into. "The weather is supposed to be nice the entire weekend," he announced after a moment or two. "Rhonda is happy about that. She said it would be a sign of bad luck if it were to rain on her wedding day."

"What time is the ceremony Saturday?"

"It'll start at five o'clock sharp. My mother and Max are strict about time. And because they're footing the bill for the small ceremony, they are holding Mrs. Pollard, the coordinator, to task. I expect the wedding to be short and sweet, followed by a small, intimate reception with just our family and closest friends."

Royce shifted in her seat and turned her head in the opposite direction. Father Gregory picked up on her stiff and defensive body language right away. She was closer to him than anyone else in the world, including his parents, yet she wouldn't be allowed to attend Rhonda's wedding. She *couldn't* be there. Their complex circumstances wouldn't allow it.

"How long will I be stuck in the hotel room alone with nothing to do, Nicholas?" she asked in an emotionless voice.

"I'll hang around at the reception long enough to eat and to greet the people I haven't seen in a long time. I'm the bride's big brother. Heck, I'm her only brother. It's a standing tradition that I dance with her at least once. After that, I'll fake a headache or tell everyone I'm tired. I promise I'll be back in time to take you out on the town."

Chapter Thirty-four

"Something fishy is going on, Andra. And I believe you know all about it. I can feel it deep down in my bones. Tell me what you know about Royce's new man."

The younger cousin released a breath and counted to ten. Zora had always been bossy, judgmental, and meddlesome as far back as she could remember. It was really time for her to get a life so she could stop trying to control Royce's.

Andra was not a fool. She knew Royce was involved in a secret affair with some mystery man. She had picked up on the warning signs weeks ago. But Royce was a grown-ass, independent woman. She had a right to sleep with whomever she wanted to. And it wasn't Zora's business. If Royce was on a lovers' getaway to Chi-town with a man, it was perfectly all right with Andra.

"I don't have time to play private eye and snoop around in Royce's personal life," Andra finally said. "She's an intelligent, successful woman. She works hard, Zora. I think she has the right to play just as hard. Anyway, I have to run now, cuz. Like Royce, I'm a single lady. I'm on the prowl for a good man who's willing to put a ring on it. The nightclub is calling me. I'll talk to you later."

Andra hung up the phone before Zora had an opportunity to go into one of her infamous rants. She didn't have the time or patience to listen to all of her screaming and outrageous accusations this evening. Happy hour had just begun at Masai's on Peachtree, and Andra's girlfriends were waiting for her to join them at the bar.

After applying one last coat of copper lipstick and a couple of strokes of mascara to her eyelashes, she was satisfied with her appearance. "It's show time, baby. Brothers, beware."

Andra left her studio apartment prepared to mingle, but she filed a brain note to warn Royce as soon as she returned to Atlanta that Zora was up to her nosy-Rosie routine and had attempted to solicit her help in her scheme.

"The food was amazing, and the ambience was incredible. Thanks for a lovely evening." Royce pecked Father Gregory on the cheek as they walked hand in hand through the swanky downtown Chicago restaurant.

"Nicholas? Nicholas Gregory, is that you?"

They stopped in midstride and turned toward the booming voice. Royce became nervous as the heavyset man with a wild beard and mustache made steps in their direction. She could tell that Father Gregory was a bit uneasy. He rubbed the back of her hand with the pad of his thumb.

"It's me, Shadow Henderson. We were altar boys together back in elementary school at Covenant Life Cathedral. I was the chunky kid who always had licorice sticks stuffed in his pockets. And you were going to be a priest and serve the Catholic Church for the rest of your life." The man's grayish brown eyes inspected every inch of Royce's body. He smiled at his childhood friend. "I see you changed your mind. I never understood why you wanted to punish yourself with such a boring life. I'm glad to see you turned out to be smarter than you looked."

Father Gregory blinked his eyes a few times as if he were recovering from a wicked spell. He extended his free hand to Mr. Henderson. "It was good to see you again after so many years. Take care." He walked away, pulling Royce along with him.

"Are you okay? I'm sure that was very awkward for you."

"I'm fine."

It was not true. He wasn't fine. It was obvious to Royce. The whole scene had unfolded like the most frightening horror movie. A fellow altar boy from his past had misjudged his life in only a matter of seconds, and he'd been too embarrassed and flustered to correct him about it.

"I don't feel like going for a walk downtown. Let's turn in early tonight. We'll have all day tomorrow to hang out," Royce reminded him.

There were over ten cars parked in the driveway and along the street in front of the two-story brick house. Father Gregory immediately reflected on the many fun-filled memories of hanging out with his older sister, Michelle, Rhonda, and all of their friends. Their house had once been the spot to be because his mother was always there cooking and watching over them while Max was at work. Most of their friends had been products of families wherein both parents were employed or the children of single, working mothers.

Father Gregory got out of his rental car, slamming the door behind him. He thought about Royce on his trudge up the walkway. She should've fallen asleep by now after an afternoon of extensive sightseeing. Right after breakfast, they'd visited and laid flowers on the grave of Edward York, Father Gregory's biological dad. Their next stop was the DuSable Museum of African American History and then on to the Chicago Riverwalk, where they'd eaten lunch at a quaint café. Royce had refused to return to the hotel for a room-service dinner without first doing a little bit of shopping at the Water Tower Place.

The sounds of animated voices talking and laughing floated through the front door. Father Gregory rang the doorbell, excited about seeing his parents, sisters, and the rest of the family. Judging by the extra cars, he was expecting to see some of their old friends as well. The door swung open.

"Get on in here, son."

A pair of strong arms grabbed him and pulled him into a warm embrace. The familiar scents of pipe tobacco and top-shelf brandy surrounded him. Father Gregory relaxed in Max's arms and pulled his stocky body close.

"You look good, Pops," he said, taking a step back. "I see you're celebrating early."

"My baby girl is leaving me. I'm not celebrating, Nick. I'm trying to drown my sorrows." He released a hearty laugh from his protruding stomach.

"Nick, is that you, baby?"

Father Gregory's mother pushed through the crowd until they stood face-to-face. She threw her short arms around him and reached up high to kiss his cheek. "Come on in, baby. Everybody was waiting for you to get here so you could offer the blessing over the food." Lillian Gregory turned around and sashayed her petite frame down the hallway. "It's a shame you're staying in a hotel like a complete stranger," she threw over her shoulder to her son. "I got your room ready, but you have the gall to be spending your money on a fancy hotel room. Shame on you."

"I figured other relatives might've claimed my old room before I got here. I didn't want to be a bother."

Michelle and Rhonda, the bride-to-be, ran from the den and yanked their brother into a group hug. They started laughing and talking over each other exactly the way they used to do when they were little girls. Relative after relative came forth to greet Father Gregory soon afterward. He eventually ended up in the dining room, standing before a table covered with scrumptious-smelling, good-looking food.

He folded his hands in front of him. "Let us bow our heads and close our eyes for the grace."

***

"You're back early." Royce sat up in bed and turned on the lamp on the nightstand.

"I missed you."

"How is the family?"

"My parents look great. Mama is just as stubborn and feisty as ever, and Max is having a hard time letting Rhonda go. Although he never treated Michelle and me any different, I always believed he loved Rhonda more because she's his biological child."

"Is that for me?" Royce asked, pointing to the saucer covered with aluminum foil in his hand.

"Yes. I brought you a piece of my Aunt Zelda's award-winning double-chocolate cake."

"Thank you, sweetheart. That was very thoughtful of you. We'll share it tomorrow. Tonight the only thing I want is you."

Father Gregory stripped bare in record time and joined Royce in bed. Running into Shadow Henderson the night before had dampened their romantic mood, so there had been no intimacy. Their last lovemaking session had been two weeks ago, on a night when they could no longer control themselves. The senior priest, in his horny state, had left the parsonage in the middle of the night out of sheer desperation. Luckily, Tyler had turned in early, exhausted after track practice. The secret lovers had wasted no time satisfying each other from midnight until the break of dawn. If the walls in Royce's all-white living room could talk, they would've had an erotic story to tell. Soon, the same could be said of their executive suite at Chicago's Four Seasons.

Their kisses were hot and urgent as if two years had passed instead of two weeks. Crazed and in need, Father Gregory flipped Royce over onto her back with more force than necessary. In his condition, his strength had obviously increased unbeknownst to him. Royce took pleasure in his roughness and aggression. She met his feverish kisses with intensity. She relished the feel of his hands all over her body, kneading her flesh, setting it on lustful fire.

Royce tore her lips away from his and spread her legs wide. "Now, Nicholas, right now."

Father Gregory lifted her legs higher and rested the backs of her knees on his broad shoulders. His rigid penis entered her drenched vagina with ease. Royce tightened her inner muscles around his rock-solid dick and watched his eyeballs roll to the back of his head. Pump for pump and thrust for thrust, they gave to and received from each other at an urgent, quick pace. Streams of sweat dripped from Father Gregory's face as he pushed deeper and more vigorously inside of Royce. She hummed and lifted her hips, bucking in orchestration to his steady rhythmic motions. Royce reached around and gripped his butt with both hands, pulling him closer to that spot within that would blast her into orbit.

"Right there, keep it right there, baby. That's it. That's it," she encouraged. And then the rapturous sensations seized her entire body. "Mmm . . . mmm, Nicholas!"

Her climax undoubtedly triggered his. Royce felt the explosive release of warm semen swooshing inside of her walls. Father Gregory trembled and groaned from his soul moments before he collapsed fully onto her perspiration-covered body. He rolled over onto his back slowly with Royce in his arms. She rested her head on his chest and inhaled the potent scent of sweet sex wafting in the air. Her eyelids became droopy, and her body was sated, causing sleep to come quickly.

Chapter Thirty-five

"Let me help you with that." Royce reached up and secured a perfect knot in Father Gregory's blue and red paisley-print tie.

He turned away to examine the results in the mirror. "Not bad. Who taught you how to tie a men's necktie?"

"My father did, of course. He challenged me once when I was in middle school, and I shocked him with my skills. You should've seen the expression on his face."

"Well, you did a fine job with my tie too, baby. Thank you." He walked to the closet, removed his navy suit coat from a hanger, and put it on. "You've never seen me in a regular suit before. I'm usually dressed in clergy attire."

"Or nothing at all," Royce teased him and grinned.

"Be serious, woman. How do I look?" Father Gregory struck a simple pose with his hands in his pants pockets.

"You look so handsome that I'm almost tempted to hold you hostage in this room. Every single woman at the wedding will have her eyes on you. Please don't run off and leave me for some trollop."

"Girl, you're stuck with me. There ain't a woman in all of creation who could take your place." He took Royce in his arms and looked directly into her eyes. "Remember the plan. I'll meet you at Les Nomades at eight o'clock. Enjoy a glass or two of some fine French wine until I arrive."

"All right. I'll be the sexy chick in red."

"I don't want you to look too sexy. Some man may come along and sweep you off your feet before I get there."

"That'll never happen, sweetheart."

Father Gregory gave Rhonda a forehead kiss and held her in his arms a few seconds after the song ended. The small crowd of family and friends clapped and cheered.

"I love you, Nick," she whispered. "I want you to be happy for Walter and me. You're not losing your baby sister. You're gaining the brother you've always wanted."

"I know, but you need to explain that concept to our father before you guys leave for Hawaii in the morning. Tell him he's gaining a son and you'll always be his baby girl."

Father Gregory released Rhonda and watched her float like an angel walking on clouds over to her new husband. The moment was bittersweet. He had always been the man she depended on besides Max since she was a baby. From this day forward, it would be Sergeant Walter B. McKissick, the man who had given her his hand in marriage. As her only brother, Father Gregory was very happy that Rhonda had found true love with a good man, but he would miss her calls asking for money and advice. He was no longer needed.

Father Gregory checked his watch and panicked on sight. He had only twenty minutes to say his goodbyes and make it from Joliet, Illinois back to Chicago to meet Royce at the restaurant by eight. He was doubtful that he would make it in time. It was unfortunate because he'd been mindful of the time throughout the reception. But some unexpected things had popped up, prolonging the short program. Max's toast to the bride and groom had transformed into a lengthy emotional tribute to Rhonda. It was evident from his slurred speech and frequent outburst of tears that he had paid the bartender a visit before taking the microphone. Most wedding guests had found Max's words touching, but Father Gregory's patience had begun to wear thin midway through the toast. By some miracle, his stepfather had run short on stories about Rhonda's eventful childhood around the time the catering staff started serving mango parfait, the bride's favorite dessert.

The bouquet and garter tosses soon followed. Rhonda and Walter then sliced their wedding cake and fed each other small pieces to boisterous cheers and applause. Moments later, the wedding guests were entertained by the traditional father-and-daughter dance. After some time, Father Gregory had boldly tapped Max on the shoulder, signaling that it was his turn to take Rhonda for a twirl on the dance floor. Now, it was time for him to leave his family and join the woman he loved for their final romantic evening in the city. Father Gregory wanted to make it a magical night that Royce would cherish forever.

"Would you like to order an appetizer now, ma'am?"

Royce shook her head and drained her wineglass. She placed it on the table with a slight thud after the server walked away. It was nine thirty, and Father Gregory had yet to arrive. Royce refused to call his cell phone again. He hadn't answered the first ten times she'd tried to reach him, and she was livid.

"Why is a gorgeous woman like you sitting here all alone?"

Royce looked up and got lost in the piercing eyes of a very tall and handsome man. "I was waiting for someone, but apparently I've been stood up."

"May I?" the towering, good-looking stranger asked, gesturing toward the empty chair across from Royce.

"No. I'm about to leave. I wouldn't be very good company for you anyway. Enjoy your evening." Royce removed a few bills from her clutch bag to cover the two glasses of Bordeaux she'd drunk. She tossed the money on the table carelessly and stood.

"Please allow me." The gentleman picked up the bills and pressed them tenderly into Royce's palm. Then he placed a single bill on the table. "He's a damn fool for standing you up. Maybe he doesn't appreciate you or realize how lucky he is. If you were mine, I would never disappoint you." He kissed the back of Royce's hand, which was still holding the money, and walked away.

***

Father Gregory slipped inside the dark room as quietly as he could and closed the door softly behind him. He tiptoed over to the bed and stood. The silhouette of Royce's hourglass figure was clearly visible underneath the covers. Her body was flawless, and he'd had every intention of feasting upon it on their last night in Chicago. But the ever-unpredictable Windy City traffic had thrown a monkey wrench in his plans. It had taken him more than two hours to drive from the Pristine Chapel in Joliet to Les Nomades on East Ontario Street. The slow-moving traffic into the city and the downtown area had almost driven him to curse and spit. And he'd had no way of calling Royce to tell her what was going on because his phone's battery had died at some point during the festivities.

Father Gregory undressed quickly and eased under the covers next to Royce, thinking of ways he could make up for missing their dinner date. He had tried his best to get to the restaurant before she left. God knew he had. But Max's long speech and his mother's insistence that he bid each of his aunts and uncles a personal farewell had used up a lot of his travel time. And then there was the traffic jam, which had only made matters worse. Surely, Royce would understand that he'd had no control over any of that. He would explain everything first thing in the morning.

"Royce, please talk to me, honey. You pouted around the hotel room all morning long as if you didn't understand why I was late last night. You barely said two words to me on the drive to the airport, and you totally ignored me on the flight home. I'm sorry I didn't make it to the restaurant on time last night. The traffic was at a standstill for more than an hour. And I couldn't disrespect Rhonda, my parents, or the rest of the family by leaving the reception early. I got to the restaurant as fast as I could, but it was too late. You had left. Baby, I'm sorry. Please forgive me."

Royce pulled away from Father Gregory, struggling with her bulky carry-on bag as they rushed to catch the train to the baggage claim area at Atlanta's Hartsfield-Jackson International Airport. She needed his help, but she didn't want it. She wasn't sure if she even wanted *him* anymore. The love she had in her heart for Father Gregory was still very much alive, but reality had slapped her in the face hard. Love simply wasn't enough. Royce wanted it all. She always did. But because she loved him more than life, she had somehow convinced herself that she could live without the total man. If Father Gregory couldn't give himself completely to Royce, she didn't think they could go on.

On the short train ride to the baggage claim area, Royce sat quietly next to the man she loved with a battered spirit. She willed her tears not to fall when she imagined her life without him. Once they reached the carousel and retrieved their bags, she turned to Father Gregory.

"I need some time, Nicholas. I'm not sure if I can do this anymore."

"What are you saying?"

"I don't know if I can continue this shell of a relationship. It's too painful and confusing. I will never have all of you. I thought I could handle you loving me behind closed doors while treating me like an ordinary person in public. I have tried, Nicholas, but now . . ." Royce sniffed and succumbed to the warm tears stinging her eyes.

"But now what? You've changed your mind? Royce, I love you more than I thought was humanly possible. I can't live without you. We can work this out. Let's talk about it."

She shook her head. "I need some time to sort things out. I'll call you."

"Royce, please don't do this," he begged, tugging at her arm gently. "I need you. We can fix this. Just talk to me, baby."

"I can't think right now. My mind is all over the place. I need some time and space away from you."

"Royce!" he called out when she walked away, pulling her rolling suitcase behind her. "Royce, come back here! Royce!"

Chapter Thirty-six

"Come in!"

"Good morning, Father. How was your trip?" Sister Ellen Marie had entered the office and allowed the door to close slowly on its own behind her. She walked farther into the room.

"My sister's wedding was lovely. She was the prettiest bride I've ever seen. I enjoyed spending time with my family. I hadn't seen some of my relatives in years."

"Well, you were certainly missed around here."

"I assume Father Schmidt and Father Rivera kept everything afloat in my absence."

"They did. Father Schmidt's noonday homily was quite inspiring."

"Great. Is there anything we need to discuss, Sister?"

"Yes, sir, there is. Don't forget about the luncheon this coming Wednesday."

"Luncheon? What luncheon?" Father Gregory honestly had no idea what the nun was talking about.

"The group of aspiring priests from the Boston College School of Theology will be stopping by the church Wednesday morning for a tour and fellowship. It was your idea for them to have lunch with you and the other priests at the parsonage. In fact, you requested that Mrs. Ellison prepare rosemary chicken, kale greens, and wild rice. I reminded her yesterday before noonday mass."

After the trip to Chicago and his unexpected troubles with Royce fresh on his brain, Father Gregory wondered how he had managed to rise early, dress, and make it to the church without falling apart. There was no way he could've remembered the luncheon. His life was in shambles. He hadn't slept very much the night before, worrying about his relationship with Royce, if they still had a relationship. Father Gregory truly loved her, and although their relationship was a forbidden one, he had fully devoted his heart to her. But Royce wanted more. She wanted his soul, but it belonged to God. He'd made a vow that he simply could not break.

"Father, are you all right, sir?" Sister Ellen Marie walked closer to his desk. "You seem troubled, distant, as if you're someplace far away."

Father Gregory rubbed both hands over his face. Exhausted and upset, he attempted to sound normal. "I'm tired from the trip. That's all. I'll leave here early today and go home to rest."

"Very well, sir. I'll leave you to your work now."

Alone and surrounded by quietness, Father Gregory still was unable to concentrate on his sermon or any of the memos in his inbox. Royce's sad face damp with tears at the airport was all he could think about. He had never meant to hurt her.

Life was so unfair. She certainly deserved a commitment from him, and he was worthy of a wife. If Baptist, Methodist, Presbyterian, Pentecostal, Episcopal, and other Christian ministers were allowed to marry and father children, why couldn't he? Non-Christian holy men like Imams of the Islamic faith, Hindu pujaris, and some Buddhist monks, depending on the sect, were permitted to wed as well. Were these men of faith any less committed to their gods than he was just because they had wives and children? Father Gregory thought not. If he could marry Royce, he believed he would be better able to serve the church. There wasn't a doubt in his mind that he'd be much happier, and his needs, both emotional and physical, would be thoroughly met. But the rule had been made over 2,000 years ago, and he and every other Roman Catholic priest were bound by it.

Father Gregory looked at the phone on his desk as if willing it to ring. "Call me, Royce. Just pick up the phone, darling, and call me."

Tyler walked into the dark den and flipped the light switch on. He dropped his backpack on the recliner. "Seriously? You're not going to work again today, Auntie?"

"I'm still recovering from my trip, sweet pea."

"But it's Wednesday. You've had two and a half days to rest. And what's up with all the ice cream? I know you like pralines and cream and all, but too much of that stuff will make you sick." Tyler laughed. "I should know."

"It makes me feel better," Royce mumbled. "After this carton, I won't eat any more. I promise."

"I better get to the bus stop. Old man Sanders will leave me if I'm not there at ten minutes 'til seven sharp. I'm so happy this is my last week of school. I'll see you later."

"Have a good day, sweetie."

Royce got up, turned off the light, and plopped back down on the sofa. She preferred the darkness because it matched her state of mind. Her favorite ice cream was her medicine, although it wasn't working so well. She wanted to talk to Father Gregory, but she didn't really need to right now.

The few days they'd been out of contact had given her lots of time to search her heart and come to grips with some important facts. Zora was right. She had been deluding herself. She and Father Gregory had no future together. He did love her, though. Royce felt it every time he entered her, joining their two bodies together as one. No one, not even Zora, could convince her otherwise.

And it wasn't just the way he made love to her. Royce felt Father Gregory's love whenever he sat quietly and listened to her talk for hours about her businesses. He comforted her whenever she was sick and often surprised her with special gifts just because. The time he spent with Tyler was priceless, and it was all because of his love for her. Above all, Father Gregory had sacrificed his soul, sinning against God and the Catholic Church every day just to be a part of Royce's life. But it still wasn't enough. No matter how much of himself he gave to her, she wasn't satisfied.

The telephone rang. More than likely it was Tabatha calling with an early morning report. Royce lifted the phone from its cradle. "Hello?"

"What's up, cuz? I just hung up with Tabatha. Why aren't you at work? Are you sick?"

"I'm under the weather today, Andra. How are you?"

"Were you under the weather yesterday and the day before too? For a woman who just returned from a trip to Chicago with her secret lover, you sound horrible."

Royce's back stiffened. "What are you talking about? Who said I went to Chicago with a man?"

"I'm not stupid," Andra said, snickering like she'd just heard a good joke. "I know you're seeing someone, cuz. Why are keeping him under the covers? I want to meet him."

"It's complicated and . . . and . . ." Royce started sobbing. "My life is so screwed up, Andra. I feel like I'm about to lose my damn mind."

"I'm coming over."

"What about the midday news?"

Andra smacked her lips. "Girl, that's why I have an assistant producer. I trained Dreyfus well. He can handle it. I'm on my way. Do you need me to bring anything? Maybe a bottle of wine?"

"Can you bring me a carton of pralines and cream ice cream?"

"I'll bring you two."

"That was a mighty fine meal, Mrs. Ellison. And the peach cobbler was the best I've ever tasted. Thank you."

The older woman smiled and continued gathering empty plates from the table. "It was my pleasure, Father Gregory."

"We certainly enjoyed it. We don't get good Southern cooking like this in Boston," one of the young future priests said.

"We sure don't," another one confirmed.

The other young men nodded in agreement. Father Gregory and his housemates smiled. They were blessed to have Mrs. Ellison as their cook. But Father Gregory preferred Royce's cooking.

"I would like for all of you to see our garden," Father Rivera told the young men. "It's in the back of the house. We have rows and rows of all kinds of vegetables. There're rosebushes, too, on the other side. Come with me."

Father Rivera stood and left the room with Father Schmidt and seven of the eight theology students following him. The other young man remained seated at the table with Father Gregory.

"Father, can I talk to you about something?"

"Sure," he said, folding his hands on the tabletop.

The young man looked around the dining room nervously. "It's a very private matter, sir."

"I understand. Let's go to the study. No one will disturb us there."

Father Gregory led the aspiring priest to the spacious study and closed the door. He took a seat behind the antique cherry-wood desk. "What is your name?"

The young man sat in the vacant chair facing the desk. "I'm Darius."

"How may I help you, Darius?"

"How old were you when you received the call from God to become a priest?"

"I was quite young actually. Seven years old to be exact."

Darius's bright green eyes widened with shock. It amused Father Gregory.

"I was fifteen. Since that day, I've been preparing for a life in the priesthood. I truly believed it was my calling to serve God and humanity through the Catholic Church."

"Are you having doubts now, Darius?"

He nodded and lowered his eyes to the floor. "Yes, Father, I am."

"Tell me why."

"I met a wonderful young lady. Her name is Millicent. I literally ran into her at the bookstore on campus. At first, we were just friends, but then we started hanging out and having fun. Then one day I woke up and realized that I'd rather be with her more than anyone else in the world. She makes me laugh, and she understands my quirkiness. We just click."

"Have you been intimate with her?"

"Oh, no, Father," Darius said, shaking his head. "We haven't done that. We kiss a lot, though." He lowered his eyes again. "And I've thought about making love to her. Sometimes I want to desperately."

"I'm happy you've remained pure, because once you cross that line, your life will change forever." *No one knows that better than I do,* he confessed inwardly. "If you love Millicent and you want to spend the rest of your life with her, now is the time to walk away from theology school and chart a new path. Do not make the vow of celibacy or make any other commitments to God or the church if you're having second thoughts about becoming a priest. This is a very difficult life to live. Don't enter into it if you aren't certain, because once you make the vow, God will expect you to keep it for life. Pray about it and search your heart. I'm sure you'll do what is right."

"Thank you, Father. I will."

Chapter Thirty-seven

Andra sat across the kitchen table from Royce with her mouth wide open. Seconds passed as she stared at her older cousin, shocked and speechless.

"Say something, Andra, anything."

"You and your priest are sleeping together? I don't know what to say. Damn!"

"We're not just sleeping together. We're in a relationship. He loves me, and I love him."

"Now I understand why you've been so secretive over the past few months. You've got Zora calling and harassing me."

"Are you serious? She called you to ask questions about me?"

"Yeah, your nosy sister called me while you were in Chicago, asking a bunch of questions. I didn't tell her anything, though. Hell, I didn't have any information to tell her. And if I had, I still wouldn't have told her your business."

"Thank you, Andra."

"No problem, cuz. Is Father Gregory going to leave the priesthood so he can marry you and knock you up with a choir full of babies?"

Royce shook her head slowly.

"So, what's the plan?"

"I don't know. I thought we would be lovers for the rest of our lives, but I'm not so sure anymore. I love him to the moon and back, but I'm not completely happy being his secret lover. I thought I could handle it, but now it's driving me crazy."

"If it's real love, I think you should hang in there. If you continue to love that man and take care of his every need, he may walk away from the pulpit and make you his wife. Give it some time, cuz."

"Did you just advise me to continue my affair with my priest?" Royce asked teasingly.

"I sure did. I know you, cuz. You wouldn't be involved with Father Gregory if you didn't believe what you share with him was real. Trust your heart."

"I'm going to call him and invite him over tonight, so we can talk after Tyler goes to bed. I love that man, Andra, and I don't want to lose him."

***

Royce checked the caller ID on her cell phone. Her pulse quickened. "Hello?"

"How are you?"

"I'm much better now that I'm talking to you. I was going to call you later today to invite you over. I think we need to talk. Thanks for giving me the time I needed to clear my head."

"You're welcome."

"So can you visit me tonight after Tyler goes to bed?"

"Yes. I'll be there."

Royce hung up the phone and did a little happy dance around the den. She was excited and refreshed. Confiding in Andra had been a good idea. Who knew that her younger cousin could give her such sound advice?

Royce ran into the kitchen and searched the wine rack for the vintage bottle of Riesling she'd been saving for a special occasion. Reuniting with the love of her life after a major misunderstanding was special enough. It was so special in fact that Royce felt like going to her favorite boutique to buy a few new pieces of sexy lingerie. Just the thought of being in Father Gregory's arms again caused her body to shiver. Three days had been too long. Royce regretted that she'd been so angry about the situation in Chicago that she'd acted like a spoiled brat. But tonight she would make it up to Father Gregory in every way possible.

***

Father Gregory perused Royce's curvaceous body from her braids down to her shiny purple toenails with lustful eyes after the front door closed behind him. She looked sexier than ever in a lavender satin camisole that stopped an inch above her belly button and matching boy shorts. Father Gregory licked his lips and smiled. The sensitive member between his thighs became fully erect, pressing ever so stiffly against the zipper of his customary black jeans. "Hi," he finally whispered and placed a chaste kiss on Royce's lips.

She threw her arms around his neck and pulled his body snugly against hers. "I've missed you. Let's go into the living room."

Father Gregory followed Royce across the foyer toward the room where they had shared many intimate moments late at night whenever Tyler was in the house. As usual, he removed his shoes before he walked through the double glass doors. No one was allowed to walk on the plush white carpet with their shoes on. The candles, the wine, and the chenille blanket spread across the floor caused Father Gregory's heart to beat triple time.

"Let's sit on the sofa and talk," he said, taking Royce by the hand. He led the way. Sitting and still holding her hand, he looked into her eyes. "I love you from deep within my soul. I never dreamed of meeting a woman like you and falling madly in love. You're my heart, Royce. You mean everything to me."

"I love you too."

"I know you do. That's why my heart is bleeding right now. I came here to tell you we can't continue this relationship. It has to end, Royce, tonight."

"No, Nicholas. I'm sorry for the way I acted in Chicago. It was very childish of me. I believe you tried to get to the restaurant on time. I overreacted. Please forgive me."

"My decision has nothing to do with what happened in Chicago, sweetheart. I'm a broken man," he croaked with tears flowing from his eyes. "I love you, but I love God more. I've been living this double life, trying my best to please you and the Lord. I preach to others about living righteously while my life is filled with sin. I've abandoned the most sacred vow I've ever made. My conscience has caught up with me. I'm going crazy. We have to end our affair. I'm so sorry."

Royce wiped her tears and sniffed. "You promised to love me forever. You said we would always be together no matter what. I believed you."

"I will always love you. Nothing can change that. I want you in my life, but I can't have you if I want to please God. I made a vow to Him and His church."

"You made one to me too, but I guess breaking vows and promises means nothing to you." Royce stood up with tears still spilling from her red, swollen eyes. "You've said what you came here to say. You can leave now. Get the hell out of my house!"

Father Gregory did as he was told. Leaving Royce was the most difficult thing he'd ever had to do. He loved her. He wanted her. But he couldn't have her. His tears continued to fall as he guided his motorcycle over the familiar route back to the parsonage. His heart was filled with grief over losing the one and only woman he had ever loved. There would be no other. Hurting Royce caused Father Gregory the most pain. He would learn to live without her, and within time, his wounded heart would heal. But he would never forgive himself for the emotional pain loving him had caused her. It was a burden he would carry with him throughout eternity.

If only Royce could understand the agony Father Gregory had experienced when he looked into Darius's peridot eyes and spoke words to him that he, himself, no longer lived by. He had broken his vow to God and the church, and he was deliberately living in a sinful state. He wasn't worthy of offering Darius or the other theology students any advice about sanctification, but he had, and emphatically so. The blatant hypocrisy of it all had been sobering. Father Gregory wasn't able to face himself in the mirror after admonishing the young man. The Holy Spirit had convicted him, causing him to become overwhelmed with guilt and shame. It was his sorrow of turning his back on God and the vow he had made to Him that had influenced his decision to end his romance with Royce. Nothing else.

"Tabatha, I'm going to take the rest of the week off, so I need you to continue to man the ship and crew. I hope you don't mind."

"I don't mind at all. Are you okay?"

Royce stuffed a spoonful of pralines and cream ice cream in her mouth and swallowed. "I've been better. Hopefully, a few more days of rest and relaxation will cure me."

"Would you like me to email you the midweek numbers and the expenditure report?"

"That won't be necessary. I'll look over everything Monday."

"Okay. I'll call you later. Take care."

"I will."

Royce had no idea what to do with so much free time on her hands. She had no place to go, and there wasn't anyone in particular she wanted to see. It would be her luck to run into Father Gregory at Walmart if she dared to venture outside. Thoughts of him twisted her stomach into knots.

"I'm not going to cry. I refuse to cry. I knew better. I gambled with love and lost."

Royce left the den and went upstairs to her bedroom. She hadn't slept very much the previous night. Maybe the sandman would have mercy on a weary, lovesick woman right now.

Chapter Thirty-eight

"Father Gregory offered to drive me home today after summer camp."

Royce looked at her nephew with her peripheral vision, careful to avoid a fender bender in the early morning traffic. "When did you speak with him?"

"Last night."

"Did you call him, Tyler?"

"No, ma'am. He called my cell phone to ask how we were doing. He wanted to know why we skipped church yesterday, too."

He has some damn nerve! "Look, honey, now that you're out of school on summer vacation, I don't think you need to spend as much time with Father Gregory as you used to. You finished the year with good grades and a satisfactory behavior report, so I think you're okay now."

"Yeah, I did improve, but I still want to hang out with Father Gregory some days after I finish volunteering with the little kids at summer camp. He's my friend, Auntie Royce."

Royce sighed in frustration. She didn't want to disappoint Tyler. He had bonded with Father Gregory while Eric was away. It wouldn't be fair for her to demand that the child stop spending time with him just because he had dumped her. "Okay, you may hang out with him twice a week after camp, but I'll transport you to and from the church."

"Oh, he doesn't mind driving me home."

"I do."

"Huh?" The boy looked at his aunt, visibly confused.

"Father Gregory was more than nice to you when you were acting a fool at school with those thugs. He helped you improve your basketball skills, too. Let's give him an opportunity to help another child who may need him. Okay?"

"Okay."

Father Gregory's body jerked backward and out of view. He peeped at Royce's SUV from behind the curtain in the front window of the multipurpose building. Over 200 small children were at play, shouting and laughing in the background, but he heard nothing. The vision of loveliness outside the window had seized all of his senses.

Royce was a sweet treat for Father Gregory's eyes but a torturous blow to his ailing soul. He would never get over her.

Alfred Lord Tennyson was a damn fool! He had deceived romantics worldwide for more than a century with his famous quote:

'Tis better to have loved and lost
Than never to have loved at all.

Nothing could have been further from the truth. Father Gregory had learned firsthand in the most painful way possible that a man under a divine calling such as his would be much better off if he never loved a woman or shared his body with her.

Tyler waved to Royce before she drove away. He turned toward the building, bearing his backpack on his shoulders. Father Gregory left the window quickly and made swift footsteps down the hallway in the opposite direction.

"What's up, Father? I'm here on time like you asked."

The priest did a slow about-face. He glanced down at his watch, smiling. "Good morning, Tyler. You're early actually. I'm impressed. You'll be assisting Sister Eva and Mrs. Amica with the six- and seven-year-old boys and girls. Come with me. They're expecting you."

***

Andra looked out the restaurant window in time to see Royce exit her SUV. She watched her put on her designer sunglasses to protect her eyes from the bright late June sun before she locked the door and sashayed toward the entrance of Shiloh's Grill. Andra hadn't seen her older cousin in a few weeks when she'd made the emergency visit to deliver ice cream to her house. That was the same day she had advised her to continue her relationship with Father Gregory. Andra grimaced and took a long swig of her electric lemonade. She wished she could take back every word she'd said that day regarding Royce's secret love affair. How wrong she had been.

"I'm sorry I'm late. Traffic was crazy."

Andra gave Royce a thorough once-over. "Somebody's been eating too much pralines and cream ice cream. Girl, look at your hips."

"Is it that noticeable? I've gained ten pounds since the disappointing Chicago trip. I haven't exercised or taught a single class since I returned to work. I'll get back on my regimen after Tyler leaves for the summer."

"When will that be?"

"Eric called Monday. The mission in Sierra Leone will be officially over Thursday. He and Zora will arrive in Atlanta Monday night. They'll be here a couple of weeks before they leave for the West Indies on another mission. It'll be a brief assignment, so they're taking Tyler with them."

Andra nodded. "Cool. How are you doing, Royce?"

"I have days when all I do is cry. Then some mornings I wake up and feel like I can conquer the world. Working helps me. When I'm busy, I don't think about him."

"Have you seen him?"

Royce shook her head and reached for a menu. "I've been lucky. Every morning on the drive to the church, I whisper a prayer that he's not outside when Tyler and I arrive. So far, God has had mercy on this pitiful soul."

"In time you'll get over him and move on. Then you won't be afraid to face him, because he'll mean nothing to you. You may even start attending church again."

"That'll never happen. I will always love him, Andra. And he will always mean the world and beyond to me. Eventually, I'll learn to live without him and find another church."

"Hopefully, you'll find yourself another man, too."

Never, Royce's heart whispered. If she couldn't have Father Gregory, she didn't want anyone else.

***

"All I'm asking you to do is be mindful of your words, sweetheart. You should be happy that Royce ended her relationship with the priest. Isn't that what you wanted?"

"I wish she had never gotten involved with him at all."

"It's too late. She already did, and now it's over. Therefore, I don't see any reason why you should bring it up."

"I want to know what happened. Aren't you the least bit curious, honey?"

Eric looked at his wife when he paused briefly at the stop sign. "It's not my business. It's not yours either, Zora. The only thing Royce told me was that she is no longer seeing Father Gregory. If she had wanted me to know the details, she would've told me the whole story. She didn't."

Zora watched her husband greet the attendant in the guard shack at the entrance of Royce's community. She wanted the entire scoop on her sister's breakup with the priest. Inquisitiveness was gnawing at her. They would talk about it one way or the other, even if she had to interrogate Royce.

The car rolled to a stop in front of the house. Eric turned to Zora and placed his hand on her knee. "Please don't go inside asking your sister a bunch of questions. I'm sure her feelings are still raw and she doesn't want to talk about it. Let's spend some quality time with her before we take Tyler home. We haven't seen them since the day after Christmas. Let's have a happy reunion."

Royce hugged Zora and released her quickly. "Welcome home."

"It feels good to be back. How are you, little sister?"

"I'm fine." Royce turned and smiled at her handsome brother-in-law. "What's up, Doc?"

Eric wrapped his arms around her and squeezed. "I missed you, sis. Thanks for taking good care of my son while I was off saving lives. I owe you." He kissed her cheek before he dropped his arms.

"Mom! Dad!" Tyler screamed, running down the stairs. He sprinted toward his parents. He hugged his mother first and then his father. "I'm glad you guys are finally home."

Royce walked away, leaving the Bensons in the foyer. She went to the kitchen and grabbed a spoon from the draining rack. Then she walked straight to the refrigerator, opened the freezer, and grabbed the carton of ice cream. Royce peeped over her shoulder. Tyler didn't need to know that she was still on her binge. The first scoop slid down her throat and hit the spot like a drug. *One more will do the trick until they leave,* she reasoned with her conscience.

"Is that why you've gained weight? Have you replaced him with ice cream?"

Royce spun around fast, spilling ice cream on the floor. She closed the carton and replaced it in the freezer. "I've been eating more often than usual, and I haven't had the energy to exercise," she explained, reaching for a paper towel on the counter. Royce bent down and wiped the ice cream from the floor. "How was your flight, Z?"

Zora pulled out a chair from the dinette and sat down. "It was long. We had a five-hour layover in Brussels. Eric insisted that we go sightseeing, so I made him hand over his credit card. I put it to good use on a few souvenirs." She paused as if gathering her thoughts. "What made you finally come to your senses, Royce?"

"I don't want to talk about it."

"Why? Are you afraid I'm going to say 'I told you so'?"

Royce folded her arms across her chest and raised her chin in defiance. "It's not your business, and I don't give a damn what you say. I will not have this conversation with you, Z."

"He called it quits, didn't he? That lowdown, dirty dog used you for his satisfaction and disposed of you like stinking garbage. Who the hell does he think he is? I will—"

"You will do nothing, Zora. Leave it alone. It's over. I'll be fine."

"I sure hope so, but I'm worried. You have always taken pride in your physical appearance and your good health. I've never known you to carry extra pounds around or eat junk food. He drove you to this."

"I'm an adult, and I make my own decisions. No one drove me to do anything. So I've put on a few pounds. What's the problem? I'll lose the weight in no time at all. I'm a fitness expert. Remember?"

"Well, hurry up and get yourself together, Royce. You're still young and pretty. You'll find another man, one who will love you and cherish you forever. As a matter of fact, there's a very nice doctor who traveled with our group to Africa. He's handsome and single. He lives in metro Atlanta, too. I'm going to give him a call tomorrow."

"You'll do no such thing, Zora," Eric growled as he entered the kitchen. "You're meddling again, and I don't like it. The car is loaded, and I'm tired. Let's go to our house and mind our business."

Royce followed Eric out of the kitchen without another word to Zora. She had mentally dismissed her the moment she started trying to play matchmaker.

Tyler was in the foyer with his backpack in tow. Royce ran her fingers through his hair and smiled.

He was such a handsome kid with skin the color of cocoa just like hers and his annoying mother's. Royce was going to miss having him around. She felt like bawling and begging Zora and Eric to let him stay. But it was time for the child to reunite with his parents. It was also time for Royce to move on with her life. She wasn't sure what the future had in store for her, so she had to keep living to find out.

Chapter Thirty-nine

"So, you're leaving the country for the rest of the summer, huh?"

"Yes, sir. I'm going to the West Indies with my mom and dad. They're going for another medical mission on a teeny, tiny island called Dominica. Mom says most people get it confused with the Dominican Republic."

"I'm familiar with the Commonwealth of Dominica. It's near Barbados. I spent the day sightseeing there once when I was serving in the Caribbean. It's a beautiful island. The people there are very warm and friendly."

"Did you know that the second and third *Pirates of the Caribbean* movies were filmed there?"

"Yes, I did."

"Dad says we're going on the movie location tour. It's a popular tourist attraction. We're going deep-sea fishing and maybe snorkeling too."

Father Gregory chuckled. "It sounds like you're going on an adventure. I'm sure you'll have lots of fun."

"I will, but I feel kind of guilty about leaving Auntie Royce here all alone." Tyler leaned forward and rested his elbows on Father Gregory's desk. He lowered his chin into the palms of his hands. "I'm going to miss her."

The mere mention of her name hit the priest in the stomach like a sucker punch. Last night's dream of him and Royce holding hands walking through a botanical paradise, happy and content, took his mind prisoner. Mercy, how he loved that woman. "How is Royce?"

"Okay, I guess. I call her every evening, but she's always tired and sleepy. So we don't talk very long. I just like to hear her voice every day to make sure she's all right. She's thinking about opening a new center in another location. I heard my dad telling my mom about it."

"Your aunt is a very astute businesswoman. She's smart and quite successful. You and your family should be extremely proud of her."

Tyler's eyes sparkled like a pair of brilliant chocolate diamonds. "I am proud of her. Dad, my grandparents, and cousin Andra are too. It's just that my mom thinks . . . I mean she wants Auntie Royce to—"

"What is it, Tyler?" Father Gregory asked. "What does your mother want your auntie to do?" He leaned in closer to the boy from across his desk, curious and concerned.

"Mom wants Auntie Royce to find a good man, get married, and have babies. She says my auntie keeps getting her heart broken because she gets involved with losers. My mom told Dad the last guy Auntie Royce dated used her and had no intention of ever marrying her."

"Your mother was referring to Marlon, wasn't she?"

Tyler shook his head. "No, she wasn't. It's some other dude I've never heard of before. I don't even know his name. I just heard my mom telling my dad that Auntie Royce was a fool to get involved in a secret affair with a man who couldn't be seen with her in public. That's why they went to Chicago together. Mom said the guy has a very important job here in Atlanta, and it's against the rules for him to have a girlfriend. But Auntie Royce loved him so much that she dated him anyway. Now, she's sad and embarrassed because the dude broke up with her. His job meant more to him than she did. If I ever meet that buster, I'll punch him in his face!"

Father Gregory was stunned and stricken to silence. He couldn't believe that Royce had confided in her sister about their affair. It was supposed to have been their secret. No one else was ever to know. But she was hurting just like he was. Fortunately for her, she had someone she could trust and pour her heart out to. Zora had no doubt comforted her as any big sister would have. Father Gregory couldn't blame Royce for reaching out for consolation. He wasn't as privileged.

"Violence is never the solution to a misunderstanding," he finally said to Tyler.

"I know, but he hurt Auntie Royce. I'm tired of men mistreating her. I don't understand why she can't meet a man who'll love her, respect her, and treat her special."

She already did, Father Gregory wished he could tell the boy. He closed his eyes instead and sent a silent prayer to heaven for Royce's wounded heart.

"My auntie is fine and smart," Tyler added. "Plus she owns her own businesses, and she makes globs of money. Any man would be lucky to have her, but she always ends up with a dog. From now on, I don't want her to date anyone else."

A knock at the door drew their attention away from the conversation. Father Gregory thanked God for the interruption. He felt guilty and uncomfortable discussing Royce with her nephew. And the sheer thought of their breakup brought about a sharp pain in his chest that felt like someone stabbing him unmercifully with a dagger. The throbbing became more intense when

Tyler described Royce as sad and embarrassed because of what he had done to her.

After the second knock, Father Gregory called out, "Come in." He spoke in a calm voice although a tornado of emotions was tearing him apart on the inside.

Sister Ellen Marie entered the office, smiling as usual. "Tyler's father is here to take him home. He's waiting in the vestibule."

"Cool! Thanks, Sister Ellen Marie."

"You're welcome. I will see you tomorrow, dear."

Tyler turned to Father Gregory after the nun left the office. "I want you to meet my dad. I've been telling him all about you. Come on."

"Um, I . . . I'm sure your father is tired after curing sick people all day. Let him hurry home to eat dinner, spend time with his family, and rest. I'll meet him some other time."

"If you don't meet him today, you won't get another chance until after we come back from Dominica." Tyler walked around the desk, grabbed Father Gregory's hand, and tugged. "Come and let me introduce you to the best doctor in the world."

Tyler would have it no other way except his way. Father Gregory had grown accustomed to his persistent and somewhat stubborn nature. He realized he had no other choice than to meet the boy's father. To refuse would be rude.

He stood and followed Tyler out of his office and down the hallway. As they walked closer to the towering male dressed in green scrubs, Father Gregory inhaled and exhaled slowly. Dr. Benson was in good shape. If he suddenly decided to punch him in the face to defend his sister-in-law's honor, he would probably succeed. And Father Gregory would take his beating like a man out of love and respect for Royce.

"Dr. Benson," he called out, approaching him with his right hand extended.

Eric turned around and smiled at Tyler, but his expression became unpleasant in a matter of seconds. Father Gregory sensed that Dr. Benson wasn't happy to see him. If looks could kill, a homicide was definitely on the good doctor's evening agenda. But hopefully, Tyler's presence would serve as a buffer to spare his mentor's life.

"You must be Father Gregory," Eric said after an extended and very awkward pause. He shook the priest's hand. "I've heard a lot about you."

"I hope Tyler has said as many good things to you about me as he has to me about you and your wife."

"My son has spoken very highly of you. But there's another source very close to me who knows you quite well also. I don't suppose we need to dig into that discussion at this time."

"Of course not, Dr. Benson."

Eric smiled, seemingly satisfied that he had put the fear of God in Father Gregory. "Thank you for mentoring and counseling Tyler while my wife and I were away on a mission. I'm sure you've heard that we're taking him with us to Dominica in a few days."

He nodded. "Tyler told me he's going away for the duration of the summer. I'm going to miss him."

"You'll have more time to spend saving souls with fewer opportunities for anything else after he leaves. I understand you spent lots of time with my son and his aunt while Zora and I were in Africa."

"I . . . I did," Father Gregory stammered and shifted his weight from one foot to the other timidly.

Eric walked closer to him and whispered sternly, "Now that Tyler will be leaving the country with us, you have no other reason to visit Wind Song Estates. Your priestly duties have been discontinued there." He walked away in the direction of the exit door.

"Goodbye, Father Gregory," Tyler said, hugging his friend and mentor. "I'll see you tomorrow. Remember the kickball tournament starts right after lunch. I can't wait!"

***

"Mama?" Royce sat up in bed and rubbed her eyes. "Is that you, Ma?"

"Yes, it's your mama, baby. How are you? You've been on my mind lately."

"I'm fine. I've been working hard, trying to expand the business to a new location. By the time I get home most evenings, I'm dog-tired."

"Your father and I are very proud of all you've accomplished, but I worry about you sometimes."

Royce laughed softly. It felt good to be loved. "You sound like Tyler. He calls every day to check on me. I love that kid. I miss him so much. This house isn't the same without my little love bug."

"Yeah, my grandson is worried about you too. I spoke with him an hour ago. He told me you work like a slave, eat ice cream all the time, and you go to bed before the sun goes down. I'm concerned, sweetie. Why don't you come and visit your father and me for a few days so we can make a fuss over you?"

"That's not necessary. And I don't have time to take off from work anyway." Royce sighed. "Mama, please don't be concerned about me. I'm doing great. I feel wonderful," she lied smoother than silk.

"Okay. I reckon I'll have to take your word for it. It's just that I remember how thirty-two years ago my daily routine sounded a lot like yours. I worked hard, ate too many sweet treats, and slept every chance I got."

"Wow! Really? Were you sick?"

"No, sweetie pie, Mama wasn't sick. She was expecting."

Chapter Forty

Father Rivera's snort-filled laughter reminded Father Gregory of a wild hog. It, mixed with Father Schmidt's throaty chuckles and slurred speech, would've been entertaining any other time. But this evening it held no humor for the senior-ranking priest of the group.

Although Father Gregory had agreed to join his housemates in the parlor to watch a comedy movie and sip cocktails, his mind was somewhere else. Thoughts of Royce, her sister, and her brother-in-law had taken him prisoner. His brief encounter with Eric Benson had been awkward, but no hostile altercation had taken place. However, Royce's brother-in-law had confirmed that he indeed was aware of their past involvement. And he'd made it crystal clear that under no circumstances should the relationship be rekindled. Father Gregory couldn't exactly accuse the doctor of threatening him, but he had spoken to him quite candidly out of concern for Royce.

The two other priests suddenly howled at a funny scene in the movie. Father Gregory abandoned his thoughts of Eric Benson, the overprotective brother-in-law, to concentrate on Royce. He wondered what she was doing at that very moment. If she was as miserable as he was, she was damn near pathetic. A glass of wine and an all-star cast of talented comedians clowning through an outrageous plot couldn't cure his ills not even for a night. Even though Father Gregory wasn't alone, he was lonely and on the brink of tears. He didn't want Royce's life to be reduced to loneliness, teardrops, and sleepless nights. He loved her so much that he wanted her to be happy. He prayed that God would bless her with a wonderful husband who would love and honor her and give her the children she desired. She deserved that kind of life and so much more.

Tears found their way through Royce's closed eyelids. She wiped them with the back of her hand and sniffled. She stared at the wick of the digital home pregnancy test, which guaranteed 99 percent accuracy, one more time. Its results were the same as the first three she'd taken. Royce was pregnant. It should've been the most joyous moment of her life, but that wasn't the case. How could she be happy? There she was almost 32 years old, unmarried, and pregnant by a man with whom she had no future. Today was not a day of celebration. Royce was sad and ashamed. She was a registered nurse, for heaven's sake! How had she been so irresponsible?

Royce picked up the phone with every intention of calling her mother to tell her that her out-of-the-blue prediction had been dead on point. She was expecting. She hadn't planned to get pregnant, but she and Father Gregory had not been as careful as they should have been on a few occasions. Royce could recall a couple of times when they'd acted like two reckless teenagers in heat. She hadn't been overly concerned because her cycle had the tendency to be irregular from time to time. Over the years, she'd missed a period here or there without alarm. But during those times she'd either been celibate or very cautious with her partner.

Through a heavy flow of tears, Royce noticed the time on her cell phone. It was much too late to call her mother. Andra was in Los Angeles at a television producers' conference, and Royce had no intention of sharing her delicate situation with Zora. She needed compassion, not a lecture on stupidity and irresponsibility. Royce dialed the number of the person who had been her rock during her messy breakup with Marlon. The phone rang several times before the familiar, deep voice answered.

"Eric, it's me, Royce. I'm sorry I woke you, but I really need to talk to you."

"You didn't wake me, little sis. Believe it or not, I just left Smitty's Bar. I was hanging out and catching up with the fellows. I could swing by if you need me to."

"I'll make a pot of tea."

"Would you care for a glass of wine also, ma'am?" the petite flight attendant with a cute pixie hairstyle asked Royce and smiled.

Eric held his breath, hoping that Zora wouldn't make a big deal out of Royce's beverage selection. Everyone in the family knew her to be a passionate lover of white wine. But she couldn't drink alcohol in her condition. She had just entered her second trimester of pregnancy, according to his calculations. It was safe for her to travel to Dominica with the family and assist the medical team with pediatric checkups, but boozing it up was totally out of the question. Eric had invited Royce along on the mission only because she was so distraught about her unexpected pregnancy. And he believed she needed a break from Atlanta, where memories of her life with Father Gregory were still fresh.

Royce returned the flight attendant's smile. "I would love a glass of orange juice, ma'am."

"What?" Zora snapped, whipping her head in her sister's direction. "You have never refused a glass of wine since the day you turned twenty-one. What's going on with you, Royce Dominique?"

"You've been calling me fat ever since you and Eric returned from Sierra Leone. Now that I'm trying to watch my weight, you have the nerve to question me? Give me a break, Z."

Royce's smart and speedy response seemed to have quieted Zora for the time being. Eric was relieved. In a few weeks, it would be virtually impossible for Royce to hide her pregnancy from his ever-meddlesome wife. If she chose outfits that made her seem more slender and laid off of the ice cream and cookies, she could possibly buy herself some more time. Regardless, Eric was determined to protect Royce and support her until she was ready to tell the family about the baby. It was a day he was not looking forward to.

Tyler, who was sitting on the other side of Royce, removed his earplugs and smiled at his aunt. "I'm glad you decided to come with us. You and I can go swimming in the ocean, jet skiing, hiking in the mountains, and jogging on the beach. I can't wait, Auntie Royce."

"Neither can I," she told the child with a straight face.

Royce and Eric's eyes met. He offered her his most encouraging smile. Her baby was growing and developing fine, and Eric did want Royce to be as active as possible during the pregnancy. He would allow her to swim and jog as long as she was up to it. But there would be no jet skiing or hiking in the mountains.

Eric closed his eyes and reclined his seat. There was more on his mind at the moment than he was ready to deal with. Royce was pregnant by her priest, and they were keeping it a secret from Zora, his wife. He had never withheld anything important from her in the entire thirteen years they'd been married. The guilt was choking the life out of him, but he had made Royce a promise, and he was going to honor it. Then there was the issue of leaving his in-laws in the dark. Once again, he had given Royce his word that he wouldn't utter one syllable until the time was right.

Eric found it strange that out of all of the promises Royce had coerced him to make, she never once asked him not to contact the baby's father to tell him she was carrying his child. He wondered if he had the green light to give the priest a call to inform him he would have more to celebrate in January besides the New Year and Dr. Martin Luther King Jr.'s birthday.

Eric felt that Father Gregory needed to know what his carelessness had caused. He was as much at fault as Royce. And it wasn't fair that she was bearing such a heavy burden alone. Father Gregory may have been a priest, but his title didn't excuse him from his duties as the father of Royce's child. His inborn, sinful nature, like that of any other human being, had led him astray. No clergy collar, crucifix, or holy water had prevented his penis from popping out of his pants. And he would not be granted a pardon for his sexual misconduct. An innocent child would soon make his or her debut to the world. Every little girl and boy deserved the love and support of both of their living parents. Eric had no clue about Royce's plans to deal with her baby's father. He, on the other hand, had plenty of ideas and colorful words to say to the man. But he would wait to speak with Royce about his concerns privately after they'd settled in Dominica.

"I placed Father Gregory's dinner plate in the microwave. His garden salad is in the refrigerator," Mrs. Ellison told Fathers Schmidt and Rivera. "Please let him know when he wakes up from his nap. Enjoy your evening."

Father Rivera nodded and smiled.

"Goodbye, Mrs. Ellison."

Father Rivera turned to Father Schmidt as soon as the older woman left the dining room. "He hasn't eaten in two days. I'm very concerned. It's unhealthy for him to skip meals and spend so much time alone in his room. It appears that he's depressed or in mourning."

"I know exactly how he feels. He's suffering emotionally and physically. It's quite painful to lose the love of a woman."

"I'm grateful that I will never experience such mental anguish. If falling in love causes so much pain, I consider myself blessed to have avoided it. Praised be to God for His mercy."

"Falling in love can be a wonderful thing, my friend. There's nothing more gratifying than giving your heart to a woman and have her give hers to you in return."

"But when something goes wrong in the relationship, one suffers to the point that they seem suicidal like Father Gregory."

"His case is different," Father Schmidt pointed out, wagging his finger at his fellow priest. "He must suffer greater than ordinary men because he broke the sacred vow. Sin brings about tragedy. But when an ordained priest dishonors his ultimate commitment to the Lord and the church, he will reap God's wrath tenfold."

"I pity him."

"I feel sorry for him as well, but he'll recover in time. And hopefully, he will never get involved with a woman again. His unfortunate circumstances will serve as a reminder to him, I'm sure."

Father Rivera frowned with confusion. "A reminder? What reminder is that, Father?"

"It will remind him why all Roman Catholic priests are avowed to a life of celibacy and bachelorhood. We are married to the church. She is our bride. Marriage or a romantic relationship with any woman is adulterous. It will hinder our ability to serve and minister to God's people. The vow is not a punishment as others may believe. It is a commitment to God that sanctifies and strengthens us for His service."

"Amen."

Chapter Forty-one

"She's such a beautiful baby," Royce told the young mother. She handed the infant back to the woman and reached for the chart on the counter. "You're doing an excellent job with her. She's very healthy. The rash behind her ears appears to be eczema. The doctor will give you an ointment for it."

"Thank you, ma'am."

Eric entered the treatment room, smiling. "I'm Dr. Benson. And who is this princess?" He gently pinched the baby's chubby cheek.

"Her name is Natalie, and she's nine months old."

"Hello, Natalie. May I hold you?" Eric asked, reaching for the baby.

Royce was exhausted. She took a seat on a metal stool and watched Eric examine Natalie from her tiny afro to her stubby toes. She had seen twenty-three little ones over the last eight hours. She was glad that Natalie was their last patient for the day. Royce was ready to return to the modest three-bedroom house in the small town of Glanvillia where they were staying during the mission. She was hungry and in need of a long, hot shower. Her back was hurting terribly, too. She wondered if there was a masseuse anywhere on the small island. The last time Royce had had a massage, Father Gregory had done her the honor. It seemed like a lifetime ago.

"This cream should take care of the eczema," Royce heard Eric say to Natalie's mother. "Rub it behind those little ears twice a day until the rash disappears completely." He handed the woman the tube of cream he'd removed from a cabinet above his head.

"Thank you, Doctor."

"You're welcome."

Royce smiled and waved to the woman and her baby before they left the treatment room. Eric sat on the examining table with a flat expression on his face. His eyes revealed his serious mood. Royce lowered her eyes to her hands, which were folded on her lap, and she waited for her lecture.

"I want you to take the rest of the week off to rest, sis. You're tired, and your back pains haven't eased up. I can tell by the way you walk. I know you want to stay busy to keep your mind off of your situation, but I'm putting my foot down."

"Okay. I'll stay home and relax for the rest of the week. But if I'm refreshed by Monday morning, I'll be right here with you, Zora, and the rest of the team. I came here to work. This is not a vacation." Royce laughed softly.

"While we have privacy and a little bit of time, I need to ask you something."

"I'm listening."

"When are you going to call Father Gregory and tell him you're pregnant with his child?"

"Never."

"Royce, don't be foolish. You have to tell him. He's the baby's father. He has a right to know. It's only fair that he share the responsibility of raising and providing for the child along with you. He enjoyed helping you make the baby, so I want him to help you care for it."

"Women raise children every day all over the world as single mothers. I can do it too. The situation is too crazy. He will never leave the church and the priesthood, so how the hell do you expect him to be a father to my baby? He was my secret lover, Eric. I don't want him to be a secret father to his son or daughter. It'll never work."

"Atlanta is a big city, but it's not big enough for you to hide from Father Gregory and the entire congregation forever. Someone will see you sooner or later. He's bound to find out that you're expecting, and he will know the child belongs to him. What do you plan to do when he rings your doorbell someday in the near future and demands to see his little boy or girl?"

"I don't know. I'll handle the situation if it ever comes down to that."

"Oh, it's going to come down to that, Royce," Eric warned with certainty. "There is no doubt in my mind that it will. If I were you, I would think long and hard about the decision you've made. It's not a very smart one, sis. Come on. Let's go home. You need to feed my niece or nephew and get some rest."

By Sunday afternoon, Royce felt like a brand-new woman. Three days of rest, relaxation, and good food had done the trick. She decided to join the family for shopping and a sightseeing tour of Roseau, the capital city of Dominica. The cab ride was an hour long, which gave them the opportunity to take in the beauty of the island's mountain range, coastline, and the small towns along the way. Once they reached Roseau, the real adventure began.

Eric led the family to many historic sites and popular attractions with the help of a tourist map. After visiting Middleham Falls, the Roseau

Museum, and walking the shore of Champagne Beach, they headed for the Old Market Square to shop. Eric and Tyler weren't too thrilled about that. They bought tropical drinks and found a bench in the middle of the square where they chilled while the ladies splurged on souvenirs.

"Look at this hat, Royce. Isn't it pretty?"

"I like it. I'm going to buy one for Mama."

"I want to stock up on T-shirts. I see some over there."

Zora took off toward the T-shirt stand with Royce a few steps behind her. The sun was shining brightly in the sky, and the air was muggy. After the long ride and lots of walking, Royce was starting to feel light-headed. Her back pains had returned, too. It was time to take a break and have a cool drink. Royce reached the table where Zora stood looking through a stack of T-shirts in every color and size.

"Can we sit down for a few minutes after you're done here? I'm getting overheated."

Zora looked at her sister. "Are you okay? You look a little flushed." She placed the shirts on the table. "Let's go and find Eric and Tyler." She took Royce by the hand and led her away.

Father and son were laughing and talking on the bench while sipping their drinks. Royce could see them a few yards away. The pain in her back and the heat made it seem as if miles and miles separated them. Royce felt woozy, and her breathing was labored. She leaned on Zora for support. Eric looked up and saw the sisters walking in his direction. Apparently, he sensed that Royce was in distress. He jumped up from the bench and sprinted toward them. Royce's eyes rolled to the back of her head seconds before she collapsed in Eric's arms.

"Yes, Mama, the doctor said she's fine. She's resting now." Zora looked over her shoulder at her sister lying in the hospital bed. She allowed her tears to fall freely, but she spoke calmly because she didn't want to upset her mother. "I'm going to stay here with her tonight. She'll be released in the morning. I'll call you when we get back to Glanvillia. I love you, Ma."

Zora sat down on the bed next to Royce. She stroked her cheek tenderly. "My baby sister is going to have a baby." She smiled through her tears at the thought.

There was a tap at the door before it swung open. Eric walked in with Tyler on his heels.

"Is Auntie Royce going to be all right, Mom?"

"She'll be fine, sweetie. She got overheated and dehydrated after walking too much under the Caribbean sun."

"We're about to catch a cab back to Glanvillia, but I need to speak with you in the hall before we leave. Tyler can watch Royce for a few minutes."

Zora followed her husband out of the room and closed the door.

"I'm sorry you had to find out this way. Royce had every intention of telling you soon, but she was afraid, Zora. You've been so hard on her lately. She didn't want to be judged or belittled. Royce needs your love and compassion now more than ever before. Please be nice to her when she wakes up."

"I will. After all, I'm not angry with her. I want to kill that priest who got her pregnant and broke her heart."

"She loves him, honey. And no matter how bad he hurt her, she doesn't want to hear anything negative about him or their relationship. I'd like to strangle him to death too, but it wouldn't solve the problem. Our family will soon welcome an innocent baby into the fold. Regardless of the circumstances of its conception, we should all be happy for the life God is about to bless us with."

"I guess you're right. Babies are precious gifts from God. I'm grateful and excited about finally getting a niece or a nephew. But I am not happy about how it all came about. I'm going to call Father Gregory and tell him he's going to become a daddy."

Eric shook his head. "You can't do that. It's not your responsibility. And Royce doesn't want him to know."

"Why not?"

"She has her reasons. I don't agree with her, and she knows it. But it's her life. I've been trying to talk her into changing her mind. I haven't had much success, though." Eric took Zora by the hand and looked at her directly. "Promise me that you'll respect your sister's wishes. Swear to me that you won't call Father Gregory and tell him anything."

"I promise not to call Father Gregory and tell him about the baby."

"Thank you."

Chapter Forty-two

Father Gregory entered the confessional with tears streaming down his cheeks. He kneeled and waited.

"What brings you here today, child of God?"

"I have n . . . not sinned," he stuttered over sobs. "I came for a . . . a word of comfort. I need . . . need spiritual guidance, Father."

Even through the crying and sniffles, Father Kyle recognized the voice. It was the young man who loved the woman he could not marry. It had been several months since he had sought help. Father Kyle was pleased that he had come today, but he was concerned about his state of mind. He sounded deeply troubled. "What can I do for you today, my son?"

"I'm no longer involved with the woman I love. I ended our relationship a few weeks ago. I didn't want to continue dishonoring God by fornicating with her, so I did what I believed was best. I know God is pleased, but why does doing what is right hurt so much? I was happier when I was fornicating and constantly asking for forgiveness than I am now that I'm celibate again. I don't understand. I feel like I'm dying. Have I lost my mind, Father?"

"No, my son. You are indeed sane, but you are human. The spirit inside of you will forever war with the flesh. You love this woman with all your heart. That is why you could not abstain from being intimate with her. You wanted to stop, but your flesh was weak. Your decision to end the affair was influenced by your love for God and your commitment to Him. You did the right thing for your soul, but the human side of you still yearns for her. That's understandable."

"Dear God, I love her so much. I miss her. I can't function without her in my life. I'm beyond miserable. This is not the abundant life the Bible speaks about. I have no life without her!"

Father Kyle's heart was heavy for the young man. He whispered a prayer as he listened to him weep out loud on the other side of the confessional. His whimpers were heart-wrenching. Tears pooled in Father Kyle's eyes as he waited for God to give him a word of comfort for the pitiful soul crying on the other side of the screen.

Time passed as the young man wept and the priest pleaded with the Lord for a word of consolation. At last, the Holy Spirit spoke to him.

The older priest cleared his throat. "God loves you, my son. He will always love you no matter what. God is love, and He created us in His image in love. We are His children, and He loves us in spite of our sins. And because He loves you, it is His utmost desire that you are happy. God ordained love between man and woman. He will honor the love you have for the woman you desire in marriage . . . Father."

The sniffles on the other side of the confessional ceased abruptly. Several seconds of complete silence lingered between the two priests. Father Kyle waited patiently for a response. He did not want the young man to leave angrily as he had done before. It was important that he receive adequate counseling for his ongoing spiritual problem today once and for all.

"Who told you? I mean, how did you figure out my dilemma, that I'm a priest?"

"The Holy Spirit revealed it to me while you were crying."

"Now you understand why I can't marry the woman I love."

"I do."

"I think I should ask to be reassigned someplace far away. Eventually, I'll forget about her, and my life will return to normal."

"There is no distance in love, Father. No matter where you go in the universe, she will always be in your heart. You carry her in your spirit. Your souls are connected."

"Then what do you suggest I do?"

"Follow your heart."

"Are you advising me to abandon the priesthood and marry her?"

"I am telling you that God knows your heart. Even before you were born, He knew this day would come. Our God is a very loving and forgiving God. He will love you regardless of the decision you make. His love for us has no end, and His mercy endures forever. Follow your heart, Father."

"You better stop spoiling me. I could get used to this." Royce leaned back on the stack of fluffy pillows and bit into another chocolate chip cookie.

"Mama told me to take good care of you. I'm just being obedient."

"Thanks, Z."

"It's my pleasure to look after you. I've been taking care of you since you were a little girl. I don't mind. You need special treatment now that you have a bun in the oven."

"I'm not talking about that. Thank you for not flipping out when you found out about the baby."

Zora sat down on the bed and rubbed Royce's growing baby bump. "I must admit I was pissed off at first. I wanted to whip your butt. But when I saw you lying in that hospital bed exhausted and helpless, it brought back memories from our childhood. You were my sweet and innocent little sister again. I just wanted to hold you, protect you, and let you know that everything would be okay."

"Will it?"

"What are you talking about, sweetie?"

"Will everything be okay?"

"Of course it will. Eric and I will be there to help you every step of the way. I bet Father Gregory would be there for you too if you would tell him he's going to be a daddy."

"I don't want to force him to choose between fatherhood and the priesthood. If he ever finds out about this baby, he will want to be a part of its life. The only way that'll be possible is if he steps down from the pulpit. I don't want this baby to be the cause of that, Z. Nicholas could live to resent me someday and blame me for ruining his life. I'm going to raise this baby alone."

"I disagree with you, but it's your decision. I'll have to respect it." She kissed Royce on the forehead. "I'm going to bed now. Sleep well."

"Good night."

"Damn it, Royce! Where are you?"

Father Gregory walked down the three steps from Royce's stoop, angry, confused, and frustrated. It was the third day in a row he'd hopped on his motorcycle and sped to her house. He couldn't imagine where she could be. He had called her dozens of times and left countless messages on her cell phone, her land phone, and both job voicemails. He knew she was hurt because of their breakup, but she was taking her game of hide and seek a little too far.

Father Gregory guided his bike to the pavement and mounted it. He sat for a moment, unsure of his next move. He thought about riding to the Royalty facility in midtown, but he quickly changed his mind. It was possible that she had banned him from both locations for life like she'd done Dr. Marlon Burrell. Father Gregory didn't want to be dragged away from the building in handcuffs.

He took in his surroundings. Royce had never spoken to him about any of her neighbors, so he didn't think it was a good idea to bother them. Tyler's face suddenly floated through his head. Surely, he knew where his aunt was, but he was out of the country. He hadn't spoken to the boy since he'd left for Dominica, although Tyler did leave him a message assuring him that he and his family had arrived on the island safely.

Father Gregory removed his cell phone from his pocket and dialed Tyler's number.

The faint buzzing of the phone stirred Zora from her afternoon nap. She sat up on the sofa and looked around. Tyler had left his cell phone on the coffee table while he went swimming with his father.

"Who the hell is calling him?" Zora picked up the phone and pushed the power button. Before she could greet the caller, he started talking fast and frantically.

"Tyler, I'm so glad you answered. This is Father Gregory. I've been trying to reach your aunt for three days. I really need to talk to her right away. Do you have any idea where she is?"

"My sister is here in Dominica with her family. What could you possibly want to speak with her about?"

"Mrs. Benson, how are you?"

"I'm wonderful now that Royce is no longer sleeping with you."

"I know I was wrong to get involved with your sister, but it just happened. The next thing I knew we had fallen in love. Things got complicated, and I ended the relationship. But I never stopped loving Royce and I never will. If I could just speak with her please, I would be appreciative."

He actually sounded sincere to Zora. He was practically begging for a chance to talk to Royce. But Zora wasn't sure if she should allow it. She didn't want him to say anything to Royce that might upset her. He claimed to love her sister, yet he had ripped her heart from her chest and left her pregnant. Zora decided to test the priest.

"Do you really love Royce?"

"Yes. I love her more than I love myself."

"What are your intentions at this point? You're still a priest. You can't marry Royce or even date her."

"I left the priesthood. I submitted my resignation to the archdiocese and to my church. I asked to be relieved of all my duties immediately. I had to follow my heart."

"Oh, my God! You're serious, aren't you?"

"I'm very serious. I can't live without Royce. We were meant to be together. I've prayed about it and sought counsel. God has forgiven me and granted me His blessing to leave the priesthood so I can marry your sister. I'll continue to serve the Lord as a layman in every way I can. There's still a divine calling on my life, and I'll fulfill it with my wife by my side."

"I think you should come to Dominica and tell Royce face-to-face about the decisions you've made. A man needs to look a woman in her eyes when he declares his love for her and asks for her hand in marriage."

"I'll come as soon as I can. I'm in the process of moving out of the parsonage and into an apartment. I need your direct number so I can call you next week with my travel itinerary. I'd like to surprise Royce if it's possible."

"She's going to be surprised all right." *And you will be too,* Zora wanted to add, but she kept it to herself. She smiled because she now had a secret . . . a very pleasant secret.

Chapter Forty-three

"I'm going to miss you, Father Gregory." Father Rivera threw his short, meaty arms around his former fellow priest. He released him and took a backward step. "What will you do now that you've left the priesthood?"

"I could always teach at the college level. I've thought about writing my memoires. I'm a former Roman Catholic priest who left my flock to get married to a woman I've been involved in an affair with for several months. It sounds like a *New York Times* bestseller to me." He grinned.

"Will you keep in touch with us?"

Father Gregory nodded and stuffed more items inside the nearly full box. "I don't see any reason why I shouldn't. I'll be right here in Atlanta. You, Father Schmidt, and I will get together for pool and drinks from time to time."

"I would like that."

"I'd rather learn how to ride your motorcycle," Father Schmidt announced as he entered the master suite.

"I'll give you lessons, although I don't think you'll need them. Riding a Harley is easy."

"You're one brave and lucky man, Father Gregory."

"How so?"

"You've done what many of us have contemplated but lacked the courage to do. I know your decision didn't come easy, but you took God at His word. He promised to never leave us nor forsake us. He'll be with you in your new life because He loves you." Father Schmidt patted Father Gregory's shoulder. "I wish you well, sir."

"Thank you. And from now on, I want both of you to call me Nicholas."

The small clinic on Ross University School of Medicine's campus had closed two hours ago, but Eric, Zora, and Tyler still hadn't returned home. The sun's brilliance had been replaced by the darkness as the stars appeared one by one scattered around the moon. Royce waddled to the huge bay window in the parlor and opened the blinds. The slow-paced lifestyle of the native

Dominicans left their tiny neighborhood quiet and uneventful. There was no one walking up or down the street, and the children had retreated indoors for the evening after playing outside. She left the window and returned to the comfortable recliner to watch television.

Royce gasped and rubbed her protruding belly in response to her baby stirring in her womb. The tiny kicks fascinated her every time. It was an amazing feeling that Royce didn't think she'd ever grow tired of. Regardless of her present circumstances, her baby was a blessing from God that she was grateful for. Her little girl or boy would always remind her of the one and only man she had ever truly loved. Nicholas Gregory had given her the most precious gift ever, although he was clueless to the fact.

The sound of a car's engine and flashing bright lights startled Royce. She was relieved that the Benson crew had finally decided to come home. They'd probably gone out to dinner at the Purple Turtle, their favorite restaurant on the island. Eric had no doubt devoured a few lobster tails. He loved them prepared in the Dominican spices.

Royce frowned at the round of light taps at the door. Everyone had been given a key to the house by the landlord the first day they moved in. Even

Tyler had placed one of the keys on his Atlanta Hawks ring. The tapping continued, irritating Royce to no end. She was comfortable and didn't want to leave the recliner. She struggled to her feet, hurried to the door, and snatched it open.

"Royce," the familiar, rich baritone timbre rumbled.

A pair of long arms enfolded her. She wiggled free from his embrace with her mind reeling from shock. It had to be a dream or maybe an apparition even. There was no way the love of her life, the father of her unborn child, was standing before her.

Royce's eyes locked with Nicholas's. He smiled at her, and she nearly fainted. His eyes left her face and traveled lower to her new curves. She saw the astonishment in his deep ebony orbs the instant realization kicked in. Royce couldn't speak. She couldn't move. She watched Nicholas lower his body to one knee. The feel of his hands caressing her belly brought out deep emotions she couldn't contain. Teardrops streamed down Royce's face as the baby kicked and squirmed in response to its father's gentle touches.

Nicholas massaged and kissed Royce's belly repeatedly before he stood again. "We're having a baby?" he asked with his eyes glistening with unshed tears.

Royce, much too overwhelmed to speak, simply nodded and covered her tearstained face with both hands.

Nicholas turned around and lifted his suitcase from the porch and closed the door. "Come. Let's sit and talk. There's so much I need to say to you."

Royce allowed him to lead her to the sofa. They sat quietly for a few moments, each obviously sorting through their thoughts and emotions. Royce had a million questions to ask him, and she knew he had just as many for her.

"Why did you come here?"

"I wanted to apologize for hurting you. It tore a hole in my soul the day I ended our relationship. I haven't enjoyed a moment of peace since that night. Please forgive me."

"I accept your apology, but I was partly to blame for the mess we made. I didn't enter the situation blindly. I knew you were a priest and you always will be."

"I left the priesthood. I resigned from all my duties. I couldn't live that lifestyle anymore, sweetheart. My season in ministry had come to an end. Many people will never understand or accept my decision, but I don't care. I'm at peace with it, and I'm at peace with God."

"I never would've asked you to choose, Nicholas. There were more times than I can count that I wanted to, but I couldn't bring myself to do it."

"You don't ever have to worry about that again. I'm free to love you completely the way Christ loves the church, if you'll have me as your husband."

"I love you, Nicholas. You know that. Of course I'll marry you."

"Thank God! I never dreamed I would have a wife and a child. It's hard to believe this is really happening to me."

Royce wrapped her arms around her man's neck and kissed his lips. "How long will you be here?"

"I'll be here long enough to get married and have a honeymoon. Then I'll take my beautiful pregnant wife back to Atlanta where we'll wait for the arrival of our baby. I'll have to look for a new job, of course, and learn how to be a father. But right now I would love to practice for the honeymoon."

Royce giggled like a silly schoolgirl. "We can't. I'm expecting Eric, Zora, and Tyler any minute."

Nicholas gave Royce a smile so sexy that her heart skipped a couple of beats. He shook his head. "The Bensons aren't coming home tonight.

As a matter of fact, they went to Roseau for the weekend. We have the house all to ourselves thanks to your lovely sister."

"Who? Zora? I don't believe you."

"She's my new best friend. By divine intervention, we spoke on the phone two weeks ago. We had a serious conversation about everything concerning you and me. At the conclusion of the matter, she gave me her blessing to come here. We've been in constant contact ever since. You're fortunate to have Zora for a sister. She would move heaven and earth for you."

"I love her too, even though she gets on my nerves sometimes."

Nicholas rubbed Royce's belly. "Let's go to bed."

Nicholas tossed the magazine on the nightstand when Royce entered the bedroom. She was voluptuous and sexy as hell with a bright prenatal glow. He couldn't remember her looking more desirable. Without warning, she lifted the pastel pink caftan over her head and allowed it to fall to the floor. Her naked pregnant body was exquisite. Nicholas opened his arms to her, and Royce did not disappoint him. She stretched her body out fully on top of his, and he cradled her to his chest.

"Am I dreaming or are you really here with me?"

"I'm here, baby." He kissed her passionately to prove it and pulled back. "I have something for you," he said, reaching toward the nightstand. He opened the drawer and picked up a small jewelry box. "After all of the excitement of seeing you again and learning about the baby, I failed to give you a proper proposal." He opened the box, revealing a humongous emerald-cut diamond surrounded by a halo of small round diamonds set high on a platinum band. "Royce Dominique Phillips, will you marry me?"

"Oh, Nicholas, it's the prettiest ring I've ever seen in my life. You chose well, baby. Thank you. And yes, I will marry you."

He took her left hand and eased the stunning piece of jewelry on her ring finger. "It's a perfect fit just like you and me." He sealed the official proposal with another sizzling kiss.

Royce returned his passion in the heated manner she always had whenever they were together. Her soft body, familiar but yet so new, shuddered under his caresses as he reacquainted himself with every inch of her smooth flesh. Too many days and moments in time had kept them apart. The reunion with the woman he loved, now the mother of his unborn child, was sweet.

He fondled her growing and noticeably more sensitive breasts until the nipples hardened. He licked each rigid peak repeatedly, and Royce whimpered out her pleasure. He eased her onto her back and kissed a path from her bosom to her stomach bulging with his child. His finger found the hairy, wet spot at the apex of her thighs. The heat between its folds was hotter than normal, and it caused more blood to rush to his already erect penis. It throbbed with anticipation to be buried deep inside of Royce as he slid his fingers in and out of her drenched vagina, teasing her stiff clit with every stroke. Their foreplay released the distinct aroma of sex into the air inside the small bedroom. The glow from the full moon shining through the window washed over their naked bodies.

Royce rolled over onto her left side with her knees bent, and she raised her right leg. "We'll have to do it this way because—"

"I understand. We can't hurt the baby," he whispered, fully comprehending.

Nicholas positioned himself at an angle behind Royce and penetrated her slowly with care. He stroked her gently and cupped her full breasts, kneading them to heighten her pleasure. She pushed backward into his body to meet his thrusts in a moderate and easy rhythm. And even as the pace quickened and the urgency intensified, his motions remained smooth and tender.

"Ah . . . I love you, Royce."

She cooed and hummed out her response and continued rocking her hips and rubbing the large hand massaging her right breast. The rhythm of their lovemaking increased. They continued feeding each other's passions until their bodies were completely satisfied and energy had betrayed them both.

Just before dawn, Royce woke up and discovered she was in bed alone. She sat up and looked around the room and smiled when saw her fiancé staring out the window. "Come back to bed."

He turned to face her. "Your body needs a break. I don't want to overdo it and end up harming you or the baby."

Nicholas's concern for her and their baby warmed Royce's heart. "I wanted to ask you a question many months ago," she began, "but I was too embarrassed."

"Go ahead, sweetheart. You can ask me anything." He sat on the bed next to Royce, took her by the hand, and kissed her palm.

"You had never made love to a woman before I came along, so how did you know what to do the first time we were together and every other time after that?"

Nicholas threw his head back and belted out a laugh. "I was a pretty good biology student in high school and college. And although I was going to be a priest, it didn't stop Max from giving me the classic lecture on the birds and the bees. And like you once said, some things just come natural."

Chapter Forty-four

A love that had endured more sorrow, complexities, controversy, and limitations than most was rekindled and reaffirmed that night under a Caribbean moonlight. It was a forbidden romance deemed punishable by hell's fire and damnation in the hearts of millions all over the world. Not even the sanctity of marriage could validate Nicholas and Royce's coming together as one. A sacred vow had been broken, and for that, love could offer no spiritual or moral excuse according to the Roman Catholic Church. But for the two lovers, love indeed was the ultimate justifying premise that superseded the traditions and interpretations of God's law by mere mortal men.

Tyler sat and watched his father and grandfather escort Nicholas to a corner in the small reception hall. From the looks on their faces, he could tell the conversation they were about to have with his buddy wasn't going to be a very friendly one. Sure, both men had smiled through the rehearsal dinner and appeared touched by Nicholas's sweet and romantic vows he'd recited to Royce with tears in his eyes during the wedding ceremony. But now they reminded the boy of a pair of vicious thugs prepared to do bodily harm. Tyler actually felt sorry for his mentor.

The child squinted, trying to read his grandfather's lips as he talked and jabbed his finger forcefully in the air only inches away from Nicholas's nose. Tyler believed he could see beads of sweat forming on his poor friend's forehead. Whatever his father was whispering in Nicholas's ear had caused his face to turn a fiery shade of red. It had to be a threat. Tyler could feel it in his gut. Knowing his dad, he'd probably promised to break both of the man's legs if he wasn't a good husband to Royce. And the flash in his eyes said he meant every threatening word.

Tyler wasn't concerned about Nicholas cheating or being mean to his aunt. He believed he truly loved her and would always respect her and treat her like a queen. That was the promise he had made to Tyler the evening he and Royce had sat him down to tell him about their engagement and the baby. At first, he was totally confused and upset, but by the end of the conversation, during which the boy had asked a ton of questions, he understood that sometimes certain things in life don't turn out the way we plan them. And he learned a valuable lesson about love. Royce and Nicholas had explained that it was a powerful emotion that often made strange things happen that we can't even begin to understand.

Tyler breathed a sigh relief when Nichols was released from the corner unharmed. He made a lightning path to the bar where his stepfather, Max, sat nursing a drink. Tyler wanted to run over and talk to him to make sure he was okay, but he figured it wasn't a good time. Nicholas more than likely needed to spend some time with his stepdad, and he probably could use a drink too.

The small reggae band suddenly broke out into an upbeat tune. The lead singer invited everyone at the reception to the dance floor. Tyler jumped up, snapping his fingers and bobbing his head to the funky beat. He noticed Andra standing alone, wiggling her hips to the rhythm of the music. He half walked and half danced across the room and took his older cousin by the hand. Together they joined their family members on the dance floor. Tyler smiled when he looked to the front of the room and saw his aunt and brand-new uncle in each other's arms, swaying from side to side with smiles on their faces. They were happy, and Tyler was too.

"Be totally honest with me, Nicholas. Do you have any regrets?"

"Absolutely not," he answered without hesitation, shaking his head. "I didn't plan it nor did I foresee it. But if I had to do it all over again, I would do almost everything the same."

"Oh, yeah? What would you differently?"

"I would have gone to my superiors the day I realized I'd fallen in love with you. In the back of my mind and deep in my heart I knew we would end up together, but I fought it. I was stupid to think I could live in two worlds for the rest of my life. And it was so unfair to you. But I was afraid, Royce. I didn't want to fail or be ostracized."

"Do you believe God is disappointed or angry with you?"

"No, I don't. A very wise, holy man assured me that God knows my heart and He had ordered my footsteps even before I was born. You, our child, and the life we now share were all a part of His plan. My destiny has come to fruition. God loves the spirit of love, Royce. God is love. He loves you.

He loves me. And He loves the love we have for each other."

"So you're not going to hell?"

Nicholas laughed and massaged his wife's back. "No, I'm not going to hell, and neither are you."

Royce rested her head on her husband's chest and listened to his strong heartbeat. She allowed his words to settle deep in her spirit. It had been her fear since the first time they made love that they had brought a curse upon themselves without any hope for salvation. She had actually been more concerned about the man she loved than herself. After all, God's expectations and requirements of him were far greater than those of an ordinary person like her. But it didn't matter now. Their days of lies, fornication, and secrecy about their relationship were now a part of the past. They were happily married and bound by the vows they had made to each other in the presence of God and their families. It wasn't a fairy tale, but it was the life Royce had always envisioned. She had a husband who adored her, a baby on the way, and a supportive family. Business was booming. Her third fitness and health center was only weeks away from its grand opening. What more could a girl ask for?

"Our mothers want to know the gender of the baby," Royce announced out of the blue. "How do you feel about that?"

"We don't want to know. It's our baby and our decision, sweetheart. Case closed."

"Are you comfortable living in this house? We could move and find another one together if you'd like."

"We shared our first kiss in this house. I received my one and only adult spanking in this very room. Our child was more than likely conceived in this bed. Why would I ever want to move? There are too many unforgettable memories in this house, honey. If you don't mind, I'd like us to make many more right here in *our* house."

Nicholas folded the single sheet of paper and slid it back inside the envelope. It was a letter from Darius, the young theology student he'd met last spring. There was a "save the date" card inviting Nichols to his ordination next year enclosed in the envelope as well. The young man was on the path to a life in the priesthood. Nicholas was happy for him. He'd obviously made the decision he believed was best for him and the young woman he'd been involved with.

Nicholas was certain that Darius had not arrived at his decision without lots of prayer and extensive consideration. Nevertheless, he had chosen to stay on the course he had begun as a teenager. According to his letter, he was excited and ready to serve God and the Catholic Church. He had fully embraced the divine calling on his life and turned his back on love and marriage. Nicholas was proud that Darius had decided to do what he believed was right instead of what he desired. His prayer was that he would honor the vow he had made and become a priest who would honor God and His people forever.

"Royce, are you ready, baby girl? There're a whole lot of people out there. Tabatha said the program will start in exactly seven minutes. Your mama and I are going out there to claim our seats with the rest of the family before somebody steals them."

"Okay, Daddy, we'll be out there soon." She inhaled and exhaled as her husband stood above her chair, quietly massaging her back and shoulders.

Estelle Phillips leaned over and pushed her daughter's long braids away from her face. She pecked her on the cheek. "I'm so proud of you, sweetie. You were always ambitious when it came to your professional life. Now you have everything you've ever wanted. You almost gave me a heart attack by the way you came about it. But I'm fine now because I realize how happy you and Nicholas are."

"Thank you, Mama."

"Knock! Knock!" Zora drawled out as she suddenly appeared at Royce's office door at the new Royalty location in Stockbridge, Georgia. "It's almost that time," she announced. "The mayor, the chief of police, the fire chief, and several TV cameras are here. The room is jam-packed. You did it, sis!" Zora blew Royce a kiss and then vanished into the hallway.

Mr. and Mrs. Phillips smiled and waved to their daughter and son-in-law before they left the office to join the crowd that had assembled for the grand opening of Royalty Fitness and Health Center and Spa's new south location.

"Are you okay? You look like a million bucks, but you seem tired, sluggish even. How is your back?"

"I feel fine. I'm a little nervous, and your baby refuses to be still. But overall I'm having a good day." Royce stood with her husband's assistance. "The crowd is waiting for us. Let's go and cut that ribbon, Mr. Gregory."

Chapter Forty-five

"Mrs. Gregory, I am so impressed with your facility. Your staff, the modern state-of-the-art equipment, and the services you offer are absolutely amazing. This is just the kind of health club I've been looking for since I relocated here from Los Angeles."

"Thank you. I hope you'll take advantage of our new membership enrollment specials. The twenty-five percent discount is valid until New Year's Eve."

"You better believe I did. I signed up for the platinum membership plan. I'll be here early Monday morning for a consultation with my new personal trainer and nutritionist before I head to the studio to tape my show. I'll be discussing the 'Stand Your Ground' law currently on books in Florida, Georgia, Kentucky, and sixteen other states, including my home state, Michigan. Too many unarmed brown boys and men are losing their lives for no good reason at all."

"That's true. I'll make sure I tune in."

"Great. Again, congratulations on your grand opening. It was nice meeting you." The stylishly dressed woman offered Royce her hand.

"The pleasure was mine," she said, shaking the offered hand firmly.

As soon as the woman walked away, Royce turned to Nicholas. "Do you know who that was?"

He shook his head. "Nope."

"That was Kyra Alexander! She's a major talk show host. And the sista gives lectures all over the country, empowering women and youth. She's like the new Oprah. I can't believe she came to my grand opening *and* she joined my center."

"That's wonderful, and I'm excited for you," Nicholas said, rubbing Royce's back. "But it's time for me to take you home. You've had a full day, and now it's time for you to get some rest."

"I just need a few more minutes to greet some other people and check in with Tabatha."

"You have ten minutes, baby, and not a second more."

Royce waddled around her new, magnificent building, shaking hands and mingling with her supporters. Once in a while, she would turn to look at her husband to assure him that she was aware of the time limit he had placed on her. The clock was ticking. With moments to spare,

Royce made her way to the office area. She found Tabatha talking to one of the facility's maintenance engineers.

"I don't mean to interrupt, but I wanted to let you know I'm about to leave. The hubby says I've been on my feet too long. He's a bit overprotective. I don't know why he insists on treating me like I'm a fragile porcelain doll. I feel great with the exception of a little back pain here and there. Anyway, I'll see you early tomorrow morning."

"Yes, ma'am. I'll be here no later than seven forty-five. Take care."

"Nicholas."

His eyes popped open the moment Royce nudged him and whispered his name. He sat up in bed and instantly turned on the lamp on the nightstand. He looked down and studied Royce's face. She appeared to be in pain. "What's wrong?"

"I don't know," she moaned through choppy breaths. "The baby is moving a lot, and it hurts. The pain is unbearable. I feel wet, too, but I can't be in labor. It's too early. I have eight weeks to go."

"I'm calling Dr. Ayobami," he told Royce and snatched the cover from their bodies. "Oh, dear God!"

The sight of bright red blood covering Royce's lower body and the bedsheets terrified Nicholas. He was paralyzed briefly, but he quickly shook it off and sprang into action. He called 911, gave the dispatcher the details of the emergency, and demanded an ambulance in a composed yet insistent voice while holding Royce's hand. Then he got dressed with lightning speed.

"They don't want you to move, baby. Try to breathe and stay calm until the medics arrive. You're going to be fine. The baby is going to be fine," he assured her, although he had no idea if his words were true.

After a brief span of time, Nicholas heard the ambulance's siren wailing as the vehicle drew closer to the house. He ran downstairs to let the medics in.

"Where is your wife, sir?"

"She's upstairs. Follow me."

Nicholas left his seat in the waiting area as soon as he saw Eric emerge from the double doors. Zora followed him.

"What's happening? How is Royce?"

Eric raised both hands. "She's stable, but—"

"But what, Eric? Just tell us. How is my sister?"

"Placental abruption is a very serious condition. Although the separation is partial, Royce has lost a lot of blood. She's undergoing a transfusion right now. She's strong, healthy, and in tip-top shape, so I'm sure she'll pull through this."

"What about the baby?"

Eric sighed and scratched his head. "I've got to give it to you straight, Nick. The baby may not make it. If Royce were closer to her due date, the baby would be bigger, stronger, and further developed. Right now, it's in distress. The heartbeat is weak, and its oxygen level is nowhere near where it should be. It's touch and go. After Royce's blood transfusion, Dr. Ayobami will perform an emergency Cesarean section. A neonatal specialist and his team will begin critical neonatal care on the baby as soon as it's born. If anyone can save your child's life, it's my buddy, Dr. Felix Murat. The dude is a genius."

Zora broke down in tears, but Nicholas remained cool. He stood in place quietly as Eric tried to comfort his wife. The situation was scarier than his worst nightmare. Royce was young and physically fit. With the exception of her nightly bowl of ice cream, she had been very conscious of her diet during her entire pregnancy. They'd walked their tranquil neighborhood four evenings a week, every week since returning home from Dominica as husband and wife. This wasn't supposed to be happening!

Sin . . . The broken vow . . . The departure from the priesthood . . .

Those thoughts and a million others floated through Nicholas's psyche like a parade of bad words. Guilt assaulted him. It was his fault that his wife and baby were fighting for their lives. Royce's only transgression had been falling in love with him, a priest. But their baby, conceived in love yet through willful fornication, was totally innocent. The tiny, pure, and perfect little boy or girl did not deserve to die because of the sins of its father. And death was too harsh of a punishment for a woman who'd only done what had become natural at the beginning of time when Eve offered her body and soul to Adam in the Garden of Eden.

Royce was worthy of bearing a child and nurturing it until adulthood even though she'd conceived it out of wedlock with a priest who had been overcome by lust. If anyone deserved to die, Nicholas believed it was him.

"How soon will Dr. Ayobami deliver the baby?"

Eric, still hugging Zora and trying to console her, peered at his brother-in-law over his shoulder. "Thank God Royce was still alert when she arrived. She was able to tell the medical team her blood type and everything else important they needed to know. Because of her, the emergency physician was able to start the blood transfusion right away. Dr. Ayobami is prepared to begin the C-section as soon as he's given clearance. In my professional opinion, that should be in an hour or so."

"I'll be back," Nicholas told Eric. "I want to be in the operating room with Royce when our baby is born. Do whatever it takes to make it possible," he insisted, walking away.

"Hey, man, where're you going?"

"Nicholas, come back here! What am I supposed to tell my sister when she asks for you? Please don't leave! Come back!"

Nicholas completely tuned them out. He had to ignore them because time was not on his side. He followed the directional signs to the hospital's chapel, where he had met with the grieving Strozier family when its patriarch was transitioning to eternity. It was the most sacred place in the building. Nicholas knew he wasn't the best Christian in the world, and he believed his sins had come full circle. But he was holding on to the words of Father Kyle. *"Our God is a very loving and forgiving God. He will love you regardless of the decision you make. His love for us has no end, and His mercy endures forever."* Nicholas could hear the elder priest's voice as if he were right there with him.

He rode the elevator down to the first floor. When he stepped out, he rushed inside the chapel where a few people sat scattered in the pews, praying and meditating. Nicholas took a seat in the very last pew on the left side of the aisle. If he had learned nothing else from his years as an altar boy growing up in the Catholic Church, he knew how to pray. And he would rely on the same faith that he had studied, nurtured, and affirmed over the course of his days in seminary and as a priest.

"God, please spare Royce's life and let our baby live. Neither of them deserves to be punished. I abandoned the priesthood and reneged on my oath and calling to you and the church. I knew what I was doing was against your will, but I was too weak and sinful to abstain. I believe in my heart that you have already forgiven me and you've blessed me with two special gifts I'm unworthy of. Please, I beg you, don't take Royce and my child away from me. I will do anything if you allow them to pull through this crisis, anything, God. I would give my life for them. Just tell me what to do. Give me a sign or show me in some way, please. I promise I will do anything you want me to do if you'll have mercy on me one more time."

Nicholas wiped his tears away and sat quietly thinking about Royce and their baby. His burden was so heavy. He felt totally helpless. Never in his wildest imagination had he ever entertained the thought of becoming a father. But now that he had come so close to welcoming his child into the world, his soul ached at the possibility that death would rob him of holding his son or daughter.

"I'd rather die." He whispered his heartfelt sentiment.

The chapel door swung open. Nicholas turned around and saw Eric.

"Hey, man, I figured you were in here. Royce is asking for you. Zora is trying to keep her calm, but she wants you. We've got to hurry so you can scrub up and change. Dr. Ayobami will begin the procedure in thirty minutes."

Epilogue

Two Years Later

"Good morning, my brothers and sisters."

"Good morning." The congregation returned its pastor's greeting in unison.

He smiled and lifted his Bible in the air. "This morning I want you to join me in reading one of my favorite scriptures on forgiveness. Please flip to the one hundred and third division of Psalms. We will concentrate on verses eight through twelve. I'll give you all a few moments to locate that passage."

"Daddy! Daddy!" The angelic voice of a little girl rang throughout the sanctuary over the faint sound of pages turning.

The congregation erupted with laughter. Many of the members looked at the toddler sitting on her mother's lap and smiled affectionately.

Reverend Nicholas Gregory smiled also and lowered his head. "You all will have to forgive my two-year-old daughter, Nicolette, for her outburst. She's her daddy's number one fan. Everything I do seems to excite her. Even when I'm delivering a sermon in the pulpit, she feels the need to cheer for me. My wife and I hope she'll settle down when her baby brother arrives in three months. Then again, I'm a realist. Nicolette is our miracle baby, and she has way too much spunk. She had to fight to survive a very complicated premature delivery, and she spent several weeks in the neonatal intensive care unit. I think you all better prepare for more outbursts until she grows out of her rambunctious stage."

Another round of laughter filled the moderate-sized church in response to Reverend Gregory's remarks. His eyes locked on his wife and daughter. God had truly blessed him. He was grateful for every dark valley and rocky mountain he had overcome. Despite his fall from grace, he had been forgiven, restored, and reassigned to another season of ministry. The newly elected pastor of Grace Fellowship Christian Church in East Atlanta was thankful for such an amazing opportunity. He considered it his rebirth, an undeserved second chance.

Nicholas's love for God had never been in question, and neither had his commitment to serving the church. The dilemma he'd faced and had eventually overcome as a Catholic priest was his natural desire to love a woman and make her his wife versus his wish to fulfill a vow he no longer believed in. In the end, he chose both.